LILITH

Book III
The Illusionist Series

by

Fran Heckrotte

2016

Lilith

Third in the Illusionist Series

Mobi: 978-1-939950-15-4
epub ISBN: 978-1-939950-16-1
Print ISBN: 978-1-939950-18-5

First Edition eBook 2008
First Print Edition: January 2010

Publisher: Novel Ideas Publishing, LLC
Beaufort, SC. USA
Web Site: www.novelideaspublishing.com

Cover Design by Patty Henderson
Email: pattyghenderson@aol.com

Copy Editor: Cindy Burke
Email: cindyburkeoriginals@gmail.com

Note: This edition has no major changes or additions to the story. The story has been revised for continuity purposes.

Acknowledgments

I want to thank my beta readers who have stuck with me through my journey in telling the stories of my world of characters in the Illusionist series. Although they haven't seen the finished product, they were instrumental in getting me to my destination. Thank you Alex D'Brassis and Lee McLean, my betas...and Mary K. Bosshart, my alpha reader.

Patty G. Henderson, my cover artist, does an amazing job. She knows how to capture the essence of a story.

Cindy Burke, my copyeditor, who catches those annoying errors that I make.

A.L. Lamarre, who inspired me to write.

And, Howie. One day he'll figure it out.

Prelude To Lilith

The Illusionist (First of The Illusionist series)

YEMAYA LYSANNE is The Illusionist, a woman as mysterious as her shows. Dakota Devereaux, a journalist, decides to attend her performances hoping to discover her secrets. When the show goes horribly wrong and Yemaya is injured, the accident provides the perfect opportunity for the two women to meet. Little do they know that the encounter will begin a series of adventures that forever changes their lives. The Illusionist is a story about two women who find each other through adversity and love with the help of ancestral spirits – but is love enough to defeat the powerful darkness dwelling within the Illusionist?

Bloodlust (Second of The Illusionist series)

WOMEN ARE BEING attacked in Yemaya's hometown and not even science can determine who or what is behind it. The survivors remember little. The dead provide few clues. The locals fear the drac, an ancient evil, has returned. Even the spirits are at a loss. From the Carpathian mountains to New Orleans, Yemaya, Dakota and their ancestral spirits follow the trail of the murderer, only to discover that he isn't what he seems. Nor is he their greatest threat.

Characters from The Illusionist and Bloodlust

Yemaya Lysanne: The Illusionist, descendant of Mari, the Earth Mother and creator of land and seas.

Dakota Devereaux: Investigative journalist, descendant of the spirit of great-great-grandma Dakota, also known as Maopa by the other spirits.

Mari: Earth Mother Spirit

Grandma Dakota/Maopa: Human Spirit

Sarpe: Serpent Spirit

Vyushir: Wolf Spirit

Arbora: Spirit of the forests

Ursa: Bear Spirit

Ladyhawk: Bird Spirit

Intunecat: The Dark One, Spirit of darkness

LILITH

Part I

CHAPTER 1

SNICK! Click...SNICK!
"Damn!"
Click!
SNICK!
"Son of a bitch!"
The sound of a dull splash quickly followed.

"It's a conspiracy," Dakota grumbled, looking around for something else to write with. She was sitting by the pool, scribbling on a notepad resting on her lap, when the inevitable happened. The tip of her mechanical pencil broke and continued to break, leaving her frustrated. One of these days she was going to finish an article on the Illusionist without having to throw away pens or pencils.

The thought of Yemaya brought her back to the present. Conceding a temporary victory to the powers-that-be, she glanced at the swimmer in the pool and wondered how many more laps the woman could do before quitting from exhaustion. Just watching her lithe body moving smoothly through the water tired Dakota out. She shook her head and went back to her writing.

A low grunt caused her to look up. The sleek form of Yemaya pushed effortlessly up from the edge of the pool.

Groaning, Dakota squeezed her knees together trying to control the tingle developing between her thighs.

Long black hair clung damply to bare shoulders and firm breasts as rivulets of water ran down the semi-naked body before pooling on the cement. Dakota wished she was one of those drops trickling slowly between the well-rounded breasts concealed beneath the silver and blue bikini top. Stomach muscles rippled when Yemaya picked up a towel and rubbed her hair vigorously. As she dried her arms, chest, and then legs, the journalist's eyes followed the towel's movement. Those same legs had straddled her hips earlier in the morning while those same lips had kissed her passionately.

Remembering what had followed, Dakota inhaled deeply, and clamped her knees together. Her arms grew limp from the intensity of the orgasm. She was unaware of being watched or the worried look that Yemaya was giving her.

"Are you all right?" Yemaya asked, kneeling beside her.

Dakota kept her head down, taking deep breaths. The throbbing subsided to a bearable level.

Yemaya sat down next to Dakota, wrapped her arms around her and pulled her close. Neither spoke.

"Whew! That was intense," Dakota gasped, her voice weak and shaky. Pushing slightly away, she looked into Yemaya's eyes and blushed.

"What happened?" Yemaya pushed strands of blonde hair behind Dakota's left ear.

"Oh, ummm..."

"Dakota, are you okay?"

"Oh, yeah, I'm fine...really."

"Are you sure? You seem bothered."

"I am...was bothered. Have you ever seen yourself climbing out of a pool? Water streaming down that...that perfect body of yours? You're like some wild, exotic animal. Sleek, muscular...beautiful." It was Yemaya's turn to blush. "Just the sight of you standing there like an ancient goddess. If you affect me like this every time we go swimming, I'm in trouble!"

"Trouble? Oh! I see!"

Yemaya couldn't think of an adequate response. Dakota leaned in and gave her a quick kiss.

"Sorry if I embarrassed you."

"Oh! No, I am glad, I think. I mean, I know! You just surprised me. I had no idea."

"Sweetie, I had no idea until a few minutes ago and, believe me, I'm looking forward to many more episodes." Wiggling her eyebrows suggestively, Dakota grinned. "Instant orgasms and no work involved."

"Does that mean my services are no longer needed?"

"Good grief, no! Nothing compares to a hands-on experience."

"Just hands?" Yemaya murmured, her voice dropping to a husky, seductive whisper.

"Damn! Keep that up and I'll be too tired for anything."

Slowly unfolding her long body and standing, Yemaya gazed down at the woman who had captured her heart the year before. Her pale sapphire eyes burned with desire. Holding out her hand, she offered it to Dakota.

"Would I be wasting my time if I suggest we retire to our room?"

"Oh, I don't think so," Dakota replied impishly.

Yemaya sprinted away, letting out an uncharacteristically girlish, "Whoo hoo!"

"Last one there gets the top," she yelled, glancing back at Dakota and winking.

Gathering her notepad and belongings, the journalist shook her head slowly, muttering to herself.

"Damn! I hate losing like this!"

By the time she entered their hotel suite, Yemaya was in bed with the sheet pulled up to her chin, pretending to be asleep. Dakota decided to play along. Yawning, she undressed, slipped in next to her and turned on her side, her back toward Yemaya.

For several minutes they lay still, each wondering if the other was faking exhaustion or really feeling it. Just as Dakota was about to cave in to her urges, she felt an arm wrap around her waist and pull her backward.

"I guess you are too tired to play," whispered a husky voice. A warm breath caressed her left ear. Shivering, Dakota turned over and stared into the heated icy-blue gaze. Passion burned behind the steamy eyes.

"Tired?" she asked, her voice slightly squeaky. "I don't think so!"

"I would not want to take advantage of your weakened state."

"Since when?"

Groaning, they pressed into each other, both writhing in an effort to mold their bodies tightly together. Legs pressed against each other while knees nudged thighs apart. Hours later, they collapsed, exhausted from their lovemaking.

* * *

The two were peacefully snuggling under the sheets when Dakota's cell phone chirped. Reaching lazily over Yemaya's naked body, she grabbed it.

"Hello?"

"Daks?"

"Mom? What's up?"

Her mother rarely called unless it was important.

"It's Grams. She's very sick, honey! I'm not sure she has much time left."

"How much longer?" Dakota asked sitting up.

"A few days. Maybe a week if the spirits are kind."

"I'll be home tomorrow!"

"I'll pick you up at the airport."

"No, I can rent a car. It'll make things easier for everyone. You stay with Grams." She forced her voice to sound matter-of-fact. "Give her my love. I'll see you soon, Mom."

"I will. Be safe, Daks. Oh, and bring Yemaya along. It's about time she met the family, don't you think?"

"I'll let her know. Bye."

"Bye."

Turning to Yemaya, Dakota was about to say something when she was pulled into strong arms.

"I heard. Sonny will charter you a flight. I am so sorry."

"She's old, but she's a wonderful person," Dakota said in a tremulous voice. "Grams taught me a lot about life and about me. Between mom and her, they encouraged me to believe I could be anything I wanted."

"Well, no one can predict the future. Maybe it is not as bad as it sounds."

"Mom's a good doctor. She'll do everything she can, but I can't take my chances by not going."

"Of course not. I wish I could go with you, but my business in New York cannot wait. I can fly down afterward to meet this special grandmother of yours."

"That would be great."

Picking up her own phone, Yemaya called Sonny and explained the situation.

"Well, our vacation is officially over," she said after hanging up. "How about we get some sleep?" Nodding, Dakota settled into Yemaya's warm embrace.

6

Placing her cheek against Dakota's blonde head, Yemaya combed her fingers through the short strands. "It will be all right," she murmured.

CHAPTER 2

"**CHILD, IT BE** time to wake up."

Grumbling, Dakota burrowed deeper into the covers, enjoying the feel of the warm body beneath her.

"Go away!"

"Wake up, hon. We need ta jaw a bit."

Opening one eye sleepily, she stared at her great-great-spirit-grandmother, Maopa. Although her real name was also Dakota, the spirit chose to use the name given her by the Lakota, her adopted people.

"Hi Granny. It's been awhile."

"No need to be a botherin' you younguns' if'n we don't hafta. Yah two gettin' ta know each other better is a good thang."

"Yeah. Seems like every time we get a few weeks of peace and quiet, something happens to ruin it."

"That be how it is."

"I suppose. Granny, Pashna is dying! Mom said she doesn't have much time!" Dakota sobbed, unable to hold back tears.

"I knows, chile. That be one reason why I's here. She done had a good life. Her mind be as sharp as bear claws but her body is tarred. She done earned her rest."

"What if she dies before I see her again? You have to do something!"

"It ain't mine ta do. When yer time comes, it comes. Pashna is a stubborn old coot. She won't go without biddin' goodbye to her favorite granchile. The devil hisself couldn't win that battle."

"I hope so. I need to tell her how much I love her and to thank her for being there for me."

"Patience, youngun'. Don't go frettin' over somethin' yah can't do nothin' 'bout. Won't do you or her no good. If'n it'll make yah feel good, I give my word Pashna will be awaitin' for yah, even if I has to drag her cantankerous ole soul back to that withered carcass of her'n and shove it back inside."

Laughing at the image, Dakota hugged her ancestral spirit.

"I believe you would. You said Grams was one of the reasons you're here. Is there something else going on?"

"Well, I hate for yah to be passin' bad news on to Yemaya, but Dalnos be dead. He done gawn and kilt himself."

"Dead? What happened?"

"He hanged hisself. Made a noose from his beddin' and done it durin' the night."

"Damn! She's going to blame herself for this."

"He done what he wanted. Twern't no way he was gonna live with hisself wonst he knowed what he become. His dyin' thoughts were of his mama and the magic woman so she don't have nothin' to feel bad 'bout."

"I know, but she'll still think she could have done something to stop him. We haven't spent much time at home lately. She already feels guilty about not being at the trial. You know how she is."

"That I do. He knowed what he were. She gived him back the only one who ever loved him, his mama."

9

"I hope so, Granny. I can't say I'm sorry he's dead. Killing and raping those girls, and then trying to do the same to me didn't exactly endear him to me. Still, I feel sorry for him. No child deserves a father like his." Maopa nodded.

"Thanks for letting me know, Granny."

"Twern't nothin'."

"It means a lot to me. How are you and Mari doing?"

Grinning sheepishly, Maopa turned a strange shade of pink.

Must be a spirit thing, thought Dakota.

"Doin' fine. She be somethin' else, that Mari. Ain't never come acrosst anyone with so much...energy. She keeps me busy and she's puuurrre honey."

"I get the point. I'm happy for you two, but too much information. I need to go, Granny. Tomorrow's going to be a long day."

"Not to worry, chile. Get yerself home pronto. Say hello ta that magic woman."

Dakota closed her eyes. Two arms drew her close to a warm body.

CHAPTER 3

HUNDREDS OF miles away a lonely figure huddled near a street corner, the security light barely providing enough illumination for the intersection, let alone safety for anyone waiting beneath it. The woman leaned against the grimy wall of the old brick building, glancing hopefully at the cars as they passed in front of her. Shivering slightly from the cool breeze, she occasionally straightened up and walked toward the curb to watch the approaching vehicles. Most didn't stop. A few slowed and then sped off. Occasionally, one would pull over.

Leaning down, knees slightly bent, she engaged a driver in a conversation barely above a whisper. This one was graphically obnoxious. The woman stepped back and yelled an obscenity, before giving him the finger. Then she walked back to the building, which provided some protection against the wind.

Dressed in clear plastic platform boots, a short silver miniskirt, and a dark gray jacket over a skimpy tank top, she was a poster child for the stereotypical hooker. Her age was anyone's guess. The dimly lit area and thick makeup concealed numerous small wrinkles around her eyes and forehead. But nothing could hide the bitter disillusionment of a hard life filled with abuse and alcohol.

Belinda rarely thought about her past. The pain of betrayal had dulled over the years, leaving her with nothing more than the painful realization that she could have been more than just a whore. If her mother hadn't caved in to the pressures of the church when she discovered the priest was molesting Belinda, she could have made something of her life.

No one back then blamed Belinda for what happened. The church, however, advised her mother it was best to forgive the priest for his indiscretions of the flesh. The *unfortunate* incident became history.

The Bishop's offer of employment went a long way toward buy her mom's forgiveness. Belinda's suffering was irrelevant. Besides, suffering was good for the soul.

At seventeen, Belinda escaped her religious chains by running away. The only thing she had of value was her youthful body, and the hope for something better. Hope died quickly. By nineteen, she was a hardened prostitute. At twenty-one, a forced alcoholic. She didn't crave the booze so much as the high. It was a good way to drown out the memories that plagued her.

Only recently had she begun to feel almost human again, instead of a plaything. She was still a prostitute, but she had put her past behind her, thanks to the Sisterhood.

Tonight had not been very profitable. A few johns stopped by, wanting her to give them blow jobs. One was an old man. She actually considered doing him the favor until he called her a fucking whore.

An undercover cop tried to get her to initiate an offer. Over the years she had developed a sixth sense for cops. Growing tired of his game, she threatened to call the police. His expression was priceless. Cursing, he sped away. Belinda suspected he was a dirty cop looking for a freebie.

Taking out a cigarette, she lit it and inhaled deeply, holding her breath to prolong the warmth of the air filling her lungs. Eventually, she exhaled slowly. The smoke drifted away in the breeze.

Another car approached. Throwing the cigarette on the sidewalk, she stepped on it before walking over to the waiting vehicle. Leaning down, Belinda looked inside the darkened compartment. All she could see was the shadowy figure of a man.

"You lost?" she asked.

"No, I know where I'm at. I saw you standing here and thought you might be cold," the driver replied, his voice low and deliberate.

"So, you're offering me a ride? How thoughtful! Thanks, but I'm fine."

"How much?"

Surprised by the question, she hesitated, looking closely at the plush interior and then glancing up and down the street.

"Excuse me?"

"How much? What do you charge for your services?"

"I think you have me wrong."

"Oh! I thought...never mind. I apologize."

Again caught off guard, the prostitute wasn't sure how to respond.

"Look. Maybe I have the wrong idea. What exactly do you want?"

"Someone to talk with, nothing more. I thought perhaps you would like an easy night."

"And you think a whore is the person you need?"

"Let's just say some things aren't meant for normal people's consumption."

"Normal people. I like that. And what am I?"

"No offense intended, but you're a prostitute. Are you interested? I'll pay you $250 now and another $250 when I drop you off in a few hours."

"That's a lotta money for just listening," Belinda said, growing suspicious.

"I can afford it. Are you interested or not?"

Shrugging, she climbed into the car and buckled the seat belt.

"Your money, your time. I ain't doing nothing more than listening though."

When the driver nodded, Belinda leaned back and closed her eyes for a few seconds.

At least the car's warm, she thought as they pulled away from the curb.

"Where are we going and what do you feel like talking about?"

"Some place quiet...secluded. We'll talk then. Do you want to pick a spot or should I?"

Belinda shifted sideways and stared at the man. She could barely make out his features. Gloves concealed his hands, making it impossible to tell if he wore a ring, particularly a wedding band.

"You decide, as long as you bring me back here."

"As you wish."

They rode in silence while the mysterious man drove through partially abandoned streets. He turned down a narrow dirt road and they eventually ended up in the driveway of a small brick house with a wrap-around porch.

"My place."

"You don't think that's a little dangerous, bringing a stranger to your house?"

"Do you remember how we got here?"

"Not really."

14

"Then I don't see the problem. Is there one?"

"No, it doesn't bother me."

"Good! Come on in. I'll make us a warm drink."

Belinda followed the strange man into the house. A small fire burned brightly in the hearth, protected by glass doors. Without turning on the lights, he removed his jacket and walked toward a closed door.

"Kitchen," he said. "Make yourself at home. I'll be right back."

Removing her own jacket, Belinda tossed it on a chair and walked over to the fire. The faint smell of burning wood and the crackling was seductive, making her temporarily forget where she was. Only the sound of quiet footsteps brought her back to reality. Turning, she watched as her host put a tray on the coffee table. He still wore tight brown leather gloves.

"Coffee. I hope you don't mind. I never drink alcohol."

"That's fine. I've had more than enough for both of us." Belinda laughed.

"Good! Please have a seat. There's sugar and cream on the tray if you want them."

As he motioned to a recliner near the fire, he turned to face Belinda. It was the first time the prostitute had gotten a good look at the man.

Handing her a cup, he sat in his chair and leaned back, staring into the flames. The prostitute waited for him to start talking, but soon realized that the man was lost in thought. Glancing around, she noticed the room was sparsely furnished. There were no pictures or paintings on the walls, no items on the tables, nothing to give away anything personal about him or his life. It was almost as if he had no identity.

Minutes passed into over an hour. Belinda felt drowsy. Shifting her position, she leaned her head against the headrest. Blinking several times, she rubbed her eyes wearily. The man hadn't spoken since offering her the coffee. She decided a short nap wouldn't hurt anything. He'd wake her up when he was ready to talk.

Looking up from the flames, the man stood and walked over to the prostitute. Assured that she was asleep, he left the room, only to return a few moments later carrying something in his gloved hand. Holding the object up toward the light, he squirted a small stream of fluid from the tip. Then he pressed the syringe against the sleeping woman's arm and pushed the plunger, forcing the clear fluid into a small vein.

Belinda stirred and tried to push the man's hand away. Her tongue felt thick when she opened her mouth to speak.

"I'm sorry. I need you," the man apologized.

Picking up the phone, he dialed a number. Within minutes, two large men arrived. Motioning to the woman, the man left, leaving her future to them. They would remove any evidence of her presence in the house and lock up.

CHAPTER 4

THE FLIGHT HOME took a few hours. Yemaya arranged for a Jeep to be delivered to Dakota. The journalist had to admit that money made life a lot easier. She made a mental note to talk to her about that later. Dakota refused to live off her lover's wealth.

Driving down the almost deserted highway, she pulled out her cell phone and punched the number one, silently thanking the powers-that-be for speed dial. Listening to the familiar clicks, she scanned the mountain peaks, hoping for good reception. Until two years ago, very few cellular phones worked in this part of the country. With the new towers installed, it had gotten better.

"Hello?"

Dakota shivered and unconsciously squeezed her legs together at the tingling sensation building between her thighs. "Hey," she replied, her voice slightly breathless.

"Hey to you too! Are you okay?"

"Yeah! You caught me by surprise."

"You were the one that called," Yemaya said, laughing softly. "How was the flight?"

"Bumpy. The Jeep is cool. I'm not sure black is the best color, though."

"It was the only one available with all the bells and whistles. I know how you like to play with gadgets."

"Not while I'm driving. The satellite radio is nice."

"I can drive when I get there. Then you can play with the radio and the GPS system."

"GPS? In this car?"

"Like I said, bells and whistles."

"That's so cool! How long will you be in New York?"

"No more than a week. Andrei is arranging the funeral for Dalnos. He will be buried in our family cemetery until we can locate his mother's gravesite. Then we will transfer her remains and lay them next to his."

"That's a nice thing to do. I'm not so sure he deserves it."

"He did not deserve his childhood. That does not excuse what he did to those girls but it may give him and his mother peace. Other than that, Sonny and I need to finalize the details for the next tour. I will fly down afterward."

"So, you've decided not to retire, then?"

"I want you to be a part of the decision process. Until then, I might as well do one more show. It is the least I can do for my crew. If I do retire, their future must be assured. Ours too."

"You have doubts about us?"

"Not about my feelings. I want to make sure you are comfortable with our relationship."

"Listen, sweetie. If there's one thing you can bet your life on, it's that I'm comfortable. I love you. I intend on being in your life for a very long time."

Dakota could actually feel the relief on the other end.

"Thank you," Yemaya said. "I needed that."

"Me too. We'll talk more about this later? I'm almost to mom's place."

"Sounds good. Say hello to Tee for me. And Dakota? I miss you."

* * *

Tee was sitting on the porch of the old farmhouse anticipating her daughter's arrival. The trail of dust kicking up in the distance signaled the approach of a fast moving vehicle. Shading her eyes from the bright sunlight, she watched as a black Jeep sped toward her small farm. When the car stopped in front of the gate, Tee stood up and walked down the steps. Dakota climbed from the Jeep and hurried to embrace her mother.

"Hey, Mom. How's Grams?" she asked, anxiously.

"She's stable. I think the spirits are watching over her."

"I can believe that," Dakota agreed, mentally thanking Maopa for keeping her promise. "Is she awake?"

"She was about an hour ago."

"Can I see her? We can talk later."

"That's fine. Your grandmother is a stubborn woman. She said she wouldn't sleep until you got here. Come on in. I'm sure she's chomping at the bit. The old coot will be climbing out of bed if we don't head her off."

"Mother! Be nice!"

Her mother gave her a cheeky grin and opened the screen door, motioning for Dakota to go ahead.

Pashna was sitting up in bed, working on a needlepoint picture of two wolves in the snow. An old quilt lay across her lap and a cheap pair of glasses rested precariously on her nose as she squinted at the images in front of her. Glancing up when the door opened, the wrinkles of concentration turned into lines of joy as Dakota closed in to give her a hug.

"Hey, Gram, how are you feeling?"

"I'm still here, child. Spirits watch over the wicked." Chuckling, she patted an area of the mattress next to her. "Sit! It's about time you came home!"

Seeing the weariness in her grandmother's eyes, Dakota decided it might be better to let her rest for a while. Leaning over and kissing her cheek, she patted her hand affectionately.

"I feel grungy from the flight. Let me take a shower and get a quick bite to eat and I'll be back."

"Why of course. I'll just rest my eyes a bit."

"Thanks. Yell when you wake up. I have so much to tell you."

"So I've heard. I can't wait to hear about that young woman of yours. Tee says she's a looker."

"That she is! She might be here in a few days. You can judge for yourself."

"As long as she makes you happy, I don't care if she looks like an old dog, but it shore don't hurt none to be pleasing to the eye. Now run along. I ain't going nowhere."

Giving her a tender hug, Dakota left to look for her mother. Tee was sitting on the porch. A tray of sandwiches and iced tea sat on the small table between two rocking chairs.

"Food! You're a saint, mom."

Grabbing two halves, she plopped down in the chair and threw her left leg over its arm.

"Daks, that's no way for a lady to sit."

"Ahhmmm no lay...dy," Dakota replied, chewing a mouthful of food.

"You were when you left here! What kind of manners are you learning out there?"

Swallowing, Dakota stuck her tongue out.

"None! That's what's so great about being an adult."

"Well, I hope you don't act that way around Yemaya. I know she's better bred than that."

"Naw. I'm all prim and proper around her. I only act this way around you and everyone else."

Shaking her head, Tee laughed loudly.

20

"That's what I thought. No respect."

"Aw, you know I love you."

Both women fell into a comfortable silence while Dakota finished her sandwich and grabbed another half. As the sun slowly settled beyond the horizon, the sky turned an orangish-red before fading into darkness.

"I've forgotten what it's like to watch a sunset in these hills." Dakota spoke softly, not wanting to disturb the quietness of the night.

"We're lucky to live so close to the land. I sometimes feel our people have abandoned their old ways and their ancestors for today's modern conveniences. They miss out on the most important things in life, the simple things."

"I know. For a while I was one of those people. It's easy to get sucked into materialism."

Tee watched her daughter's face for a few moments. She was different from the restless daughter who had left home several years ago. More mature, and more comfortable with herself.

Yemaya! she thought.

"I have to admit I worry about you, but your grandma keeps telling me you need to spread your wings. Only then will you feel a closeness with the land."

"She's right. I know you love this place, mom. So do I, but...well, it's too small a world for me. There are things out there I never could have imagined. It's exciting and wild and wonderful, and I'm happy. *Really* happy."

"I know. I don't think I've ever seen you this relaxed. Yemaya has a lot to do with it, I imagine."

"She has everything to do with it. What it feels like to be near her or away from her, I...I—."

Patting Dakota's knee, Tee nodded her understanding.

"You don't have to explain; I can imagine. When is this wonder woman coming for a visit? You aren't keeping her away from us, are you?" Her mother teased. "I promise not to show her your baby pictures the first day."

"God, I hope not. Please?"

Noticing her daughter's pitiful look, Tee reluctantly agreed, but conditionally.

"Okay, as long as she doesn't ask."

"Thanks. I'll make sure she doesn't. I'm hoping we can both spend some quality time here later this year. She may be down in a few days, though, if she can break loose from business. I should check on Grams. Ummm...mom...is she going to be okay?"

"Yesterday, I would have sworn she had only a couple of days left. Today, I'm not so sure. Her heart sounds better and her blood pressure has dropped quite a bit. Maybe the spirits heard my prayers."

"I'm sure of it! If anyone deserves their help, it's you and Grams. I don't know anyone who's been more dedicated to our people or to keeping the old beliefs alive than you two. I used to think the spirits were just imaginary people like the mythology we learned in school, but..." Dakota let the sentence die.

Tee looked closely at Dakota.

"You have changed!"

The journalist shrugged, not sure what she wanted to say.

"Life does that."

"Daaakkkoooottttaaa!" cried a voice from inside the house.

"She certainly hasn't lost her voice. Later."

Jumping up, Dakota dashed inside.

"Hey Gram, did you get some rest?"

"Sure did, child. Come on over here and tell me what you've been doing. I want to hear all about this illusionist of yours. Don't leave out the juicy stuff, either."

"Graaamms!" Dakota exclaimed, slapping her grandmother's knee lightly and blushing.

Chuckling at her granddaughter's embarrassment, Pashna decided to give her a break. Later, she would wheedle more details about the mysterious woman.

"Well, how about we save that for another day. I don't think my heart could take that sort of excitement just yet. Start with the tamer stuff."

"There isn't anything tame about my life, especially since I met Yemaya. We've been together for almost a year and I've had more adventures in that time than in my whole life."

Launching into the details of how she and Yemaya had met, and describing the events that followed, Dakota talked for almost three hours. Occasionally, Pashna would interrupt to ask a question or make a comment, but mostly she lay quietly in bed, content to listen to the stories.

"Those are wonderful adventures. It sounds like the spirits are watching out for you."

"More than you'll ever know. Grams? I know you and mom have honored the spirits all your lives. Have you ever really seen or talked with any?"

"I don't need proof of their existence. I know they're real. They give life to the plants and the animals. I feel them all around me in the winds and the waters and here," thumping her chest with her closed hand, she smiled confidently, "inside of me."

"I know. I've felt the same things lately."

Dakota's words revealed more to Pashna than anything else she could have said. Nodding her head wisely, she looked into the green eyes so much like her own and saw that there was truth in her words.

"You are blessed. They have shown themselves to you as they have to me in times of need. I don't speak of this often.

Many of our people have forsaken our traditions and think me a crazy old woman. I'm happy for you."

"Me too. Now, it's time for you to rest. I'll bring you in one of mom's sandwiches and some juice. Tomorrow, if you behave, I'll tell you about my visit to the spirit world."

"I can't wait. It's good to see you, Daks. I've missed you," Pashna said, sliding a bit further down onto the bed. Pulling one of the pillows from behind her grandmother's head, Dakota placed it next to her. Then she leaned down and kissed one weathered cheek as she gently touched the other with her fingertips.

"You too. I'll be right back with some food."

Dakota hesitated by the door and looked back at her grandmother.

"Grams?"

"What, child?" asked Pashna, looking up from her needlepoint.

"I love you."

"I love you, too. Now get out of here before we get all mushy, and put mustard on that sandwich. You know how I hate mayonnaise."

"I sure do. I'll be back in a jiff," Dakota said, laughing at the scrunched up face her grandmother made when she mentioned mayonnaise.

CHAPTER 5

YEMAYA HAD JUST arrived back at the penthouse when the phone rang.

"Lysanne."

"Hey, sweetie! How are things?"

"Hey to you, too." Yemaya laughed, thrilled at hearing Dakota's voice. "Things are going well. Sonny wants me to look at some investment property. It could prove valuable for an idea I have."

"Sounds intriguing. Listen, Gram is doing better. She's almost back to her old self again. I'm thinking of heading back in a few days. Care to take a little detour to Baltimore?"

"That works for me. Let me know when and I can have Sharon fly down to pick you up."

"Cool! I can't wait to see you. I've missed you."

"I miss you, too. What are you going to do tonight?"

"Mostly hang out with mom and Grams. I might go into town to visit a few friends."

"Well, go play. I have to work on the new show."

"Gee! Thanks. I feel like I've just been demoted to a child. Listen, if I get home before you, I'll pick you up at the airport."

"Sounds good. Until then, stay out of trouble."

"Yeah, yeah. Look who's talking. Love you! Bye, bye."

"You too. Bye."

The next day Dakota caught up on the latest gossip from both her grandmother and mother. Taking advantage of her daughter's visit, Tee decided to meet a few friends she had neglected during Pashna's illness. Pashna secretly confided in Dakota that Tee was turning into a stuffy old woman.

Dakota's departure on Tuesday left everyone a little melancholy, but she promised to fly back with Yemaya before their return to Moldova.

"If you two behave, I might even be able to get you an invitation to Yemaya's castle."

"Might?" challenged her mother, crossing her arms and glaring at her ominously.

"Might!"

"Don't you worry about it, child," Pashna interrupted. "I'll make sure your mom behaves herself. I haven't met this magic woman, but I'm figurin' she's already family."

"She is that! I'll tell you when to pack. I love you two. Oh, and behave. Neither of you are spring chickens."

Looking at each other, the two women grinned.

"Children!" Tee said, rolling her eyes. "No respect!"

"Your daughter! She takes after you," Pashna teased.

Arriving in Baltimore, Dakota caught a cab to her flat and then threw herself onto her bed, exhausted. Rhonda, a close friend, had left a message on the refrigerator that a salad was in the fridge. She'd call her later to catch up on the news. Along with the note was a newspaper clipping advertising a newly discovered nightclub in town. The words "check this out" were written in the margin. She was almost asleep when her phone chirped.

"Devereaux," she replied, yawning.

"You sound tired," whispered a husky voice, sending a shiver down Dakota's spine.

"Damn you're good!" Dakota replied, rolling over on her stomach.

The soft laughter made her groan. "Are you all right?"

"No! I've gone from tired to horny. How are you?"

"A similar state and no way to scratch that particular itch. How was the flight?"

Dakota grimaced. "Long. I'm going to have an early night. Rhonda left me an ad about a new nightclub. I might check it out tomorrow. No use dragging you to some typical dyke hangout when you get here."

"And typical would be?"

"You know. Loud music, a little dancing, pool tables. That sort of thing."

"Well, I have never visited a typical dyke bar so I might find it interesting. Anyway, I just wanted to hear your voice. Get some rest. I should be in Baltimore in a couple of days. Call me tomorrow."

"Count on it. Bye. Love you."

"Bye...and you too." Yemaya replied softly.

CHAPTER 6

THE WAREHOUSE district north of the Bay Tunnel appeared abandoned. Except for the occasional security patrol and a few winos, few people visited the area after midnight. It was considered one of the most dangerous places to be after sunset and the perfect place to meet for private conversations. Once the patrol car had passed, two figures emerged from the shadows to continue their conversation.

"This is the last one! I'm not going after any more prostitutes!" the shorter man declared angrily, his voice echoing slightly between the two metal buildings.

"Keep your voice down!" hissed his companion, looking around nervously. "You'll do what the boss wants! She says she wants ten by the end of the month...and ten it is!"

"Well, she can do it without me! Catrina's getting too greedy and too careless. Someone's going to get suspicious and start asking questions."

"We'll worry about that if, and when, it happens. Until then, we follow orders. Now, where's the whore?"

"The boys picked her up this morning. She was put with the others."

"Good."

"What did Catrina say about the young woman I picked up two weeks ago?" the first man asked, glancing toward a movement several buildings away. He was sure he saw someone lurking nearby.

"She hasn't decided anything, yet. Knowing the boss, she's not turning the girl loose," the other man replied. "And quit fidgeting. There's no one out there, Gregori."

"Catrina's a fool. I'm telling you, right now the Lysannes aren't a problem. They will be if Catrina does something stupid. Release the girl and send her home. Buy her a ticket, give her a few bucks, and she'll forget about all of this. She's a fuckin' whore. All she wants is the money, and she sure as hell ain't going to the cops. Hell, she isn't even an American. Immigration will deport her once they find out what she's doing."

"We can't take the chance. We'll all end up in jail if she fingers you."

"Christ, Ivan! You're as paranoid as that bitch you work for. She won't remember anything, especially me. That's why I used Rohypnol. And since when has my work ever been questionable?" Gregori demanded. "I'm telling you we can't keep grabbing women off the streets. Even whores are missed by someone."

Ivan sighed. Gregori was probably right, but he had worked for Catrina long enough to know it was in his best interests to follow orders, no matter how unreasonable they seemed. His boss was ruthless.

"That's not our concern. This girl is a problem."

Gregori shook his head in disgust.

"I'm telling you, let her go."

"And I'm telling you it's not that simple! This girl's cousin works for the Lysannes. That complicates everything. The boss said to get rid of her."

"Whatever, Ivan. I'm tired of the whole thing. I told you in the beginning that the sex-trade business was a bad idea. Kidnapping and selling women overseas is too risky, even with whores. You'd think those stuffy pricks would want less experienced women."

"Why should we care why they want them?"

"I don't, but I do care about my skin. I'm finished with this shit." Gregori said, disgustedly. Throwing up his hands, he turned and walked away.

Gregori took only a few steps when something slammed into his back. Momentarily stunned, he turned to look at Ivan, confused. His companion held a small gun in his hand, the barrel covered with a silencer. When he tried to speak, he felt short of breath. Something warm filled his mouth and he coughed, swallowed and then gagged. Reaching up to wipe away the spittle, he stared at the bright red stain on his fingers. Ivan walked up to him, forcing the gun against his ribs.

"Sorry, my friend. No one quits without the boss' say so. Those are the rules."

Gregori never heard the muffled pop as the bullet punched past his ribs, ripping through a lung and into his heart.

Ivan caught the body as it slumped and gently lowered the dead man to the pavement. He had known Gregori for several years. This was the part of his job he hated. Slowly, he placed the gun on the dead man's chest, crossed his hands over it and then reached up with a gloved hand to close Gregori's eyes. The dead should never be left looking at the living. Standing, he walked away.

* * *

"Gregori didn't need to be eliminated!" Ivan shouted, slamming his fist on the desk in front of him. "He'd never have told anyone anything."

"I can't take the chance," replied the woman calmly seated in front of him, her accent very mid-European. "He knew the rules. I made an example of him to remind the others... and you, just in case you're getting too sentimental. Of course, if I really thought that, Breshni would be standing here and you'd be lying out there with your friend. Now, enough about Gregori. What about the Lysannes?"

Ivan began pacing.

"Raidon Lysanne is in Moldova. He may have heard something about the girl by now, but I doubt if he knows about us or the business. It's only a matter of time, though. As long as he remains in his country, he's untouchable. Our best chance to eliminate him is through his sister, Yemaya. If we can get rid of her, he'll come to the States to retrieve the body."

"Where is she?" Catrina asked, twirling her pen nonchalantly in her right hand.

"Last I heard, New York. My contacts are tracking her and a female journalist who's been traveling with her. They're very close. Seems the whole damn family is queer."

"Something about gays you don't like, Ivan?" Catrina's voice turned cold.

"You're damn right! Men fucking men! Women eating pussy! It's not natural."

"Well, personally, I find 'eating pussy', as you so tastefully put it, quite satisfying," she replied, leaning back in her chair and staring coolly at her second-in-command.

Ivan stopped his pacing and looked at the woman. She couldn't be more than fifty-six, slim and very attractive. Her dark brown hair was shoulder length and slightly wavy, framing an oval face with flawless olive skin. Brown eyes the color of dark honey gleamed with a sadistic humor as she patiently sat through his mental appraisal. Her right eyebrow, raised slightly, emphasized the slight smirk on her lips.

"Nothing to say, Ivan? You had a lot to say before. Don't let my position stop you. I like to know as much as possible about my employees."

"Like I said, it's not natural. I think that says everything," Ivan replied, unwilling to reveal anything more about himself. A woman like her could make him disappear, no questions asked. Ivan wasn't foolish enough to believe he was the only one in this line of business working for her.

Catrina laughed. Men were so predictable. They assumed she was straight and were intimidated when they found she preferred women. Occasionally, she'd meet a man who interested her. Her eyes roamed up and down Ivan's body, assessing his looks and build.

"Another time then," she promised. "So, what do you suggest we do about Ms. Lysanne?"

"Nothing. We don't know enough about her. She probably doesn't know about the girl yet. Whores aren't exactly close to their friends and families."

"As long as it doesn't take very long. What about the girl? Have you taken care of her?"

"She's isolated from the others until we decide what to do with her. If we kill her, the Lysannes will definitely get involved. Gregori may have been right about cutting her loose."

"I'll think about it. But I want to look at her before I make a decision. Bring her to me," ordered Catrina. Her eyes gleamed with anticipation at having a new *toy* to play with.

"Here?"

"No, you fool. To my place. Tonight. Say around eleven."

"As you wish."

"Remember that, Ivan."

Ivan left, wondering why he had ever gotten involved with this woman. The fact was, he had no choice and he knew it. Catrina Drenkova was a powerful woman. What Ms. Drenkova wanted, Ms. Drenkova got, no questions asked. He had sold his soul to the devil, and she was it.

CHAPTER 7

THE NAME OVER the entrance read 'Lilith's Den.' The sign boldly displayed on the door read 'PRIVATE CLUB, WOMEN ONLY. ALL UNAUTHORIZED MALES WILL BURN IN HELL!'

Damn, I like this place already, Dakota thought. Folding the small paper with the club's address scribbled along the edge, she tucked it into her coat pocket. From the number of cars in the parking lot, it was a popular hangout. Hopefully, the owner wasn't one of those people who posted a sign and then let guys in anyway. She'd seen that too many times.

A blast of warm air welcomed her when she entered the building. A large woman with several tattoos on her forearms and shoulders greeted her.

"ID, please," she demanded in a gravelly voice.

"Sure," Dakota said, pulling her license from her wallet. "I'll take that as a compliment," she added, jokingly.

"It's policy. No ID, no pass. Thanks."

Handing the license back, she motioned toward a side door.

"You can check your jacket there. It's mandatory. The boss thinks it's safer and friendlier that way. No surprises, if you know what I mean."

"No problem. It beats having to worry about it."

After checking her coat, she wandered down the hallway and into the main room. Gray swirls of smoke floated randomly around the bar, giving it a mysterious atmosphere. 'No smoking' signs were posted on the walls and Dakota realized the haze was produced by machines concealed in the ceiling. The smoke enhanced the laser lights flashing around the wooden dance floor on her right. Several couples gyrated to the fast beat of techno music. To her left was a long, black enameled bar lined with women talking loudly. Nowhere in sight was there a male.

So far so good.

Walking to the bar, she pulled out some dollar bills and waited for one of the two bartenders to notice her. After a few minutes, a young woman stepped in front of her and smiled.

"Whatcha having?"

"Corona and lime. Thanks."

"One Corona and lime, coming up."

Watching the woman walk to a nearby refrigerated locker, the journalist was intrigued by the bartender's appearance. Short red hair, highlighted with purple tips and combed into spikes, she was about Dakota's height but not quite as heavy. An orange tank top and brown jeans emphasized her slender physique. A chain link belt finished off the wardrobe. Bringing the beer back, she popped the cap and stuffed a lime slice into the top.

"Here ya go. Three bucks."

Dakota gave her four and took a sip from the bottle, glancing around the room at the activity.

"Nice place. You ladies are serious about the 'no guys' thing."

"Yeah. That's one thing Lilith insists on. Less trouble."

"Is it always this busy?"

"Fridays are. If you're looking for a quieter place, come on Thursday or head on down to Lazy Susan's. She has a few pool tables and caters to the country-western crowd."

"Not my style. This is perfect."

"Good! Soooo...what's a nice girl like you doing in a place like this? I can't believe you're cruising. A looker like you has to be taken."

Laughing, Dakota switched her gaze back to the bartender just in time to catch a small, fiery glint in her dark brown eyes.

"That is sooo cliché."

"Yep, but it's a good starter and always works."

"I can imagine. Actually, a friend of mine left me a copy of an ad about this place and I decided to check it out."

"By yourself? Why didn't you bring her along?"

"Rhonda? She's as straight as they come. Not that she isn't cool. She just isn't a night person."

"Well, I can't believe you're unattached. Oh...by the way, my name's Agra."

"Hi. Mine's Dakota. Agra, eh? That's an unusual name."

"It's a nickname. My real one's too long to pronounce and too odd to remember." Agra laughed. "Dakota's a nice name. So, are you or aren't you?"

"Attached? Definitely!"

"Where's the lucky lady? She can't be dumb enough to let you run around a place like this all by yourself. Too many cats on the prowl looking for kittens to gobble up."

"This kitten has teeth and claws...and my significant other doesn't control what I do or where I go."

Agra raised her brows questioningly.

"I mean, she's not the controlling type. The relationship wouldn't work if she was."

"Ah! An independent woman and in a relationship. How refreshing! Oops! Gotta get someone a drink. Be back in a few."

Waving goodbye, the bartender left to serve a woman at the end of the counter. As Agra leaned over the bar, the woman leaned in, their heads almost touching. Long, straight black hair swung forward, blocking both of their faces as they engaged in a quiet conversation.

After a few seconds, the woman turned to look at Dakota. The journalist gasped. From a distance the woman reminded Dakota of Yemaya; tall, dark and sensual-looking. The eyes were a shocking blue/black, very much like a blue onyx Dakota had seen in a jewelry store. Picking up her drink, Dakota moved to take a seat at a nearby table.

"I wonder if she's family," Dakota mumbled to herself.

"Do you always talk to yourself?"

Turning her head, she stared at the woman who had been talking to Agra at the bar. *God what a color,* Dakota thought, staring into the most amazing eye color she had ever seen. There were moments when they seemed black, and then morphed into icy blue.

"Always. It's a bad habit of mine."

"I see. We have something in common then. I'm Lilith, the owner of this place."

"Hi, I'm Dakota."

"You seem distracted. Are you okay?"

"I was just thinking."

"That's never good in a place like this. You're supposed to forget all of your troubles here. Anything I can help you with?" asked the woman, sitting down at the table.

"Not really. And actually I was just thinking about you. You remind me of someone. It caught me by surprise," Dakota confessed, embarrassed.

"Ah. I hope it's someone you like."

Laughing, Dakota smiled for the first time.

"Oh, definitely!"

"Good. Does she reciprocate?"

"Completely!"

"I see. So, where is she, if you don't mind me asking? You're too cute to be in a place like this on your own. Some of these women are very predatory."

"That's the second warning I've gotten since I walked in here. Is there something I should know about this place?"

Chuckling softly, Lilith shook her head. "Nothing beyond the norm. I like to look after my customers, especially newcomers. We get a lot of young women who want a little excitement and then get more than they can handle."

"Believe me, excitement is the last thing I need in my life. I'm here for the ambiance, nothing more."

"That you'll find in abundance. So, what do you do for a living?"

"I'm a journalist."

"Really! How exciting! Have I read any of your reports?"

"Probably not. I freelance for a magazine called Illusions and Magic...and a few others. Most people have never heard of them unless they're into that sort of thing."

Lilith smiled and leaned in conspiratorially.

"Well, between you and me, I have a subscription," Lilith confided. "You're not planning on doing something on my place, are you?" she asked casually.

Lilith stared into Dakota's green eyes as if trying to read her thoughts. Had the journalist not experienced the dark intensity of Yemaya's gaze, she would have been unable to withstand this woman's scrutiny. Realizing they were both staring, the two lowered their eyes simultaneously and then chuckled.

"Miss Lilith, do you want another drink?" asked Agra, interrupting the conversation.

"Please, Agra, and another Corona for Dakota, on the house."

"Sure thing. You warning her not to get picked up by any strangers?" teased the bartender, winking at Dakota.

"I think she can take care of herself. Besides, I hear you've already warned her."

"Just doing my job, boss. Can't have new clientele being harassed now, can we?"

"No, we can't. Thanks Agra. Now where were we...oh... the magazine. You've been doing an exposé on the Illusionist. Rumor has it you two are an item."

"I'd never have taken you for someone that listens to gossip."

"You'd be surprised what you can learn from gossip."

"I guess. You remind me of her. She's tall and dark, like you. And I think you might be just as dangerous, in your own way," Dakota observed, sipping her beer.

"Dangerous? I'll take that as a compliment. What's she like? She's quite beautiful if the pictures are any indication... and mysterious."

"Very. One day, I'm going to discover how she does those illusions."

"And then what?" Lilith asked, leaning back in her chair.

"I don't know."

Lilith glanced around the room, clearly checking out the customers.

"Well, I need to circulate a bit. Thanks for coming in. I hope you have a good time. Let me know if you need anything."

"Thanks, I will."

Getting up, Lilith motioned to Agra to bring Dakota another drink. As she strolled away, the journalist couldn't help but admire her graceful movements, and the hot glances she received from other women in the room. The red tank top and tight black jeans emphasized her long, sleek figure and sensual grace.

"She likes you," whispered a soft voice in her ear.

Jerking around, Dakota found another woman standing slightly behind her. Silver hair and amber brown eyes were an unusual combination. Smooth, pale skin was enough of a hint that she was not the outdoorsy type. Still, if she looked as good without her clothes as she did in them, she would be hot, thought Dakota. Realizing she was staring and wondering where that thought came from, Dakota smiled sheepishly.

"Lilith or the barkeep?"

"Lilith definitely, and probably Agra, too...and hi, my name's Cammie."

"Hi. Mine's Dakota."

"Dakota. Nice name. Do you mind if I join you?"

"No, not at all. This is my first visit. I really don't know anyone. Everyone seems extremely friendly so far."

"It's a great place to hang out, and it's safe."

"What's with this place? First Agra and Lilith warn me about predator women, and now you talk about it being safe. You aren't one of those predators they're talking about?"

Cammie laughed. "Trust me, I don't need to hunt for women. They find me easily enough."

"I can believe that." Dakota grinned and then wondered about her own boldness. The conversation was interrupted when Agra brought over two drinks.

"Hey, Cammie. Good to see you."

"You too, cutie. How've you been?"

"Samo, samo. You know how it is."

"Yeah. You hear anything about your girls?" Cammie asked, lowering her voice slightly.

"Not yet. I put the word out, but they seem to have just disappeared."

"Well, I'll keep an ear open, too. Hopefully, they'll show up soon."

"Thanks. Kali and I would appreciate it. Oh, the boss sent these over and said to enjoy."

"Tell her thanks."

Dakota sat quietly listening to the exchange. When the bartender left, Cammie turned her full attention on the woman in front of her and smiled. The effect was almost devastating. Dakota's hand shook as she sucked in a deep breath, struggling to collect her thoughts. Picking up the beer, she took a quick sip, hoping it would calm her unusual reaction.

Whoa, she thought, wondering what had just happened.

"Ummm...something happen to Agra's daughters?" she asked, unable to think of anything else to say.

"Daughters? Oh, you mean her girls. No, just some of her and Kali's friends. Are you okay? You're a little flushed."

"Oh. Yeah. Must be the beer. Lilith's given me two freebies. I'll be lucky to finish the second."

"That'll do it." Cammie's laughter made Dakota feel suddenly warm. Clamping her legs together, she resisted the urge to press her hand to her pubic area. *It must be jet lag.*

"They like to keep customers happy," Cammie said.

"And you?"

"I help them."

"Keep customers happy?" Dakota asked coyly, and then blushed, appalled at her brazen question. *Where in the hell did that come from?*

Cammie sat and looked at her for a few seconds without replying. Her brown eyes gleamed, speculatively.

"Not like that," she finally replied.

"Gosh. I'm so sorry. I don't know where that came from," Dakota said, turning a darker shade of red.

"Don't worry about it. It was a fair question."

Reaching over, she squeezed Dakota's hand. The contact re-ignited the warmth, causing the journalist to swallow nervously. Staring blankly at the hand covering hers, she wasn't sure what she should say or even if she could say anything.

Finally, shaking her head slightly, she looked up, making eye contact with honey brown eyes. The heat between her thighs increased. Shifting uncomfortably, she crossed her ankles and flexed her leg muscles. If she had been alone she would have rubbed herself.

If I was alone, I wouldn't be feeling like this. "I...uh...I think I need to go. I may be coming down with something," she murmured. *I know I am!*

"I understand. Maybe another night. Do you want me to drive you home?"

"No. My car's outside. Thanks, though. I'm sure it's nothing. It was nice meeting you," Dakota stammered, "and I'd like to see you again. Maybe when I feel better."

Both women stood simultaneously. Cammie walked Dakota to her car. Once she was seated, Cammie leaned down and kissed her gently on the cheek.

"Don't worry about it. It happens all the time," she whispered and walked away.

Dakota's heart was pounding so hard she could hear it. Feeling weak, she sat for a few minutes, confused and finding it difficult to breathe. Finally, almost in a daze, she started the car and drove slowly back to her apartment. Quickly undressing, she crawled into bed, pulled the cool sheets over her heated body and fell asleep, forgoing a badly needed cold shower.

CHAPTER 8

TWO DAYS LATER, Dakota watched nervously as the plane glided toward the landing strip. Crosswinds were gusting at 20 knots, creating hazardous conditions for the small charter jet. She knew Yemaya's pilot was extremely capable but could still imagine the petite woman fighting the controls to keep its descent as smooth as possible.

Finally, as if in a last desperate effort to force the plane onto the strip, she saw it drop, rise slightly and then drop again, the rear wheels making contact with the tarmac. The nose finally settled, causing the plane to fishtail a few times before slowing and coasting to a halt near the terminal.

A small door on the side of the plane opened inward and steps were lowered to the ground. When the pilot stuck her head out, she saw Dakota standing next to her Jeep and waved. Then she backed inside and Yemaya stepped out, ducking her head to avoid bumping it against the airframe.

Seeing Dakota, she smiled and gave her a thumbs up. Laughing, the journalist hurried over and pulled her head down for a quick kiss.

"That was scary," she said, her voice quivering slightly.

"If Sharon had not been the pilot, I would agree," Yemaya said, calmly. "How is your grandmother?"

"Better than ever. I think Mari and Grandma Dakota have something to do with it."

"Could be...or maybe she is just a tough lady?"

"Well, I don't care what it is. I'm not ready for her to leave either. By the way, she's looking forward to meeting you. Mom's been telling her a few things about us. I told her we'd probably be back in a few weeks. I hope that's okay."

"Pick a date and I can have Sharon reserve the plane. I look forward to hearing their stories about you," Yemaya teased.

Rolling her eyes, Dakota slapped her lover's arm. During the ride back to the apartment, she described her visit to the nightclub and her encounter with Cammie.

"I really can't believe how easy it was to talk to her. You'd have thought we were long lost friends."

"It happens like that sometimes. You meet someone and feel the connection. It happened with us."

"This's different. If you're up to it later tonight or tomorrow, maybe we can drop in for a few drinks. I think you'll find it an interesting place."

"Sounds like a plan."

* * *

Agrat-bat-mahlaht was livid. The air crackled with electricity from the anger she was unsuccessfully attempting to control.

"What do you mean she's disappeared?" she demanded, turning to glare at her business partner and long-time friend seated in the recliner near the fireplace.

"Like I said, she's gone, vanished, poof. You know!" replied the dark-haired woman, unimpressed by the fiery theatrics. She had known Agra too long to be disturbed by the colorful fireworks popping noisily in the background. "None of the girls have seen her for several days."

"No one just disappears like that, at least not from the Sisterhood. First it was Jennie, then Sasha and now her. Who saw her last?"

"Kiera."

"Get her in here!"

Taking out her cell phone, Kali quickly dialed a number.

"Shandra, tell Kiera the boss wants to see her...No, it won't wait. If she's not here in fifteen minutes, she can kiss her next paycheck goodbye...Good."

Snapping the lid shut, she grinned wickedly, her lavender eyes twinkling.

"They do love their money."

"It's the only security they have. Too bad they can't take it with them," replied Agra, sarcastically.

"Don't be so overly dramatic," Kali chastised. Picking up her glass of wine, Agra sat on the sofa across from her companion, crossed her legs, leaned against the backrest and closed her eyes.

"We've been doing this too long, Kali. No matter how hard we try, we can't protect them all the time."

"I know. Sometimes, I feel like we've wasted our lives trying to win battles we're destined to lose."

"Me too. Then I think about those we saved and it makes all of this worth it, doesn't it?"

"I suppose," Kali agreed, somewhat reluctantly. A knock on the door interrupted their musings. Getting up, Kali walked over and opened it, motioning for the plump, black woman to enter. "Thanks for coming,"

"Like I hads a choice. I can't be affordin' to lose my pay," Kiera grumbled, glancing toward Agra.

"If you saved some of that money, you could," Agra replied, coolly. "We pay you plenty."

"Oh, I ain't complainin', Miss Agra. I'm just mouthin' off a little. You know I be that way."

"Yes, I do. It's a habit I'd work on correcting. When was the last time you saw Belinda? No one's seen her for days."

"Thursday afternoon. She said she was gonna see if she could make a few extra bucks on the side. Not that you don't be payin' her plenty. She saw this real cute dress she was wantin' and was 'fraid someone would get it before she got enough money saved."

"Why didn't she just call me?" Agra asked, frustrated at hearing one of her whores had ignored a basic rule of the Sisterhood. "She could have borrowed the money if it meant that much."

"She thought you'd be lecturin' her about wastin' her money...kinda like you do me sometimes."

"Are you or the others unhappy with our arrangements?"

"Oh no, Miss Agra. You pays us well. No one else ever cared enough to give us medical coverage or the protection you do. Shit, you even gives us a savin's account so we can get off the streets if we want to. I might be able to retire in a few years now. Miss Kali and you be like family. We ain't never had no women pimps before, you know."

"Then why do you still take unnecessary chances? The rules we made are for your protection."

Kiera shrugged.

"Old habits hard to break. Before you come along, we never had no one cared much for us...not like you. The pimps, they took most everything we made. The last few months are like a dream, you know? I guess we just feels it ain't gonna last. Some of the pimps on the street, they been hasslin' us, sayin' they was gonna get you two sooner or later. Talk is it's gonna be sooner. Then the Sisterhood ain't gonna be no more."

When Agra lunged to her feet, Kiera jumped back, startled at how quickly her boss moved.

"Who's making these threats?"

"Just some small-time pimps. We know it's all talk so we don't say nothin'."

"I don't care how small the talk is. No one threatens my whores. I want to know who they are. One of them might have grabbed Belinda."

Kiera looked hesitantly at Kali and then back at Agra.

"Chicklet, mostly. He's the main mouth."

"Chicklet?"

"Yeah. He's a mixed-breed that hangs out on the strip near the bars. Thinks he's a real tough guy but he's all talk. Always poppin' gum."

"How many whores work for him?"

"A dozen. Maybe more."

"You ever hear any complaints from them?"

"Nah. Like I said, he's all mouth but he got game. He takes half their money but he make sure they got good protection. If anyone roughs up his hoes, he hunts 'em down and they pay double. Then he splits it fifty-fifty with the hen house. Most of his hoes chose him up cuz he takes good care of 'em...better than the pimps on the east side."

"A pimp with some ethics, eh?" Kali asked, interrupting the conversation. "Well, if you ever hear anything different, let us know. We'll deal with the assholes on the other side of town in a few days. Agra and I plan on paying them a little visit. Right now our girls are our main concern. Now, have you heard any street talk about any other whores that have disappeared?"

"No. Everyone's still lookin' for Jennie and Sasha. Those two, they just up and disappeared. Jennie, she was a pro. Been doin' it for years. She wouldn't break none of your rules, Ms. Agra. And Sasha, I tried to tell her not to go out by herself, but you know how kids is. There's talk about some that went missin' a few months back before you all come. We just figured they took off cuz they wanted out. Their pimp was real unhappy."

"Alright. Call us if you hear something, and put the word out on Belinda. Someone may have seen or heard something."

"I'll tell them. Maybe one of the johns know somethin' at the Mission. Me and the girls will check around."

"Good. You can go. Be careful. Until we find out what happened to her and the others, I don't want anyone working by themselves. All sisters work in pairs. No leaving the strip in anyone's car unless they know the person. If a driver wants your services, he or she can get it in the back seat, an alley or nearby motel. I'll make arrangements with a few owners to have rooms available. Also, make sure at least two girls see their customer's faces. Got it?"

"Yes, Miss Agra. I'll pass the word, but it's gonna put a crimp in our business."

"I don't care. And Kiera, anyone who breaks the rules is out of the Sisterhood."

"Yes ma'am!"

Once Kiera was gone, Kali waited patiently for her friend to calm down. The high level of energy that had been bouncing around her earlier settled to an occasional flicker. The demoness was always amazed that humans never felt the tremendous power flowing from Agra whenever she was upset or angry. Then again, perhaps it was just as well. It would probably prove fatal to most mortals.

"I don't like this!" Agra said. "You'd think after all these years, we'd be able to keep better track of them. What's happening to us? Our powers continue to weaken. There was a time..." Not wanting to dwell on the past, Agra let the thought die.

"The world has changed. I'm not so sure we're any weaker," Kali said. "Whoever's responsible for this will wish they had never been born! Hell will be paradise compared to what I'll do to them," she promised.

Agra had no doubt Kali would fulfill her threat. Her ability to inflict pain far exceeded her compassion for their prostitutes...and her compassion for them was infinite.

"What do you think of our newest customer?" Agra asked, deciding to change the topic.

"Which one?"

"You know who! The one Cammie was talking to last night."

"Oh her! She seems okay."

Agra laughed at the demoness' sulky tone.

"You can't really be jealous of her?"

"Don't be an ass!" Kali snapped. "What's there to be jealous of? She's human."

"You tell me!"

"You're just imagining it. Like I said, she seems nice enough. Besides, how would I know? You and Lilith talked with her. I was busy with the other customers."

"That's true, but I noticed you watching her and Cammie a lot. If I didn't know better I'd say you were interested in one of them."

"I don't have time for relationships!"

"If you say so."

Obviously something was bothering Kali, but she wasn't ready to talk about it.

"I suppose we should head on out to the bar. Lilith wants us in early tonight. She wants to have a few words with the ex about the whores. Dis may be involved."

"I doubt that! He's not about to piss her off. The last time nearly cost him his kingdom." Kali laughed. "And to think she gave up Adam for him."

"Did you ever meet that guy?"

When Kali shook her head no, Agra put her arm around her friend's shoulders and started for the door.

"Well, let me tell you about him. He may have been good-looking, but when it came to charisma..."

CHAPTER 9

WHEN DAKOTA and Yemaya walked into the bar, several women turned to stare at them. Tall and dark, Yemaya looked every bit the seductress in her leather jeans and burgundy silk blouse. Like a panther, comfortable in her skin, she seemed to flow across the floor.

Dakota was the perfect balance to Yemaya's darkness with her own golden aura. Blonde hair and standing several inches shorter than the Illusionist, she was dressed in designer jeans, a coral colored tank top and a black nylon windbreaker trimmed in a bright floral pattern.

"What do you think?" Dakota asked.

Laughing, Yemaya shook her head. "We just arrived. Give me time to look around."

"Aw come on. You have great instincts. At least admit it's coo-el looking inside."

"Okay. It is coo-el looking. You pick out a table and I will get us the drinks. Then we can discuss the ambiance of the place."

"Sure. I'll be over there in the corner. I know how you like to people watch."

Leaning down, Yemaya gave her a quick kiss on the lips and then ruffled her hair.

51

"Thanks. See you in a few."

* * *

Lilith saw the two women enter the club and immediately knew their souls were forever linked. The energy between them was so finely interwoven it would be almost impossible to separate the strands...almost.

Recognizing Yemaya from her pictures in the magazines, she had to admit that the Illusionist was extraordinarily beautiful. More important though, her life force was unusually strong. Had she not known who she was, Lilith would still have sensed her presence and the darkness within, something very familiar to her. She hadn't felt that in a long time.

As she watched the two women separate, she had signaled to Agra to serve the Illusionist. Yemaya now carried two drinks to the table where Dakota was waiting.

"Good evening, Dakota," Lilith said, walking over to the table. "It's nice to have you back."

"Lilith! Thanks. Yemaya, this is the owner of the club. She likes to meet all of her clientele, a very old-fashioned concept, wouldn't you say?" Dakota teased.

"A good business practice," Yemaya commented, putting down her drink. She noticed the woman's sparkling black eyes. "Nice to meet you, Lilith."

"And you, Yemaya. I hope the drinks are to your liking."

"Very much so. Would you like to sit down?"

Glancing around to make sure everything was running smoothly, Lilith lowered herself onto a nearby chair.

"Thank you. Are you going to be in the area for a while?"

"A few weeks. Dakota has personal business to attend to, and I am taking a break from my work."

"Not permanently, I hope. I've never seen any of your shows but I hear they're spectacular."

"I am not sure what I will be doing, but I am planning another tour."

"She's been talking retirement," Dakota interjected. "But that's not going to happen. I haven't figured out how she does her stunts, yet. Besides, I'm too young to retire and if she stops, I won't have anyone as interesting to stalk."

Rolling her eyes, Yemaya pretended to bitch slap the back of the journalist's head, tapping it lightly with her fingertips.

"I'm glad to hear that." Lilith laughed, amused at the unexpected playfulness of the Illusionist. "I'd like to see one of your shows before you call it quits."

"We have one scheduled in a few months. I will have my agent send you a few tickets once we finalize the arrangements."

"Wonderful! I look forward to it. Now, if you'll excuse me, one of my girls is about to have a problem with a customer."

Standing, Lilith walked away, her hips swaying gracefully beneath a long, form-fitting black dress. With only one strap and a low cut back, she oozed sensuality. Even Yemaya felt the woman's sexual allure.

"She is very interesting," she commented, sipping her drink.

"Yeah! If I didn't know you better, I'd be jealous," replied Dakota, watching the Illusionist's face.

Yemaya looked at Dakota and smiled mischievously.

"I doubt if I have what it takes to handle her."

Spewing her drink onto the table, Dakota swiped at it with her palm, and looked around to see if anyone had noticed.

"You've got to be kidding!" she gasped, slightly breathless. "She may have the looks and the moves, but no one can satisfy a woman like you can! Trust me on this one!"

Laughing softly, Yemaya tipped her head slightly, acknowledging her lover's compliment.

"I am glad you think so."

Dakota grinned smugly.

"I know so! Hey, Cammie's here!" she said looking over at the silver-haired woman who had just entered the room. Dressed in dark green slacks and a pale green blouse, she stood looking around as if searching for someone. When she spied Dakota, she waved and smiled. The journalist motioned for her to join them. At the same time, Agra showed up at the table with new drinks, including one for Cammie.

"Thanks," she said, sitting next to Dakota and looking at Yemaya. "Hi, I'm Cammie."

"This is Yemaya," replied Dakota, not giving her partner a chance to respond.

When Cammie extended her hand, Yemaya had no choice but to shake it. She immediately became aware of a warmth flowing up her arm toward her shoulder and then down into her chest. For a moment she felt as if someone was pushing on her ribs, trying to suffocate her. Releasing the grip nonchalantly, the Illusionist sat back in her chair and picked up her drink.

"Nice to meet you," she said. *Interesting*, she thought, resisting an urge to massage the area below her left breast.

"You too." Turning back to Dakota, Cammie smiled and winked. "She's a real looker."

"Yes, she is," replied Dakota, glancing at Yemaya and then shifting her attention back to Cammie. "So, what have you been doing with yourself since we last met?"

"Last met? You make it sound like an eternity." Cammie laughed softly.

"Oh...yeah. For some reason it seems longer. I'm not sure why I said that."

"Well, I helped close down the club, met with a couple of young ladies later, and sent them home a few hours ago."

"Two? You had a date with two women at one time?"

"I have a lot of energy."

"I barely have enough for this one," Dakota claimed, nodding her head toward Yemaya without looking at her.

Raising both eyebrows, Yemaya remained silent.

"I find that hard to believe," teased Cammie, giving the Illusionist a quick glance.

"She hasn't complained yet. You know I've never tried a threesome. It sounds like fun, butdoesn't it complicate things?"

"Not really. With the right partners, it can be quite enjoyable. The trick is to make sure everyone is having a good time and to know whom to focus on. Too much attention on one might make the other jealous or cause her to lose interest. On the other hand, you have to let them be as assertive or as passive as they want. Personally, I like the assertive ones best. It becomes a small battle of wills."

"Wow! I bet you come out on top all the time."

Cammie grinned but shook her head.

"Not always. I like top, bottom, front and back."

"Do you use any toys?"

Yemaya shifted slightly to get a better view of Dakota's face. The questions she was asking had nothing to do with 'inquiring minds wanting to know'. At least as far as her job was concerned. This was a completely different person. Her Dakota would never be so bold or forward on this particular subject.

"Toys? You mean like vibrators or dildos?"

"Sure, or anything else. I bet you're into BDSM aren't you?" Dakota slid her chair next to Cammie and leaned closer in a conspiratorial manner. "It sounds exciting," she whispered.

"It can be fun. I've done it a few times but only the basic stuff. Cuffs, restraints, dildos, things like that. If someone likes a little pain, I'm not opposed to acting the Dominatrix. Nothing extreme, though. It's not for everyone."

"Hey! Until I've tried it, I'll never know, now will I? I've wanted to do a little experimentation but never had the nerve."

Yemaya had just taken a sip of wine when she heard Dakota's confession. It took all of her skills not to spit her drink out on the table. Instead, she swallowed hard and then coughed, trying to clear her windpipe. Cammie looked at her and frowned.

"You okay?"

"Oh, yes, sorry," Yemaya said, her voice slightly husky from the burning in her throat. "Just...inhaled...at the wrong time."

"She's fine," Dakota said, making it sound unimportant. "Now, about those toys and things. I'd really like to hear more about them. Perhaps you could show them to me sometime. Give me a little insight into how they work."

Wiggling her eyebrows, the journalist's expression was almost comical. Yemaya wasn't amused.

"Well...ummm...sure. If Yemaya doesn't mind."

"Oh, she won't mind. She's not into that sort of thing, but who knows. Maybe I can change her mind. You know, work my own magic on her. Anyway, I'd sure like it if we could get together. I bet we have a lot to offer each other."

Cammie seemed at a loss for words. Yemaya decided that the conversation had gone about as far as it should. Whatever had come over Dakota, she was definitely going to regret this conversation later.

"I think you might have embarrassed Cammie, Dakota."

"Oh, come on! If she can handle two women at one time, she can handle me."

"We should head back to the apartment. Tomorrow is a busy day."

"I know...but what's the hurry? I'm enjoying myself. You go on back if you want. I'm sure Cammie doesn't mind keeping me company. I can interview her." Dakota grinned almost slyly.

"I think not. We only have one car, remember?"

"I'll take a cab."

"Dakota, I am sure Cammie probably has things to —"

"I'm not going anywhere!"

Yemaya sighed.

"Alright, we will stay until you are ready to leave."

"Listen, Yemaya. I don't need a babysitter. You said you want to go. Go! Right, Cammie?"

"Sorry, but I'm not getting involved in this one," Cammie said. "Look, I need to talk to Agra and then make a few calls. I'll catch you another time."

Getting up, she hurried to the bar and began talking to the bartender.

"Now look what you've done!" Dakota said, angrily. Slamming her hand on the table, she stood up and glared at Yemaya, ignoring the curious glances she was attracting. "You chased her away!"

Storming from the room, she ignored the giggles coming from several customers. Yemaya, however, didn't. Icy blue eyes stared coldly at the offenders. They shifted in their chairs and fiddled nervously with their drinks.

"Wow," Yemaya muttered under her breath, not sure what had just happened. Pulling a few dollars from her pocket, she slowly got up to leave when she saw Cammie walking toward her.

"Hey! I'm sorry about this. I should have known better, but I thought you two had a stronger connection."

"Connection?"

"I don't mean that like it sounds. Listen. Make sure she's okay. She's not going to like herself in the next few minutes.

Can you meet me tomorrow for a little while? I'll explain everything then."

"I look forward to it! I can be here around five."

"That works for me. Take it easy on her. It's not her fault," Cammie said, sounding mysterious. "Later."

The air outside was chilly. Dakota was leaning against the Jeep, her arms crossed over her chest, foot moving back and forth as she made half circles with her toe. Glancing up at the sound of Yemaya's approach, she dropped her gaze back to her toe.

"Are you alright?"

Dakota nodded.

"That is what you were trying to describe to me yesterday."

"Yeah."

Yemaya bent her knees slightly and leaned down to look into Dakota's eyes. When the journalist refused to look at her, she reached out and lifted her chin with her hand.

"Listen, honey, I have no idea what happened in there, but I know that Dakota is not you."

"I don't know what came over me. I treated you horribly."

"Not horribly. I have to admit I was fascinated by the change in your personality."

"I can imagine!"

Pulling Dakota into her arms, she held her firmly.

"How about we deal with this tomorrow. Cammie asked to meet with me. Apparently this has happened before. Would you like to come with me?"

"I don't think so. Tonight was rather humbling. If she has this effect on me every time I'm around her, I don't want to see her again."

"Are you sure? Sometimes it is better to face our demons."

Yemaya had no clue how close to the truth she was.

Torn between wanting to find out what exactly had happened and feeling embarrassed, Dakota hesitated.

"I...I don't think so. Not yet, anyway. I need time to think," Dakota said, dropping her eyes to avoid looking at Yemaya.

Yemaya leaned down and gently kissed her.

"Before you beat yourself up too much, let me hear what Cammie has to say, okay?"

Dakota sighed and nodded.

CHAPTER 10

SITTING AT THE far end of the bar, Lilith watched the two women conversing quietly in the secluded corner. Tall and dark, Yemaya was stunning. Her pale blue eyes reminded the bar owner of crystal ice. Even Lilith felt the faint stirrings of lust while looking at the woman...and she had seen thousands of beautiful women in her lifetime. Few, however, made her ache sexually. This one did! It was obvious, though, that Dakota held the Illusionist's heart. At one time, taking what wasn't hers would have been enough incentive for Lilith to seduce Yemaya.

The Illusionist's darkness was a different matter. It brought back memories she preferred not to think about. Lilith had pushed him from her life long ago. If he was interested in Yemaya, Lilith wanted to know why.

Telling Agra to close up, she decided to take a short trip. Her ex wasn't going to like the interruption, not that she cared. Besides it gave her the opportunity to ask about the missing whores.

Within moments, she appeared at his estate, entering the castle unchallenged. Lilith wasn't surprised.

The enormous oval bed was overflowing with young men and women, their bodies impossibly intertwined as they passionately fondled each other.

Worms, she thought. *They look like worms all balled up in a knot.*

Amid them lay Dis, his arms wrapped around two plump minions, one male and one female.

"I see you haven't changed," Lilith said, exasperated at the all too familiar scene.

"LILY! It's so nice to see you!" boomed the enormous male, grinning broadly. Pushing aside the writhing bodies, he patted the bed with his hand. "Come. Join us."

"I gave up robbing the cradle a long time ago. Besides, orgies aren't my style. Get rid of them! We need to talk."

"Ah. I see you're just as charming as ever...and as beautiful. Time has been kind to you, my dear, even if you are getting old. I remember when you loved indulging in these little parties. No one could beat your sexual appetites."

"Cut the flattery, Dis! Are you going to get rid of your groupies or should I?" threatened Lilith, not wanting to think about that part of her past.

"Tsk! tsk! You still haven't learned patience. I hoped the years had tempered that little character flaw." Before Lilith could respond, Dis held up his hand to stop her from commenting. "Alright. Out!" he bellowed, his voice a deep baritone. Clapping his hands loudly, thunder reverberated through the room, sending everyone scurrying off the bed, their tangled arms and legs causing them to fall on the floor in one giant heap.

Laughing and giggling, they freed themselves and waved goodbye to Lilith, unimpressed by their master's exaggerated histrionics. "You're a terrible influence. Even my minions show me little respect whenever you're around." He sighed melodramatically, "Now, what can I do for you?"

"Tell me about Yemaya Lysanne!"

"Who?"

"Lysanne. You know who I'm talking about, so don't play the innocent with me."

"Innocent? Me?" Dis laughed. "When has that word ever applied to me?"

"True. Now, answer my question!"

"What do you want to know?"

"Everything. What is she to you?"

Climbing from the bed, Dis swaggered over to Lilith, his dark red skin glowing in the dimly lit room. Letting her eyes wander lazily up and down his naked body, Lilith couldn't help but appreciate his magnificent physique...nor fail to notice the enormous penis he proudly displayed, even in its relaxed state.

"You seem tense, my dear. Would you like a little diversion for old time's sake?" Flexing his organ he smiled. "You know I'm good at taking your mind off unimportant matters."

"Not now! Not ever! What we had is over, no matter how impressive your assets."

Roaring with laughter, Dis pulled on a robe and motioned for Lilith to precede him into the den. Walking to a large black box, he opened the door and pulled out two small red cans. He handed her one and waved her toward a chair.

"Sit." Raising his can in a toast, he took two large swallows before continuing the conversation. "Too bad! We were so good in bed. No one has come close to fulfilling my needs like you. Don't tell me you've lost your appetite for sex."

"Only in your case," she replied, coldly.

"Oh well. My loss! Now, where were we? Ah, yes. The Lysanne woman! What makes you think I have any interest in her? I don't do mortals anymore."

"The darkness. It feels like you. It stinks of you."

"Stink? My dear, you have always had a sharp tongue. Apparently it has grown more so with age. Unfortunately, in her case, I have nothing to do with it. Not that I wouldn't like to. She's a very desirable human. The stench, as you so delicately put it, may be similar but it definitely isn't mine."

"And I'm supposed to believe you?"

"When have I ever lied to you, Lily? Times have changed. The world is different. Even I don't have the influence I used to, not that I need it anymore. Humans no longer believe in their gods and demons like before. They make their own destinies without my help.

Now, I simply wait until they die and let my minions collect their souls. My coffers are overflowing. Hell, I think I may have to enlarge the Underworld at this rate. As for this particular mortal, believe me, I'd like nothing better than to make her one of mine, and her little companion. Just the thought of bedding them makes me hard."

"A dog in heat would make you hard! If you aren't behind her darkness, who is?"

"Really, Lily! There's no need to be insulting...but, it's a good question. One I can't answer."

"Can't or won't?"

"Can't!"

"I thought you knew everything."

"Not in a long time, my dear." Dis chuckled. "My Twin and I have both grown lazy. We've foolishly neglected our duties by ignoring other entities that were evolving. It appears they have grown beyond our abilities to control. You'll have to look elsewhere."

"Your brother would never allow such a thing."

"You give him far too much credit for caring about the universe...and perhaps, I give him too little. We've both squandered away a lot of natural resources during our squabbles. Anyway, I assure you I've done nothing to acquire this woman's soul. Now, is there anything else I can do for you?"

"Yes. Tell me who's behind the missing whores? Is it one of your minions?"

Dis roared with laughter, his deep baritone voice shaking several paintings hanging on the walls.

"I have no use for whores! The world is full of them. Besides they're mine already. I leave them for Agra and Kali to worry about while they're alive. They waste their time trying to protect those puny little souls...although why, I'll never understand. Don't tell me they've misplaced a few."

"Misplaced? They're women, not objects, and yes, three have disappeared I want to know if you or any of your minions are behind it."

"Trust me. Whores don't interest me or my minions. If you like, though, I'll have Beelzebub check around. It'll give him something to do. He's bored to death right now."

Arching her left eyebrow, Lily stared at her ex, her eyes burning brightly.

"Okay. Okay. Bad joke. I really must get back to my guests. You know how I hate being a poor host."

"By all means. I wouldn't want you to be a poor host," agreed Lilith, her voice dripping with sarcasm. "You will let me know if you hear anything."

Standing, Dis retrieved the can from Lilith's hand and helped her to her feet.

"Upon my word. It's good to see you again, Lily. By the way, if you do find where this darkness comes from, let me know. I could use a new distraction. And don't stay away so long. I miss our little chats."

Leaning down, he kissed her tenderly on the cheek and then returned to his bedroom. Lilith smiled, amused at the courtly gesture and genuine affection he had retained for her after all these centuries.

"I don't know who's worse, you or Adam!"

Shaking her head, she left him to his lustful activities. He was right about one thing. The world had evolved. Dis and his legion of demons were being replaced by something far more powerful than them. It was possibly the one thing that would reunite the Twins. Deep down she knew both had an enormous affection for mortals, or at least the entertainment they provided.

CHAPTER 11

CLOSING THE BEDROOM door behind her, Catrina walked over to the young woman tied to the chair. Ivan stood next to her with his hands pressed into his pockets, looking bored.

"So, what do we have here?" she asked, circling their captive. Reaching down, she grabbed a handful of hair, snapping the girl's head up sharply.

"Not bad. Not bad at all, Ivan. Leave us. I'd like to interview my guest."

Shrugging, he walked from the room, shutting the door behind him.

She's like a fucking black widow spider, he thought, shaking his head. *Poor kid! I should have just killed her. It would have been a lot kinder.*

"Look at me!" Catrina ordered, pulling harder on the girl's hair. "Ahhh...much better. Gray eyes. A little too ordinary for my taste but the rest of you has potential."

Licking her lower lip, Catrina felt her arousal building. The girl couldn't have been more than twenty-one or twenty-two. Her long blonde hair hung loosely about her shoulders. Leaning down, Catrina inhaled deeply.

"You stink! What's your name, girl?"

"Sash...Sasha, miss."

"Well, Sasha. You need a bath. Go clean yourself up," she ordered, untying her and pointing to the tub in the corner.

Obediently, Sasha walked over to the bathtub and started filling it with warm water. Nervously, she looked back at her captor.

Catrina threw her a towel. Sitting on the edge of the bed, she lit a cigarette, inhaled deeply and then exhaled. Gray smoke temporarily blocked her vision and she waved her hand to dispel the swirls.

"Hurry up. I don't have all night," she said, throwing the cigarette onto the floor and stepping on it.

Sasha quickly undressed, climbed into the bathtub and scrubbed herself. Rinsing her hair, she stood and picked up the towel, rubbing first her hair dry and then her body.

"Good, now come here. I want a better look at you."

Reluctantly, Sasha wrapped the towel around herself and walked over. Catrina snatched the towel away and tossed it aside. Almost catlike, she stood and stepped close to Sasha.

"Nice," she purred, running her hand down the girl's arm. "Very nice. You have beautiful skin, Sasha."

Sasha shivered.

"Thank...thank you, miss."

Catrina smiled.

"So polite. I've never met a polite whore before."

"Please, miss. I'm not really a whore. I just wanted to make some extra cash and thought it would be easy money."

"Easy money? Since when is fucking for a living easy money?"

"I don't do that. Only hand and blow jobs...and I make them use condoms."

"I see. And why do you need money?"

"I go to the university. My friends said I could make a few hundred bucks a week. I talked to a couple of prostitutes and told them what I wanted. They taught me what to say and do, and how to dress. Their boss said I could give it a shot as long as I took all the precautions and followed the rules."

"Rules?"

"Yes. She's real strict about her rules."

"Your pimp is a woman?"

"She isn't a pimp. She's the boss."

"Right. And you're not a whore and this is all a dreadful mistake," Catrina said, running her hands along Sasha's back as she circled behind her. "Well, tomorrow we'll clear things up," she murmured against the girl's ear. "Tell me, Sasha. Is it true you're related to Yemaya Lysanne?"

"Oh no. My cousin works for her but we aren't related. She is paying for my education. Do you know her?"

"Let's just say I've heard of her. I can't believe she would approve of your...*entrepreneurial* endeavors."

Sasha blushed.

"She doesn't know. You're not going to tell her, are you? Please don't tell her."

"Oh, you needn't worry about that. She won't learn about your little indiscretions from me."

Sasha sighed in relief.

"Now, I know you're tired. Go to bed and get some rest. I'll wake you when it's time to go," Catrina promised, patting the girl's shoulder.

Nodding, Sasha obediently climbed onto the bed and began to pull a blanket over her.

"No. No blanket. The room is warm enough," Catrina said.

Too exhausted to protest, Sasha quickly dozed off.

Catrina waited patiently for the girl to fall asleep. She wasn't sure if she was in the mood to fuck the girl herself, watch or both. Both, she decided, smiling slightly. Opening the bedroom door, she motioned to Ivan, who had been sitting in a chair reading the local paper.

"Get Breshni."

"Now?" asked Ivan looking at his watch.

"Yes, now. What did you think I meant, you idiot?"

Shrugging, Ivan went in search of Breshni. No doubt he'd be snoring away in his room. Ivan detested the man. Breshni was a brute and an idiot, good for nothing more than taking orders. He never questioned anything. He just did what he was told. When they returned, Catrina motioned Breshni into her bedroom and told Ivan to make sure they weren't disturbed. Ivan nodded but said nothing.

"Breshni, how would you like to play our little game again?" Catrina asked in a low voice so as not to wake the girl.

"Sure, mistress. Whatever you say,"

"See that young woman sleeping in my bed?"

Breshni nodded.

"We're going to have some fun with her. You remember how we play this game?"

"Yes."

"Good! Now, very quietly, I want you to tie her hands to the posts. Don't wake her. Can you do that?"

Breshni nodded. He always enjoyed this game.

"When I wake her, make sure you put this ball in her mouth so she won't scream. Tape it so she won't spit it out."

"I understand. Is that it?"

"No, Breshni. That's only the beginning. If you're really good and you're quiet, I'll let you watch. I may even let you have her afterwards. First, I have a few toys I want to play with."

Breshni walked over to the bed and gently buckled restraints around the girl's wrists. Catrina was always amazed that someone his size could move so quietly and be so gentle. Although she found him disgusting as a man, he obeyed her completely. Too bad he was such an idiot.

Sasha felt her arms wrenched above her head and thought she was dreaming. Opening her eyes, she tried to roll on her side but couldn't get her body to turn. When she saw the shadowed face of a man bending over her, she tried to scream. A soft object was roughly shoved into her mouth, making her gag. Tape was then placed over her lips.

Catrina stepped into view wearing a dark green robe. Sasha struggled to loosen her arms from their restraints. Then her ankles were grabbed and pulled apart. Muffled grunts were the only sounds she could make. Her legs were not powerful enough to overcome the man's strength. Sasha's eyes widened in fear when he grinned and licked his lips.

"No need to worry, dear. Breshni won't hurt you. Relax and I'm sure you'll enjoy this as much as I will."

Taking off her robe, Catrina climbed on the bed and settled on her knees between the girl's legs, blocking Breshni's view. When he grumbled his disappointment, she turned and slapped him hard across the face.

"Cuminte!" she ordered. Breshni lowered his eyes submissively.

"Now, where were we. Ah, yes. You were saying you aren't a whore. I think I'll make sure. After all, if you're not, then you must be a virgin, right? I hope so. I so enjoy virgins. They are such delectable creatures. Untouched and so unaware of the pleasures of the flesh."

Inserting her finger into the young woman's vagina, she probed for the intact hymen. Finding it, she smiled her satisfaction.

"Bun! Very good. Well, my little virgin, since you liked playing the whore, I'll show you what it's like to be one. Hold her still, Breshni."

"Yes, Mistress."

Reaching into a drawer next to the bed, Catrina pulled out several fifty dollar bills and a large wooden dildo. Stroking it with her left hand, she ordered Breshni to spread the girl's legs wider.

"You see! I'm going to pay you for your services. Now, how much for your time? Fifty? One hundred? Two hundred dollars?" Sasha's eyes pleaded for mercy, tears streaming from her eyes as she watched her tormenter counting out the money. "Perhaps I should see how good you are first. What do you think, Breshni?"

"Uh...yes."

"There you go! A unanimous decision."

Throwing the money on the floor, Catrina nudged the girl's thighs further apart.

"This, my dear, is made from the finest rosewood money can buy. I had it especially made for little girls like you. Note the size. Impressive isn't it? And the gnarled end. I designed it myself," she stated proudly, caressing the toy as if it were a priceless artifact. "Now, let's just take care of that nasty little piece of skin and then all of us can get down to some serious fun."

Sasha screamed as much as the gag would allow her. The pain was excruciating. She could feel her skin tearing as the instrument was shoved harshly into her vagina and began moving in and out. Eventually, her blood acted as a lubricant, easing the pain slightly. She didn't know how long the woman continued to torture her with her assortment of toys. At some point the ball was removed from her mouth but she no longer had the strength to fight or scream.

Catrina clearly understood the art of pain. When one part of the body grew numb, she switched to another. Sasha was so badly torn inside, she didn't know what hurt the worst. After awhile, she no longer reacted to any of the invasive objects.

Disgusted, Catrina threw the oversized dildo on the floor and got up.

"Now you know what real whores put up with. The next time you want to play at something, you'll think about it a little more."

Laughing, Catrina turned toward Breshni.

"Of course, we know there won't be a next time, don't we?"

Walking to the tub, she filled it with water and her favorite scented oil. Climbing in, Catrina closed her eyes and settled back, enjoying the warmth.

"Mistress?" mumbled Breshni, reluctant to interrupt her bath.

"What, Breshni?"

"What do you want me to do?"

Opening her eyes, she stared at him and then glanced at the girl.

"Do whatever you want. She's yours," she replied, flicking her hand nonchalantly. "And when you're done, get rid of her."

Breshni grinned. Unzipping his pants, he crawled on the bed and stretched his large frame over the girl's body. Catrina ignored the animal grunts and the painful whimpers.

Men are such pigs! she thought. All they knew was how to rut. Still, they served a purpose and as long as Breshni was given a treat, like some dog, he obeyed her faithfully. Finally, she grew tired of the noise and got up. Putting on her robe, she walked to the door.

"Breshni. Clean up in here when you're done. And get me a new bed. That one's a mess." Her servant only grunted louder, not wanting to stop his assault on the young woman beneath him.

Ivan watched Catrina walk down the hall and disappear into her main bedroom. He tried to ignore the sounds coming from the other room. Finally, unable to stand it anymore, he walked into the bedroom. Disgusted, he slapped Breshni hard across the back of the head.

"Get off her, you bastard."

Breshni stopped, looking confused.

"The mistress..."

"The mistress nothing. I said get off her and clean up in here."

Breshni grumbled but reluctantly stood up, tucking his penis into his slacks and zipping up.

"Shit man. You could at least have washed it off," Ivan said, shaking his head in disgust.

Breshni grinned sheepishly and shrugged.

"Get rid of all this. I'll get rid of the girl."

"But the mistress said for me to do it."

"And I'm telling you I'll do it. Clean up this room. You don't want to make Catrina angry do you?"

"No. She gets mean when she's mad." Breshni glanced around nervously, afraid Catrina would walk back into the room.

"Exactly! I'm doing you a favor by taking care of the girl. All you have to do is tell her you dumped the body where it won't be found. Okay?"

"Sure, Ivan. Uh, where'd I dump her?"

"I don't know. Prost! Tell her you cut her up and dumped the parts in the bay. She's not going to want the details."

"Oh. Sure. Gotcha. Thanks, Ivan."

Ivan wrapped the young woman in a clean sheet and carried her to his car. Putting her on the back seat, he climbed

73

in and left, heading down the dark deserted highway. Several miles down the road, he heard a groan.

"Cacat!" he muttered, realizing she was still alive. "Now what?"

Pulling off the road, he climbed into the back and checked her pulse. It was barely noticeable. He sat next to her, his hand unconsciously pushing the hair away from her closed eyes. She was about the same age as his daughter, if Amani had lived. Sighing, Ivan shook his head. He'd have to make her disappear.

CHAPTER 1 2

INTUNECAT STARED into the black void at the images of the two mortals. Slamming his fist into his palm, his voice thundered through the Darkness.

"This will not be!" he declared, his anger so profound lightning forked through the black skies, illuminating the night. "I will not allow it!"

* * *

Mari was enjoying a meal of fruits and nuts near the waterfall when the raven entered her realm. Her spirit companion Maopa, Dakota's great-great-grandmother, appeared simultaneously. Mari preferred calling her by her spirit name rather than her given name.

"Today is going to be a busy day." Mari smiled at Maopa while watching the huge black bird winging its way toward them.

"So it seems. Wonder why he be comin' here."

"We're about to find out."

Circling, the raven settled on the ground a few feet away, its huge wings flapping slowly to ease the landing.

"Welcome, Intunecat. I see once again Curaco has allowed you the use of his body."

"Yes, he's most generous in that way. Your world is very bright during the day. Quite painful, in fact. Forgive my intrusion. As you know, I don't venture into the light without good reason. Nor can I stay here very long. We must talk."

"It must be important. The light can't be very comfortable for you, even in the body of your raven."

The raven dipped its head, acknowledging Mari's observation.

"Will you come to my realm? The matter concerns Yemaya and the Little One."

"You know I won't venture into the Darkness, Intunecat. If you have something to tell us, you can do so at the Eternal Flame."

"So be it."

The raven flapped its wings and rose slowly into the air. As it soared toward the horizon, it vanished.

"Guess we should see what this is about, eh?"

"Yep, must be mighty important for him to be comin' here."

* * *

Intunecat watched the two women conversing. The flames danced constantly, distorting the images slightly. Mari and Maopa appeared at the same moment and settled on the ground next to the flickering fire.

"You can't have her," Mari said, her soft-spoken voice low and deadly.

Laughing, Intunecat waved his hand and the image of Yemaya and Dakota disappeared.

"I'm not here to discuss that," he replied. "It would seem someone else is interested in your daughter."

Waving his hand in front of the fire, the vision switched from them to a man and a woman.

"These two want her dead. I can't allow that," the Dark One stated matter-of-factly.

"Why? And what do you have to do with this?" demanded Mari, her voice as cold as the Darkness itself. Intunecat tipped his head sideways and looked at the Earth Mother. Such coldness from her was unnatural.

"I'm not responsible for all of the evils of their world, my dear."

"He be right, Mari. We knows he don't want Yemaya dead," Maopa said, finding it almost humorous to be defending the dark spirit.

Intunecat chuckled at the irony.

"Then who are they, and what do they want?"

"The male is her servant," Intunecat said, pointing to the image of the woman. "She's the one who desires your daughter's death. Her death would also mean the death of her Chosen. I wouldn't consider that a bad thing if their life-threads weren't intertwined so tightly. Now I have the unfortunate task of having to protect them both if I'm to achieve my goal."

"Then that be a good thang. I'd be all over yah like stink on a pole cat if'n yah hurt our girls."

"Why didn't I see this danger?" Mari mused. "I see everything that affects my people."

"You think you see everything," Intunecat answered. "Therefore, you see nothing sometimes. You've been away from their world a long time, Mari. The connection to your Carpi has weakened. Yemaya and Dakota have never met these two, therefore you cannot know them."

"How is it you know about them?"

"I see most things dark and shadowy."

"Then why didn't you do something?"

Intunecat sighed.

"I can't interfere now that you've reclaimed her...at least not directly. Yemaya isn't mine to protect. Neither is the Little One. I could certainly resolve this quickly. Give them to me," he suggested, knowing it would inflame the Earth Mother.

"You've developed a sense of humor, Intunecat. Perhaps another time I'd find your remark funny," Mari said.

"Another time, then," chuckled the dark spirit before changing the subject. "Unfortunately, these two," he continued, pointing to the images of the man and woman, "aren't mine either. Their darkness comes from another...perhaps from the Underworld. I've heard rumors of a restlessness brewing between the demons and angels. Another battle may be coming."

Mari shook her head.

"Let's hope not. The last one spilled over into our world. We don't have the power to intervene. This is one time I wish you were the problem."

"Ironically, so do I," Intunecat agreed.

Mari's concern about another war between demons and angels was obvious. Many spirits had disappeared during the conflict. Taking sides in a battle was dangerous and their fate was still unknown. Intunecat remained silent.

"There be a solution to this if'n we can jest thank a bit," Maopa said. "Thank yah for comin', Intunecat."

"Yes, thank you. I know you didn't do it out of goodness, but we are grateful nonetheless," Mari said.

"Then I leave you to your thoughts. Until we meet again." Bowing, he vanished.

Mari and Maopa sat staring at the two figures in the flames. For the first time, neither had anything to say.

CHAPTER 1 3

SNICK! DAKOTA flung the pencil as hard as she could at the far wall.

"What the hell is wrong with pencils nowadays?" she yelled, throwing her hands up in frustration.

Since Yemaya was in another room making several business calls, the journalist decided to work on her exposé. The first part in her series of articles called 'Illusive Illusions' was almost complete. Her editor was expecting the final draft by the end of the month.

"Illusive is so appropriate." Dakota glared at the scribbling in front of her. "How come my pens and pencils only act up when I'm writing about you? I can't finish this if you don't cooperate, now can I?"

Tossing the tablet on the desk, she leaned back in her chair and stared at the blank monitor in front of her. "And you. You're not any better, so don't think I'm falling for your little tricks. I turn you on and next thing I know, I'll be throwing you out the window," she quipped. "Then I'll have one tall, very good-looking woman pissed at me."

Hearing a faint cough behind her, she swung the chair around. Yemaya was standing in the doorway, her right shoulder leaning against the door jam, arms crossed.

"Do you always talk to yourself like that?"

"I wasn't talking to myself. It's those damn pens and pencils over there," Dakota replied, pointing in frustration to several lying on the floor against the far wall. "Not one of them works. You put a curse on them or something didn't you?" she accused, looking suspiciously at Yemaya.

"Not hardly. More than likely you put too much pressure on the tips when you were thinking about me. I have that effect on people sometimes."

"Tell me about it. So, how am I going to finish this if I can't get past that effect, as you call it?

"I could help. What do you want the readers to know? Maybe I can give you some ideas?"

"It can't hurt. I'm not sure what I can tell them. I don't want to give away too much about you."

"I see. Well, a little history about my homeland might be a start. Everyone loves speculating about the supernatural."

"True. You don't mind me associating you with werewolves and vampires? Not that there's any such thing...at least I hope not."

Yemaya kissed the top of Dakota's head.

"As long as you do not make them start believing I am one."

"Oh, that sort of stuff can wait until the second part."

"Second part? How much are you planning on telling your readers?" The Illusionist cocked one eyebrow and crossed her arms, dramatically.

"Oh, nothing too personal." Dakota grinned. "I wouldn't want to shock them."

"I should hope not...although I suspect subscriptions would increase considerably if you did. Anyway, I better go and find out what Cammie has to say about last night. Are you sure you want to stay here?"

Dakota blushed.

"Yeah. I might make a fool of myself again. Lord knows what Cammie must think of me."

"I doubt that she thinks anything bad."

"Maybe not. Tell her I'll see her another time...and...never mind." Dakota knew she was taking the cowardly way out but decided she would have to be the one to apologize when they met. It wasn't right to ask Yemaya to do it for her.

"All right. I will be back in a few hours. Good luck with the article."

"Thanks. I'll keep plugging at it. Don't go getting lost."

"How can you get lost in a taxi?" asked Yemaya, ruffling her lover's hair.

"Oh yeah. I forgot."

* * *

Yemaya sat quietly, waiting for Cammie to gather her thoughts. Clearly something was bothering her. Head bowed slightly, the woman played with the drink in her hand, swishing it around the glass slowly. The Illusionist felt an instant attraction, and an urge to embrace her.

She ignored the impulse. The *beast*, however, stirred restlessly. It felt uncomfortably vulnerable.

"You do not have to tell me," Yemaya offered.

Looking up from her glass, Cammie focused on the incredibly blue eyes of the woman sitting across from her.

"I know. It's not something I like to talk about, but perhaps it will help you understand Dakota better and why she's not to be blamed for last night."

"I am not angry with her. Just curious. I feel what she must have. Maybe not to the degree she did, but it is there. It would be hard to resist if I loved her less."

81

"You're lucky. What you and she feel is a blessing. To me it's a curse."

Yemaya didn't respond, unsure what to say.

"Do you believe in God?" Cammie asked.

"I believe in some things. As for God, not really. At least not in the normal sense. Sometimes I wonder though."

"I can understand that. There are things out there..." she motioned toward the door, "beyond the wildest imaginations of humanity. Things that would terrify even the most devout."

"True."

"I've seen so much evil in my lives. Even participated in it in my own way. Maybe I'm being punished for my indiscretions. Perhaps there is a god beyond the one I know who watches us and doles out justice to things like me."

Yemaya didn't miss the use of the words *lives* or *things*. Nor the strange reference to the god she knew. Frowning, she leaned forward and placed her hand over Cammie's and squeezed it. A sensual warmth crept up her arm and through her body before settling gently in the groin area. It was disquieting, but she refused to release her grip.

"No god would punish you for something you cannot control. He or she would not be much of a god then. This energy you project, I take it you were born with it?"

Cammie nodded.

"It's unusual, but not unheard of amongst Cambions."

"Cambions?"

"I'll get to that later, but to answer your question, yes."

"Then it is a part of you. Surely you do not blame yourself for who you are."

"No, but I can for how I use it."

"That may be true. You do not strike me as a woman who would intentionally hurt someone. Why else would you be here? Your concern for Dakota is real."

"To redeem myself? I've grown weary of the way I am and want something more. Maybe I'm just fooling myself into thinking I can be someone I'm not."

"Listen, Cammie. I know we have just met. I may not know your past or the things you have done, but I would know if you were amoral. Trust me on this."

"I'm not sure exactly why, but I do," Cammie replied, quietly, smiling for the first time.

"Good. Now, tell me about this power and why Dakota acted so strangely."

"Well, as you said, it's part of me. Some would call it a gift."

"Gift?"

"Yes. I sometimes think the Fates are either cruel or have a wicked sense of humor."

"I know what you mean."

"I imagine you do. Anyway, in my first life, as a child I learned I was born from lust and hatred. My parents couldn't stand each other."

First life? "They must have felt something more."

"Only the need to dominate and possess each other, if you call that feeling. They didn't love each other. They fucked. That's how it's described nowadays. The very act defiled the meaning of love. Their only purpose in life was to seduce whomever they wanted. Neither felt compassion nor desire. In the end, they destroyed everything they touched. I was a mistake, an unfortunate combination of poor timing and bad luck, and my parents were appalled to discover that their copulation resulted in my conception."

"Surely they loved you."

Cammie's laughter held no humor.

"They don't know the meaning of love. It's not their fault. I sometimes think that's the reason I'm the way I am. Anyway, I've always believed life was a balance, good and bad, love and hate. I'm proof of the latter. Because my parents were filled with so much hatred, I was born to be loved, an immeasurable, eternal, shallow love that is fleeting at best."

"Fleeting? I am not sure I follow you—"

"I know. Sorry. Let me see if I can explain this better. You asked about my power. People around me fall in love with me quickly, and just as quickly fall out. That's what Dakota experienced."

"I see. So, this love...it is not real?"

"Oh, it's real. If Dakota were to stay by my side, I could make her the happiest woman in the world. I could pleasure her in ways you couldn't even imagine... a word, a look. She would be mine and willingly agree to my whims. I could satisfy her every desire, her every wish, her every need. I could fulfill her wildest desires and fantasies...and you could do nothing to stop me."

"I think you underestimate me," Yemaya stated confidently.

"No, I know she loves you more than life itself. I feel it, but she still wouldn't be able to resist me. You saw her last night. Was that the woman you thought you knew?"

Yemaya had to agree. Her Dakota would never have acted like she had the night before.

"Good, now you'll know how to deal with the situation whenever she's around me."

"And that would be?"

"Through understanding. No more, no less. She'll always be yours. It is both of your destinies. Besides, I would never do anything to compromise her love for you or yours for her. It's too rare a gift."

Yemaya nodded her thanks.

"Your life must be very lonely."

"Yes. Ironic, isn't it. I have had thousands of lovers. Most of them fleeting, a few lasted longer, but in the end, everyone moved on. It's a part of my life I've come to accept."

"Perhaps that is your problem...your acceptance. Obstacles are challenges to conquer or die trying."

Shaking her head, Cammie laughed. "Ah, an optimist. You surprise me. I thought you'd be more of a realist."

"I am both. I will never accept that fate controls my destiny. I make my own. It sounds like you have let it make yours. Perhaps it is time for a change."

"You make it sound so easy."

"I never said that. I cannot imagine how awful your life has been. I can only tell you what I think I would do if I were in your situation."

"Well, actually, my life hasn't been awful. Awful would be my parent's lives; to exist without experiencing love is to not exist at all. Like I said, I have never not known it. That is my future...my destiny. It may not be perfect, but I'll take it over a life of hate."

"You have a point. Who are your parents? And I noticed, earlier, you said lives instead of life."

Before Cammie could answer, Kali walked up to the table.

"You want anything else?" she asked curtly, giving Yemaya a sulky look.

"No thank you," Yemaya said, sensing an animosity toward her. Looking at the dark skinned woman, she tried to make eye contact, curious as to the reason, but the woman refused to look at her.

"Cammie, would you like something?"

The subtle change in her tone and attitude made it obvious Kali's anger was directed entirely at Yemaya.

Interesting! Yemaya thought.

"No thanks, Kali," Cammie answered. "Maybe in a little while, though, if you don't mind."

"Sure thing," Kali muttered, moving away to check on other customers.

"She likes you."

"Everyone likes me," Cammie replied.

"Maybe. But I think hers is different."

"Well, Kali is around me a lot. She's bound to suffer my effects."

Realizing Cammie was uncomfortable with this particular topic, Yemaya changed the subject.

"You were telling me about your parents."

For the first time, Cammie made complete eye contact with Yemaya.

"Was I?"

Laughing, Yemaya nodded, knowing the woman was playing with her.

"It would be cruel to leave me guessing now."

"Ah, yes. We can't have that, can we? Would you believe me if I said mom was a succubus?"

Rocking back in her chair, Cammie watched for a reaction. When she didn't get one, she tilted her head to the side and waited.

"And your father?"

"Incubus."

"I see... and you are?"

"Technically, I am a Cambion and offspring of that type of union."

"I would say that explains the lust and hatred you mentioned."

"You don't seem surprised. Most people would think I was crazy. That's if they even knew what I was talking about."

"I find it more surprising you are so open about it. As for me, few things surprise me anymore. I have seen too much in my life to jump to conclusions," Yemaya said, shrugging slightly. "I must admit, I have never heard of Cambions."

"We're rare. Incubi and Succubi normally detest each other. Just finding themselves in the same place usually ends up in a battle. The two species keep as much distance as possible unless we're called to a *gathering*. Serious dissension isn't permitted at our conclaves."

"By gathering, I assume you mean...?"

Cammie laughed.

"You know exactly what I mean."

"I am afraid I do. An orgy. I find it hard to believe you are a demon."

"We're not all as bad as you think. You'd be surprised at how many of us want nothing more than to live our lives like you mortals. Not that it was always like that. There was a time when we were ambitious."

"Time does take its toll."

"You could say that."

"So, are demons really immortal?"

Cammie shrugged.

"Who's to say? No one knows for sure. We've been around a long time, but I don't believe we are."

"Why not?"

"I can die. I have died."

"You look pretty healthy for a dead woman," Yemaya teased.

"Oh, I'm very much alive now. That doesn't mean I will always return."

"I would say you are a pretty good argument for immortality."

Cammie looked down at her glass and then took a sip.

"There was a time when this world was full of demons and spirits. Many are gone. Vanished. No one knows where. Every *gathering* is a reminder that our numbers are dwindling."

Laughing, Cammie twirled her glass playfully.

"Anyway, I've died so many times, I don't know who or what I am anymore. I take what life offers and try to enjoy the moments."

Yemaya watched the woman for several long seconds, trying to imagine what it would be like to be reincarnated. The thought wasn't necessarily distasteful, but it was unsettling. Combined with Cammie's so-called gift and...well...shaking her head, she didn't really know what to think.

"I would find your situation depressing."

"I do and have. There have been moments when I wanted to end it all, but then I wonder what would be the use. I'd just come back again or worse, I wouldn't come back at all. For all of my bitching, I'm not ready to give up living. The thought of not existing at all actually frightens me a little.

"Once, a long time ago, I almost killed myself. Not intentionally, of course. I'm not suicidal. I was sad, depressed. What good was love if it wasn't real? I isolated myself from everyone, only to discover I needed people more than they needed me.

Within weeks, I became so sick I thought I was going to die. Then an old woman found me. She told me she understood my needs. Her people carried me to a nearby village. Then they just disappeared. I never got to thank them."

"So what caused this sickness?"

"Starvation, dependency. Love is a drug. Without my fix, I have horrible withdrawal symptoms. A cruel twist, don't you think?"

"Perhaps. Then again, you do give something in return? People affected by your power may never experience the emotion without you."

Cammie laughed. "That sounds sadder than my story."

"Just a different perspective. Think about it."

"Maybe I will."

"Good. Can I ask you something?"

"You can ask," said Cammie, her amber eyes twinkling brightly.

"Why did you tell me all of this? You could have said you had some animal magnetism or something."

"Like you'd believe that. When we shook hands you felt the attraction and so did that darkness inside of you."

Startled, Yemaya said nothing. and the *beast* shrank further back into its lair.

"How did—"

"I've seen it in others. Yours is the strongest, though. It must be hard to keep under control."

"At times. Thankfully, I have someone who helps me."

"Ah, yes...Dakota. The two of you make a formidable team."

"Yes, we do."

"I envy you. It must be wonderful to know such love. I would give all of my future lives for what you have."

"I know what you mean. I cannot imagine life without her." Looking at her watch, Yemaya took a final drink and pushed her chair back. "Speaking of which, I had better get back to her. She needs to understand what happened."

"Will she be alright?"

"I will make sure of it."

"I believe you will."

Standing, Yemaya stared down at the Cambion and thought how innocent she was. For all of the lives she had lived, all of the people who had loved her, she had never experienced real love. As if the thought conjured up a vision, Kali appeared next to her, wiping her hands on a towel.

"Are you leaving?" she asked, still refusing to make eye contact.

"Yes. Did you want something?"

"No, just making sure," grumbled the brooding bartender before walking away.

"Kali. Wait a minute."

Reluctantly, Kali stopped and waited for Yemaya to reach her. For the first time, she looked up. Stunned, the Illusionist hesitated a moment and then continued on. She had never seen eyes flaming so brightly. By the time she reached the bartender, Kali had lowered her gaze and was playing with the towel in her hands.

"What do you want?"

"Just a word of advice for you. Tell Cammie the truth."

"Truth? What truth?"

"You know what I mean. Until you confront her, you will never know what is possible."

When Kali didn't reply, Yemaya shrugged and left. Climbing into her taxi, she turned to look back as it drove away. The bartender was holding the door open and staring at her. Even at a distance, her lavender eyes glowed unnaturally bright. Her nod was barely discernible before she disappeared back into the building.

An amazing color, thought Yemaya.

CHAPTER 14

IVAN WATCHED the ER entrance, monitoring the people going in and out. More than fifteen minutes passed with no activity. Picking up the girl, he carried her to a dark secluded spot near the entrance. Hopefully, someone would come out and find her soon. For sure, he didn't want to make any calls to the hospital.

Once back in his car, he lit a cigarette, drawing the smoke deep into his lungs. Ivan rarely smoked. After ten minutes, he was about to give up hope when a woman left the building and walked toward the darkened area. Within minutes several people rushed out the door to where she had disappeared.

"Now, all I have to do is keep this from Catrina." he muttered, throwing the cigarette out the window. Without turning his lights on, he pulled away from the curb and drove off.

* * *

Lonnie Sanders was tired. The trauma center had been non-stop all evening. After sending the last patient, a suspected SARS victim, to isolation, she decided to catch a breath of fresh air during the lull. Her pager would let her know if anything else came in.

Grabbing her coat, a candy bar and a cup of coffee, she told Joey she was going for a walk.

"Page me if anything happens. I'll just be outside."

"Sure Doc."

The night air was cool. Taking a deep breath, she walked around the corner of the building into a dark secluded spot. Normally, a security light lit the area but it had burnt out three days ago and maintenance hadn't replaced it.

Leaning against the wall, she sipped the coffee and bit a chunk of candy, chewing slowly. Tonight was unusually busy — car accidents, two shootings, a stabbing and the potentially deadly SARS case kept everyone scrambling. In two hours she'd be off, hopefully. As if her thoughts conjured up a vision, she heard a moan coming from the darkness. Startled, she glanced around, trying to locate the source. Another moan came from her left.

Cautiously, she walked toward the sound. Her toe hit something solid. She knelt to investigate. Discovering a body, she grabbed her two-way and called for help.

Joey and two nurses rushed around the corner carrying a stretcher and a flashlight. The light beam flashed over the body of a young woman wrapped in a bloody sheet.

"She's alive. Get her inside. NOW!" ordered Lonnie.

Gently, the four lifted the woman onto the stretcher and carried her into an examination room. As the nurses began cutting away the sheet, Lonnie ordered Joey to bring in IVs, pans of warm water and plenty of gauze and to get the lab to type her blood in case she needed a transfusion.

Although the sheet was saturated from the blood, Lonnie knew it might not be as bad as it looked. Locating the source was more important. Everyone worked furiously, trying to clean the girl's body enough for Dr. Sanders to make a thorough examination.

Checking the unconscious woman's eyes for a response, Lonnie nodded her approval.

"Good. Okay, people, let's see what happened here. Where's the blood coming from?" she demanded, running her hands along the girl's body, searching for any signs of injuries. Bruises around the wrists indicated a form of bondage. There were also several deep scratches around her breasts. "Does she have any ID?" Lonnie asked, knowing it was a stupid question.

"None," Joey replied.

"Doc, this woman's had an abortion or been raped or something," said one of the nurses as she cleaned the thighs.

Lonnie shifted down to examine the pelvic area. It was the obvious source of the majority of bleeding, although the flow seemed to have stopped.

"Call the OR and tell them we need it stat. See if Dr. Langley is still here. She's the best gyno in the hospital."

Joey, who had been standing to the side, picked up the phone to make the arrangements.

"Dr. Langley will meet you in ten minutes in OR 3, Dr. Sanders."

"Get her prepped. I'm going to clean up. I'll meet you there."

Four hours later, they wheeled the Jane Doe to post-op for observation. Dr. Sanders and Dr. Langley followed several feet behind the gurney.

"I don't know what happened to that girl but I've never seen anything quite like it," Lonnie said, pulling her face mask down.

"Wish I could say the same," Annie Langley replied. "This isn't as unusual as you think. Sometimes it's just rough sex gone wrong. Other times it's some sadistic bastard looking for a way to get his rocks off.

This is one of the worse cases of abuse I've seen, though. This girl was so torn up inside, I had to remove everything and try to reconstruct the entire vaginal area. She'll never have kids."

"You think it was someone she knew or a stranger?"

"Don't know, but it wasn't voluntary. The bruises around her wrists show she was restrained. And those around her ankles were made by hands...big hands. Someone held her legs while she was being raped."

"Well, there's no chance of finding semen or anything with all that blood and body fluid," Lonnie said.

"Yeah, from the looks of the injuries, it wasn't a penis that did all that damage. The creep took a great deal of pleasure torturing this girl. That makes him or her a very sick puppy."

"Her? You think a woman could do this?"

"I would hope not, Lonnie, but I don't discount anyone. In my line of medicine, I've seen some pretty horrific things done by women."

"I guess. Look, Anne, thanks for helping me with this."

"Anytime. I'll check in on her when I come in later, but I think she'll be fine. Call me if her condition worsens, though."

"Will do. I'll get her settled and file a report with the police."

* * *

CHAPTER 15

THE DARK ONE watched in fascination. The two mortals torturing the young woman were deriving an unnatural pleasure from their actions.

"I'll never understand this craving mortals have for such pleasures of the flesh, old friend," Intunecat said to Curaco, his raven. "It's their greatest weakness."

Waving his hand, the images vanished.

"Fly to Mari and request her presence at the Eternal Flame. I'll be waiting."

Curaco vanished from the blackness and reappeared in the light, large wings flapping slowly as he traveled the spirit world.

* * *

Mari arrived at the fire only moments after Intunecat.

"You sent for me?"

"Yes. Have you felt anything unusual this night?" he asked.

"No. Should I?"

"Maybe not. As I said, you have been away from your people a long time. Watch!" he ordered, waving his hand in front of the flame.

Mari watched a replay of the scene Intunecat had seen earlier.

95

"Is she not one of your people?"

"Yes, she is," Mari replied quietly, looking away for an instant. The dark spirit said nothing. Mari was angry...a rare event. Her quiet response, the icy look in her pale eyes fascinated him. Never had he seen anyone so beautiful. For the first time, he felt a stirring deep within him, an emotion he didn't quite understand. How wonderful it must be to love someone so completely, he thought. Shaking his hooded head, he waited for her to speak.

"When did this happen?" demanded Mari, returning her gaze to the images in the flame.

"This night."

"Yemaya must be told. She's the only one who can help this child until I think of something."

"Yes, but these mortals also want her. Do you think it wise to include her? She'll let her emotions guide her. I won't allow that."

"*You* won't allow it? Who are you to decide the fate of my daughter?"

"I'm the only one who isn't affected by emotion, my dear. Even now you seethe with anger over this child. What will you do if it's your daughter under this creature's control? Spirits have very little power in the mortal world unless we take mortal form. Then we are all vulnerable. Would you risk your realm for the life of one person?"

"For Yemaya, I would risk it all."

"That's precisely my point, and why you need me."

"And me," Maopa said, appearing by Mari's side. "He be right, yah know. As much as I hates tah side with this un', now ain't the time for chargin' in."

"What am I to do? Nothing?"

"No, this chile needs you more'n Yemaya. We'll go to her."

"And I'll make sure Yemaya's life-mate knows what's happening," offered Intunecat.

"I don't want you near Yemaya or Dakota," Mari said.

"A truce, Mari. We can save our battles for the future. I'm only the messenger."

"Very well," she agreed, reluctantly. Taking Maopa's hand, the two women vanished.

* * *

Lonnie was sitting at the nurse's desk writing her report on Jane Doe. She had already given a report to Officer Finley. He would try to locate her family. Momentarily distracted by a warm breeze ruffling the loose papers around her, she looked up and glanced around, trying to locate the source. It hadn't come from the ER doors. The temperature outside was below freezing. Seeing no one around, she went back to making notes on the patient's chart.

"Please excuse the intrusion. I'm here to see my niece."

Lonnie shivered. The voice was low and sultry. Looking up, she saw two women, one very tall and slender with pale blue eyes the color of frozen ice, but warm like a gentle flame. Her long black hair hung loosely around her shoulders. Beside her stood a smaller, blonde-haired woman with twinkling dark green eyes.

"What room is she in?" Lonnie asked.

"Now that be the—" Mari nudged Maopa with her elbow.

"We're not sure, miss. The authorities just informed us that she was brought here. Her name is Sasha. She's twenty-two and was an...an assault victim."

"Oh, our Jane Doe. Do you mind if I ask your names?"

"My name is Yemaya and this is my partner, Dakota. Sasha was to meet us for dinner, but never showed up. We decided to check the hospitals and authorities to see if she was in an accident. We just found out she was here."

"And we be a wantin' to see her," piped in Dakota.

Lonnie stared at the blonde woman.

Now that's as backwoods as it gets.

"I see. Well, Jane...Sasha is in room 403. She hasn't regained consciousness yet. I don't know how much the police told you but she's suffered very serious injuries. Not all physical, I'm afraid. I wish I could say we were able to correct all of the physical damage but we couldn't."

The two women listened as Lonnie explained the extent of Sasha's injuries and the final prognosis. When Lonnie finished, she escorted them to Sasha's room. With the oxygen tube under her nose and the IV in her arm, the girl looked frail and vulnerable.

"Any idea when she might wake up?"

"Not really. Maybe in a few hours. Everything depends on the patient and her will to wake up."

"Thank you, doctor. If you don't mind, we'll sit with her awhile."

Lonnie left them alone.

* * *

Sasha was lost. The darkness was impenetrable and cold. Panicking, she struggled to find a way out. About to give up hope, she felt a warm voice calling to her. A speck of light appeared to her right.

"Sasha, it's me! Yemaya. I have you now. Follow the light."

"Mistress?"

"Yes, Sasha. I've come to take you home. Andrei is waiting for you. He misses you."

"I hurt so bad," cried Sasha.

"I know. The pain will go away soon. You must come to me. I can't help you until you do."

"I'm trying, Mistress. She hurt me so bad. I'm afraid."

"There's nothing to fear, Sasha. I promise. It's time to come home."

Sasha followed the voice as it wrapped itself warmly around her, leading her toward consciousness. She struggled desperately to open her eyes. The room was dimly lit. When she finally focused on the two people standing by her bed, she immediately recognized Yemaya. The other woman was a stranger.

"Mistress?"

"I'm here, Sasha. This is my friend, Dakota. How are you feeling?"

"I don't know. I'm so confused. What happened?" she asked, wincing from the pain.

"I'll tell you later, dear. Sleep now. You'll feel better after you rest."

Sasha had always loved the Mistress' voice. Something was different about it, though. It was more soothing than normal, unnaturally so.

When Lonnie came to check on Sasha, the room was empty except for her sleeping patient. Satisfied she was resting peacefully, the doctor clocked out and went home. It had been a very long night. At least no one died on her shift.

* * *

Dakota awoke to blackness. Blinking she felt confused.
Damn, either I'm dreaming or I'm blind.
She felt the laughter rather than heard it. It was very cold.
"Welcome to my world, Little One."
Intunecat? God I hope this is a dream.

"No dream, and God can't hear you. I'm real, or at least as real as I can be at the moment."

"Cripeez! Just what I need. You in my mind!"

"Don't worry. I'm not in your mind. Tonight I am merely a messenger."

"Messenger? From whom?"

"Mari and Maopa, of course."

Intunecat described precisely what had happened to Sasha. It wasn't his nature to spare feelings or leave out details. By the time he was finished, Dakota was so angry she felt she could kill the woman herself.

"Do you have this woman's name?"

"Names mean nothing to me but you will find she owns a business at the waterfront where you live. She is a seller of women."

"Seller of women?"

"Yes. Mortals have needs. She provides the more perverted a means to satisfy them."

"She's a pimp?"

"No. She...what is the phrase you humans use? She...markets them...against their will."

"Shit. She's in the fucking sex-slave trade business."

Intunecat nodded.

"So, what is it we're supposed to do?" Dakota demanded, angrily. "I'll kill her her myself if I get the chance."

Intunecat laughed. Dakota was well suited as the life-mate of Yemaya.

"Keep Yemaya focused. She'll become emotional like you. In her case, it could be deadly. Carpi feel more deeply than most. That is Yemaya's greatest weakness. You know her darkness; it wants its freedom. Make sure she stays in control of herself. Until she tames that beast, she's a danger to herself and everyone around her."

"Not me. Never me."

"Even you, Little One," Intunecat replied, calmly. "You are both her strength and her weakness. Don't underestimate either."

"I'll do what I have to."

* * *

Yemaya wasn't sure what woke her. Perhaps a dream. Whatever it was, the pain was real. Wrapping her arm around Dakota, she snuggled against her side. For the moment, she could do nothing about something that wasn't known.

Dakota awoke feeling strangely disoriented. For a few minutes she lay still. Rubbing her forehead, she wasn't even sure if her conversation with Intunecat was real or a dream. She couldn't take the chance "Hey sweetie, wake up," she said, shaking Yemaya's shoulder.

Groaning slightly and burrowing further into Dakota's chest, Yemaya tried to ignore the soft voice calling to her.

"Come on. We need to talk," coaxed Dakota.

Opening one pale blue eye, Yemaya stared at her lover for a few seconds.

"It's about Sasha," Dakota said.

"What about Sasha?"

"She's been hurt. Get dressed. I'll tell you all about it while I call a cab."

By the time the taxi arrived, a cold rage burned inside Yemaya. Dakota could feel the fury. Intunecat was right. Yemaya was consumed with anger.

"Intunecat told you this?"

"Yes. At first I thought it was a dream. It's just too real...like when Mari and Grandma Dakota visit us."

When Yemaya didn't say anything, Dakota began to worry.

"Talk to me, Yemaya."

Yemaya barely heard Dakota. Her mind was on Sasha. No one harmed her people without suffering the consequences. She would enjoy making this woman pay.

"Damn it, Yemaya. What's going on inside that head of yours."

Yemaya gave her a blank look, still lost in her own thoughts. For a split second, Dakota thought her lover's eyes had changed from icy blue to coal black and was afraid. Shaking her head, she grabbed Yemaya's arm and shook it.

"What?" Yemaya finally asked, calmly. Too calmly.

"I said, tell me what you're thinking.' What are you feeling?"

"Anger, of course. I am angry. How else am I supposed to feel?"

"No different, sweetie. Just make sure it's only that. Okay? What now?"

"We check on Sasha. Afterward, I find this woman."

"And then?"

"And then I kill her." It was said so coldly that Dakota shivered.

"No!" Dakota ordered.

"No, what?"

"You won't kill her. At least not unless you absolutely have to."

"And why not?"

"Because I'm asking you not to. Promise me you won't, Yemaya."

"I cannot do that. Do not ask me to make a promise I am unable to keep, Dakota." Yemaya stared into Dakota's eyes, sensing the fear. She had known from the beginning there would come a time when she would have to choose between the Carpi way and her love for Dakota. Sighing, she lowered her eyes. "I cannot always be who you want me to be," she whispered, sadly.

Dakota closed her eyes. Tears streamed down her cheeks.

So this is it, she thought.

Fingers gently wiped the tears before they could fall.

"But I will try," promised Yemaya, her voice husky. "I am Carpi, the protector of my people, as were my ancestors. I have unique abilities. This is the price I pay because of them."

"I know...I don't want to lose you."

Yemaya gathered Dakota in her arms, holding her tightly. Pushing the rage back, she felt it reluctantly retreat.

CHAPTER 16

LILITH PACED BACK and forth.

"Surely someone down there can tell us what's happening," Agra said.

"You would think," Lilith agreed. "Apparently, they have little interest in whores."

"Since when did minions get to choose their duties?"

"Since Dis grew bored with this world. He's decided humans do enough evil on their own without his intervention."

"Well, I'm not about to let anyone harm what's mine without feeling my wrath. My Lord gave them to me thousands of years ago for fulfilling my duties to him. Those who work for me come under my protection willingly."

"Agra, you have done all you can. Dis is right. We've grown too attached to these humans. Most of them are doomed to a miserable existence as it is."

"That's not the point. And I'm not here to argue with you. If Dis or his minions won't help me, I'll go to the Twin."

"That's a little extreme," Lilith admonished.

"I agree, for now," Kali said, having just entered the room. "There are other ways of finding out. A few minions owe me favors. If they don't know anything, you can bet they'll find someone who does."

Turning to make eye contact with Agra, she placed her hand on the demoness' shoulder. "If we don't hear anything soon, I'll join you if you still want to go to the Twin. And Dis, himself, won't be able to stop us. He has felt my wrath, already. He may still be our Lord, but only as long as we permit it."

Lilith looked from one demoness to the other and laughed.

"He's lucky you two aren't ambitious. I'm not so sure he'd win in a battle against you."

"We have no interest in ruling the Underworld," Agra said. "The *damned* lead boring existences."

"As do the good," Kali added. "It's those whose fate is still undecided we find most to our liking. They are the unfinished stories of life."

"I agree. Keep me informed," Lilith ordered and vanished abruptly.

"She's so serious at times. You'd think she'd learn to relax," Agra joked.

"Like us, you mean."

"Hey, we're getting better."

Kali cocked her head sideways and smirked at her friend. Agra's newest hairdo made her look like a punk rocker from some heavy metal band. Red spiked hair with purple tips, dark green eyes and the torn jeans and tank top gave her an appearance far removed from the dark looks of her past. The change was the result of her mental evolution from the angry demoness who had rebelled against the Twin...and earned Dis' respect and gratitude...to the more fun-loving woman of today.

Had Kali not lived in the time when the Twin had cast Dis and his followers out of their Kingdom, she'd never have believed this Agra was the same person who'd married their Underlord. Of course, the marriage lasted only a short time before he decided enough was enough and begged her for his freedom.

"What are you smirking about?" Agra demanded.

"Oh, I was just remembering something from long ago."

"Care to share or is it personal?"

Laughing, Kali shook her head.

"Not really. I was thinking about those years you and Dis were a couple."

"Paleeze! I'd almost forgotten that, or at least I was trying to."

"I know, but you have to admit we wouldn't be here if it wasn't for your marriage to him. After all, it's the only reason you got the whores."

"Yeah. Everyone still claims I did him and them a favor releasing him from the contract." Agra chuckled.

"Well, whatever went on between you two, he definitely put his minions through hell while you were together."

"Not as much as I did him. All he ever wanted was sex. I don't know if you've ever seen Dis without his clothes, but he's enormously endowed...and considers himself a great lover."

"Ummm, I think maybe we can leave out the details. Anyway, you probably did make his life miserable. It was soon afterward that Lilith caught his eye."

"Not to mention you caught mine and were flirting unmercifully."

"Well, you were hot, and I was angry and ambitious."

"That's putting it mildly. When the Angels defeated us in the Great Battle, there was no one to defend the Underworld against their final assault. We would have been overthrown had you not rallied the demons."

"Threatened, you mean."

"Threatened...rallied...no difference. The light emanating from your eyes and hands was so terrible it scorched anyone it touched. They feared you more than they did Dis and it scared him so much, he still avoids you. I've always wanted to ask you where it came from?"

"I really don't know. It's just something that happens when I'm extremely angry."

"I hope no one ever makes you that angry again."

"Age has mellowed me."

"Uh huh. I'll take your word for it."

Leaning her head against the backrest of her chair, Agra closed her eyes and relaxed. Reminiscing over old times felt good.

CHAPTER 17

DR. LONNIE SANDERS caught only a few hours of sleep before returning to check on her patients at Mercy Hospital. Although it was her day off, she felt the need to make sure everyone was stable, especially Sasha. The aunt and her partner had disappeared before she could get any personal information on the girl.

Sasha was still sleeping. Checking the notes on her chart, Lonnie nodded in satisfaction.

"Good," she mumbled to herself. "She's stable and resting well."

"Are you the attending physician?"

Lonnie looked up to see Ms. Lysanne and Ms. Devereaux standing in the doorway.

"Why yes. We met earlier this morning, remember?"

Yemaya frowned and was about to reply when Dakota coughed and nudged her with her elbow.

"Sorry, Doctor..." Dakota apologized, taking over.

"Sanders. Lonnie Sanders."

"Right, Dr. Sanders. Sorry. It took us awhile to get here."

"I can imagine. Traffic is getting worse and worse. Which hotel are you staying at?"

"Hotel? Oh. We've already checked out. We wanted to see how Sasha is doing so we can make arrangements to take her home," Dakota said.

Lonnie frowned. Something about the two women seemed different. For one, the small blonde spoke excellent English with only a small hint of a mid-western accent. The taller woman remained quiet. It was almost as if their roles were reversed from earlier.

"If she keeps improving, she might be released in a few days. She's in considerable pain, but that can be handled with meds. My biggest concern is her mental state. The emotional scars from this type of abuse are far greater than the physical ones."

"My people and I will help her through this," Yemaya said softly. "She will be well cared for."

Jesus, what a voice, thought Lonnie. *What I wouldn't give to be in Devereaux's shoes if these two are partners. Then again, she's not so bad herself.*

"Good. She's definitely doing a lot better this morning. Sorry you vanished so soon, though. I could have given you the full update on her injuries."

Yemaya looked at Dakota and frowned.

"This morning?" she mouthed.

"Ummm, grandma and Mari, probably," whispered Dakota.

"Oh. Of course."

Lonnie listened to the peculiar exchange. Shaking her head, she knew something was going on but figured it wasn't any of her business.

"If you two would accompany me to my office, I'll go over what to look for while she's recovering. Like I said, the mental trauma is the bigger problem now."

"Certainly, doctor. I would like to check on my niece first."

Nodding, the doctor motioned for Dakota to follow her. Yemaya stood next to Sasha, searching for signs of awakening. When she found none, she placed her hand on the girl's cheek and closed her eyes. Slowly, the images of torture surfaced in Sasha's mind. Yemaya could feel the hatred and rage building in her own. She had never experienced evil in its purest form. The torturer's face was forever branded in Sasha's mind, every cell scarred from the ordeal. Yemaya knew Sasha would never fully recover from this tragedy. The b*east* stirred.

"Yemaya! Stop!"

As Dakota was leaving she remembered the last time Yemaya had tried to help one of her people. A mind merge, for lack of a better term, almost cost the Illusionist her soul. Walking back into the hospital room, she hurried to her lover's side and gently pulled Yemaya's hand away from Sasha's cheek. When Yemaya looked at her, a burning fury blazed in her ebony-colored eyes.

"Come back to me," Dakota pleaded.

Maybe it was only moments, but it felt like an eternity before Yemaya relaxed. The blackness receded. Deeply troubled blue eyes stared into bright green ones. Shaking her head, Yemaya wrapped her arms around Dakota and rested her cheek against the petite journalist's blonde head.

"I cannot keep doing this," she murmured, tiredly. "This thing grows stronger in me. One day it may consume me and I will do something terrible."

"Over my dead body. You aren't alone anymore. I'll go to the depths of hell to save you if I have to. Maybe we should see the doc, then decide what needs to be done."

Yemaya nodded. "Good idea," Leaning down she kissed Sasha's cheek. "Sleep! I will be here when you need me."

After consulting with Dr. Sanders, Yemaya called Sonny, asking him to arrange for the girl's transportation back to Moldova. Then she phoned Andrei. When Maria answered and told her Andrei was in town, Yemaya briefed her on Sasha's condition.

Dakota sat quietly. Although she didn't understand the language, she listened to the soothing way Yemaya discussed the situation with her housekeeper.

"Now what?" she asked when Yemaya was finished.

"Now, we find this woman and make sure she does not do this to anyone else." The lack of emotion in the Illusionist's voice frightened Dakota. She was just beginning to understand how deadly Yemaya could be if provoked.

"Shouldn't we let the police know about this?"

Yemaya's response was interrupted by the ringing of her cell phone.

"What?"

"Is that anyway to answer your phone?"

"Sorry Raidon. What do you want?"

"Well, first I think it's rather rude of you to call here and not even speak to me. Maria told me about Sasha. Will she be okay?"

"In time, and I apologize. I was thinking only of Andrei's feelings."

"So easily forgotten," Raidon said with a sigh.

"This is not the time for drama."

"You're losing your sense of humor, sister, along with your manners. Do you have any idea who did this?"

"Yes, but not a name. It might have to do with the sex-slave trade."

"I'm not even going to ask how you came to that conclusion. Is there anything I can do from here?"

"No. Just make sure Sasha is well cared for when she gets home."

"Of course. Be careful, Yemaya. If they are traders, they're extremely dangerous."

"Not as dangerous as me...but I will be careful. Later." Closing the lid of her phone, she took Dakota by the arm and guided her toward the exit. "We need to check out the waterfront area."

"Alright, but if we find something, we call the police."

"We will see," was all Yemaya said as they walked out of the hospital.

CHAPTER 18

KALI STOOD POLISHING the glasses as she stared at the silver-haired woman sitting at a corner table. She had known Cammie for a long time. Knowing the Cambion would be uncomfortable if she knew how she felt, Kali had kept her distance. Had Cammie shown even the slightest interest in her, the demoness would have taken a chance at a relationship.

"When are you going to do something about this?" asked Agra, walking up to stand behind her.

"About what?"

"About her. And don't pretend you don't know what I mean."

"There's nothing to do," Kali mumbled, glancing up at her friend. "She has no interest in me."

"How would you know? You avoid her."

"I know. Leave it at that."

"Not this time. You've been lusting after her for a thousand years. Tell her how you feel?"

"Just drop it, Agra. Please!"

Taking Kali by the shoulders, Agra turned her around to face her. Kali stared at the glass in her hand.

"Look at me, Kali."

Slowly, Kali raised her head.

"Listen. Cammie is a lost soul. We both know that. She has spent this entire life avoiding relationships out of fear they would be superficial. That's a lot of baggage. Not to mention believing no one could love her for herself. Why should she think you're any different?"

"Because I am! I'm a demon, not some weak mortal."

"I know that. But does she? How many minions and demons have fallen for her, already? Why do you think she spends so much time here? It's because she feels safe. She can pick up women who are looking for a night or two of fun. If they want something more, she hides behind us, knowing we'll protect her privacy."

"Isn't that the point? If I even thought she'd look at me... what happens if it didn't work out? One of us would have to leave, and it wouldn't be me."

"Both of you are too old and too experienced to let a failed relationship escalate. Besides, Lilith and I would intervene long before that. Worst case scenario, you go back to your old reclusive ways and she pretends nothing happened. Cammie's good at that."

"Yeah, I guess. I'll think about it," murmured Kali, glancing longingly at the Cambion.

"Good. Now, while you're thinking, take her this drink? She's been waiting quite awhile."

Placing the glass in her friend's hand, Agra walked away, leaving Kali with no choice. Slowly, she walked over to Cammie and handed her the drink.

"Sorry it took so long."

"Oh it's okay...thanks. I'm in no hurry."

"Ummm...you waiting for someone?"

"Not really, just passing the time...you know how it is," she said. Cammie glanced up at the shy bartender, who happened to raise her eyes just then. It was the first time they had ever made eye contact and, for several seconds, neither of them spoke. Kali was the first one to break the spell, looking away and blushing faintly. She was afraid that Cammie might have sensed her feelings.

"Well...look...if you need anything else...umm...just call me."

"Thanks. Hmmm...seems kind of slow here at the moment."

"Yeah! Some of the customers offered to ask around about our girls. Lilith promised free drinks for a month to anyone who came up with any substantial information about their whereabouts."

"Has anyone checked with Dis?"

"Lilith just returned. She said he doesn't know anything and doesn't really care. He's more interested in his libido than this world."

"Some things never change. Look, if you don't have much to do, keep me company for a while. It's not much fun sitting here, staring at the walls. I don't want to live in my mind for the next few hours, if you know what I mean."

Taken aback, Kali hesitated. Looking toward Agra, she saw her friend give a nod and slight smile before going back to her own work.

"Sure. There's nothing pressing at the moment, and I know exactly what you mean."

"Thanks." Cammie grinned, her cheeks crinkling with dimples. "So, where do you go from here if nothing turns up on the whores?"

"I'm not sure. Agra is talking about going to the Twin. I don't think that's a good idea."

"Neither do I. Dis would be pissed if one of his most powerful demons sought help from his brother. There would be Hell to pay...literally. Perhaps I can check around also. I have some contacts not even available to you or the others," Cammie said mysteriously.

"Really? Now you have me curious. Who?"

Laughing, Cammie gave Kali a broad Cheshire cat grin.

"You'd be surprised. Fill me in on the details?"

Shrugging, Kali told her about Jenny, Sasha and Belinda. After listening to the bartender's story, Cammie stood up.

"Okay. What time do you get off?"

"About four. Why?"

"Well, maybe we could have a drink or something once you're off duty...that is, if you want."

"Ummm...sounds good."

Cammie nodded and then left, leaving Kali behind smiling sheepishly.

"I'd say you have a date," Agra teased from across the room.

Blushing, Kali gave her the finger and then laughed. Agra smirked but decided to save the teasing for later. It was a first step for her friend and she didn't want to embarrass her too much.

* * *

When Cammie returned to her condo, she lay down on her bed, closed her eyes and slipped into a dream state. Colors flickered in front of her closed eyes and the faint smell of flowers drifted in and out. An image wavered in front of her and then solidified. Stepping into another world, she stood beside a small lake.

"It's been a long time, Cammie."

Turning toward the voice, the demoness smiled.

"Arbora! You're as beautiful as ever."

"As are you." The vibrant, purple-haired spirit grinned impishly. "What brings you here? I haven't had the pleasure of your company in over a thousand years."

"I seriously don't think Ursa would appreciate my presence now that you two have joined," teased Cammie. "She doesn't have quite the sense of humor that you and I do."

"True. It could prove awkward, but we could spice up her life a little, don't you think? We haven't officially joined, you know."

"Well, I'll still take a raincheck. Official or not, she'd hunt me down and rip the essence from my body if she thought I was with you."

"She's not that bad. More growl than bite. Once you get to know her, she actually has a great sense of humor...in a bearish sort of way."

"I'll take your word for it."

Arbora's laughter was like a warm breeze.

"Come!" Arbora ordered, patting a place on the ground next to her. "Sit and tell me what's so important you would risk Ursa's wrath to visit me."

Cammie settled on the soft green grass and gazed out over the azure blue lake.

"You're lucky," she said, relaxing back on her elbows. "My land is filled with only a few colors, mostly reds, oranges and black. It's not that it isn't beautiful, but it's very stark compared to this."

"Each place holds its own beauty, but I can't imagine a world void of every color. So, what's up?"

"Well, some friends of mine need help."

"I take it these friends aren't mortal."

"No, they're more like me, but different, if you know what I mean."

"I do. No one is like you. But why me? You have plenty of minions at your disposal."

"You would think. Unfortunately, they have no interest in anything beyond their own gratification. I only need some information and thought the spirits might have heard rumors."

"Tell me what you need, and I'll see what I can find out."

Cammie gave Arbora a quick description of her friends, Kali and Agra, and an outline of the disappearance of the whores. "So you see, this could escalate if they go to the Twin. It could bring about another battle."

"All of this over a couple of prostitutes? I'm surprised. It seems a little extreme, don't you think?"

"I agree, but Agra is fond of her whores, like a mother is for her children. I think she's beyond reason now."

"Sounds like it. Relax here for a few minutes. I'll see what Intunecat has to say. If anyone knows about events on the dark side, it's him."

"Thanks."

Seconds later, a shadowy figure in a black cape and hood appeared next to them. Red eyes glowed brilliantly within the folds of his black cowl.

"I hope this is important," he grumbled, unhappy about the summons. "The whole spirit world heard your bellow."

"Oh stop exaggerating, Tuney. You know you're the only one who heard me." Arbora grinned, enjoying his grumpiness.

Shaking his head in disgust at the nickname, the Dark One knew he could do nothing to intimidate the spirit. As the proverbial child of life, she never took anything too seriously.

"What do you want?"

"Information! Do you know anything about missing whores?"

"You called me here to ask about whores? I have nothing to do with them and you know it."

"Geez, Tuney, lighten up. I just want to know if you've heard of anything unusual going on in the land of mortals. Not if you're fornicating with them."

"Don't be ridiculous. As if I ever would. Perhaps you should be talking to Mari."

"What would the Earth Mother know about whores?"

"Well apparently, they are the hot topic at the moment. She and Maopa are checking into the abduction and torture of one of Yemaya's people, a young woman named Sasha."

"Sasha?" interrupted Cammie.

"Yes. You know this mortal?"

"Not personally, but she's one of the whores my friends are searching for."

"And what is your role in all of this?" Arbora asked Intunecat.

"A messenger, nothing more."

"A messenger who knows more than he tells, I think."

The dark spirit laughed.

"This is serious, Intunecat. If Cammie's friends don't find these women, it could ignite the old feud between the Twins."

The change in the woodland spirit's demeanor surprised Intunecat. Rarely did she give up her optimistic, carefree attitude.

"Then by all means, I'll do what I can to help. Ask your friends to meet me back here shortly. In the meantime, I'll see what else I can find out."

"I think it would be better if you met with Lilith instead," Cammie said. "She's less hotheaded and more reasonable."

"As you wish."

Before either could respond, he vanished.

"He's impressive," Cammie said.

"He can be. He likes to act the badass but he has a soft spot for Mari and a few humans. I've never known him to get so personally involved with them before. Now it's almost a habit."

"Interesting. Well, I'd better find Lilith. Thanks for all of your help, Arbora. Tell Ursa I said hello."

"I think I'll keep this little meeting confidential for now. She still thinks you and I had a thing going."

"We did. She's very intuitive, isn't she?" The demoness grinned and then vanished.

CHAPTER 19

CATRINA WAS FRUSTRATED. Sasha hadn't given her the satisfaction she craved. She needed to release some pent up energy. Calling her housekeeper, she instructed her to send up the new maid she'd hired three weeks earlier.

The girl had been a waitress at a restaurant where Catrina dined. During the meal, she teased the pretty Latina, making her laugh and blush, all the while imagining what it would be like to get her into her bed. Afterwards, she placed a large tip in her hand, along with a business card. On the back was a note offering her a job as a personal maid along with an impressive salary quote. Now the girl would earn her pay.

"What's your name again?"

"Helena, ma'am," the girl said shyly.

"Helena. That's a nice name. Do you know why I sent for you?"

"No, ma'am."

"I can't sleep. Come here!"

Catrina patted the mattress next to where she was lying. When the girl sat down, Catrina began stroking her long black hair.

"You have beautiful hair. Has anyone ever told you that?"

"Si, my boyfriend."

"Boyfriend? Such a waste. Men don't know how to treat women. Have you ever been with a woman, Helena?"

"No...no, ma'am."

"Then you're in for a treat tonight. Remove your clothes."

"Please, ma'am. I don't like girls that way."

"You don't know what you like. Do as I say."

"Ma'am, please. I don't want to do this."

"I said remove your clothes. Or do you want me to call in one of my men and have them removed?"

"No."

Catrina watched the young woman reluctantly take off her dress, slip and underwear.

"Good. Get into bed."

Frightened, Helena climbed into bed and knelt next to her employer. Catrina settled back onto the sheets spreading her legs.

"Eat me," she ordered.

"Ms. Drenkova, please. I can't."

"You can and will...and you'll do it right or I'll call in my bodyguards and give you to them. You understand me?"

"Ye...yes. What do I do?"

Tears streamed down the maid's cheeks.

"First, stop the tears. I don't like weepy little girls. Put your head between my legs and lick my pussy like it was the best thing you ever tasted. Better make me believe it, too."

Helena knelt down, looking at the curly hair. With her finger and thumb she separated the lips and lowered her head. The warm musky scent wasn't unpleasant but when she started to touch the moist skin with her tongue she gagged. Quickly, she looked up to see if Catrina had noticed. The woman's expression frightened her. Swallowing, she leaned down and tried it again, choking back another gag.

"Sa-mi Lingi Pizda, Tarfa!" Catrina yelled. "Do that again and I will have you killed."

Terrified, Helena worked her tongue harder.

"That's better. Now, long slow strokes, then quick flicks of your tongue," Catrina ordered. "I can't believe your boyfriend never went down on you."

Helena continued lapping at the woman's vulva and lips. If she held her breath and thought about her boyfriend, she found she could perform reasonably well. Hopefully, her employer would grow tired of her and let her go back to her room. Then she'd pack her bags and leave at the first opportunity.

"Harder! I want to feel your tongue. I want it buried inside of me."

When the maid hesitated, Catrina grabbed the back of her head and pushed her face hard into her groin.

"I said harder and deeper. Make me come or my boys will get to enjoy those lips and tongue of yours. Understand?"

Helena nodded and worked her tongue vigorously over the slick area. When she heard the woman moan, she increased the pressure, stroking the opening rapidly.

"Yes, that's it. There...good...yes..." groaned Catrina. "Harder...mmmm...good...good," she gasped.

When the orgasm hit, she held the girl's head tightly against her until her muscles relaxed.

"Excellent, Helena," she purred. "I knew you'd be good."

"Th...Thank you, ma'am," Helena whispered, wanting to escape as quickly as possible. The taste in her mouth revolted her. "Can I go, please?"

Catrina scowled.

"You can go when I say so. The night's still young, Helena. Rest for a bit. Then we'll try it again. Do you like the way I taste?"

"Ye...yes, ma'am," the maid lied, swallowing back the bile that kept trying to work its way up her throat.

"I knew you would. You're wasting yourself on your boyfriend. If you please me again, I might make you my special maid. Would you like that?"

"Yes, ma'am," Helena murmured, despondently.

CHAPTER 2 0

BELINDA WASN'T SURE where she was. The rocking sensation wasn't from the dizziness she was feeling. Opening her eyes, she squinted into the darkness. The room was a dull metallic gray. Two other women sat on makeshift beds, while a third paced restlessly back and forth in the small cabin. The whore knew immediately she was on a ship. By the size of the room, it was probably a freighter. Sitting up she took a mental inventory of her body, searching for signs of abuse. Thankfully, she hadn't been raped. Abduction was another matter.

"About time you woke up," grumbled the small blonde who had stopped her pacing to look at Belinda.

"Where am I?"

"Where the fuck do you think you are?"

Belinda shrugged.

"Look. I'm not into a pissing match. It's obvious we're all in the same boat so how about we try and get along?"

Laughing, a tall black woman slipped off the bed and walked over to the whore. Holding out her hand, she helped Belinda to her feet.

"I'm Smitty. It appears we're on our way to Saudi Arabia or somewhere near there. Seems there are sheiks willing to pay high prices for whores."

"What the hell do they want women like us for? They like sweet young virgins."

"Apparently not all of them. One of the guys that brings our food is real informative when you treat him right. I do him a favor, he does me one."

"You'd fuck anyone!" the blonde said.

"Shut up, Carla. I'm tired of your pissing and moaning."

Carla was about to say something when Smitty took a menacing step in her direction. Swallowing, the woman backed away and gave her a sullen pout.

"Don't mind her," Smitty said. "She's new to the business... scared silly. When she settles down, she's actually quite nice."

Belinda examined the two women closely and then looked at the third one, who had remained quiet during the exchange. Nodding her head toward her, she raised an eyebrow questioningly.

"That's Mary Beth. She doesn't talk much. I think she's a little slow, if you know what I mean."

"Yeah, I know. So why would anyone go to this trouble for women like us? It doesn't make any sense."

"Apparently, these guys appreciate our expertise. No one's gonna question our disappearance. Even if they did, the cops wouldn't do much. What's a few missing whores?"

"Well, my bosses aren't going to like this. They'll do something," Belinda declared, remembering Agra's promise when she first signed up.

"You do your job and stick to the rules and we'll protect you, no matter what," Agra said toward the end of the interview. "You screw up, you're on your own."

Belinda believed her. The look in her eyes left no doubt the woman would search heaven and earth for her. Little did she know how true the promise had been.

"What can they do? We're outside the police's jurisdiction and no one knows we're here."

"They'll find us."

"You got more confidence than I do. If your bosses are that good, they must have powerful connections. Personally, I think we're screwed."

"Maybe. I'm still betting on my bosses."

The sound of someone outside the door interrupted their conversation. When the door swung inward, a young sailor stepped inside and looked around. Pointing to Smitty, he waved his hand for her to follow.

"Captain wants to see yah," he murmured.

Winking at Belinda, Smitty strolled out the door without commenting. Apparently, the whore was familiar with the Captain.

Walking over to her empty cot, Belinda lay down and closed her eyes, feeling tired. As she dozed off, the image of Agra flashed through her mind, giving her a sense of comfort.

CHAPTER 2 1

THE TRIP TO THE warehouse district gave Dakota and Yemaya a few leads. Several companies had international affiliations. Anyone involved in the sex-trade industry would have to have connections overseas. That was the only way to smuggle women out of the States.

Writing down names and addresses, Yemaya called her brother. His partner was a genius at Internet research.

"I doubt if we can do more now," Yemaya said after she hung up.

"Me either. Let's get a bite to eat, and a couple hours of rest."

"Sounds good. "

* * *

Yemaya was awakened by her cell phone ringing.

"Lysanne."

"Good afternoon, sister."

"Good morning. What have you found?"

"As always, straight to the point. Reymone has been snooping around or at least his contacts have. We discovered a possibility. Catrina Drenkova."

"Drenkova! The Drenkova that is rumored to have connections with members of our parliament?"

"The same. There are also stories going around that she is involved in a drug ring. Possibly even the white slave trade. The woman has a very shady reputation."

"Slavery? This may be what happened to Sasha. Have any of our young women in Moldova disappeared?"

"Not to our knowledge. Ms. Drenkova runs an import/export business with offices strategically located in Europe, southeast Asia, and the Middle East. Her home office is in Baltimore. She's cozied up to a few politicians in the States and receives considerable perks for being based there. One Senator was investigated for having illegal immigrants as domestics."

When Yemaya heard Baltimore, she stiffened.

"Thanks, Raidon. What's Ms. Drenkova's address?" Raidon gave her both the office address and her home address, a small secluded estate outside the city limits. "One more thing," Yemaya said. "Send me her picture."

"As we speak. You should receive it shortly."

"Good. I will get back with you."

"Be careful, sister. Don't lose your head."

"I never do. Bye."

Checking her email, Yemaya opened the photo of Catrina Drenkova.

"Is that her?" Dakota asked.

"Yes."

"She's very attractive."

"Beauty is good at hiding evil."

"So what now?"

"We rest. Tomorrow, we check on Sasha and then Ms. Drenkova."

Dakota snuggled up close to Yemaya. Within minutes, both were sound asleep.

* * *

"Yemaya, I know you're tired, but we need to talk," whispered a sultry voice, much like her own.

"Can this wait, Mari?"

"If it could, I wouldn't bother you."

Yemaya opened her eyes. She was sitting in front of the Eternal Flame. Grandma Dakota and Intunecat were talking quietly but stopped when Yemaya appeared.

"How yah doin', Yemaya?"

"Tired. You and Mari keep strange company these days," Yemaya said, looking toward Intunecat.

"Strange?" the Dark One asked.

"He's here to help," said Mari.

"Help? Dakota said you cannot help Sasha since no spirits are involved."

"Well, that's not exactly true. We occasionally break the rules."

"Like impersonating Dakota and me? That doctor probably thinks we are psychos, but thanks for helping Sasha."

"She's one of my own. I could do nothing less," Mari replied.

"Yep. And I believes what be Mari's, be mine."

"Thank you, Grandma Dakota. Alright, why the meeting?"

"Tomorrow you and Dakota will confront the mortal who brutalized the young woman," interrupted Intunecat. "It's imperative you not give in to the rage you hide so well."

"Why do you care? I thought you thrived on dark emotions."

"Only when they serve my needs. This situation doesn't."

130

Yemaya was about to comment when he interrupted her by holding up his hand.

"This isn't the time for debate. Inside of you is a darkness all mortals carry. It has nothing to do with me. Your darkness is strong. Control your rage and you control the *beast*. Fail and it becomes yours."

"And how do I control my anger? It is a normal emotion."

"This isn't anger, daughter. This is rage. Anger serves you well. Rage serves the *beast*. We must go now. We'll do what we can to help Sasha."

"Thanks."

Turning to Intunecat, Yemaya hesitated.

"And you. One thing, though. Your help does not obligate me to you in any way."

The Dark One smiled.

"I never said it did," he replied, and vanished.

CHAPTER 22

LONNIE WAS INFORMED earlier in the day that her patient would be transferred to a charter flight and flown to Moldova.

"I really don't recommend moving her yet," she objected. "The flight is long and she still needs medical attention."

"We've arranged for everything," replied the dark-haired woman, her voice warm and silky.

"I still don't like it. She's my patient. I also have Sasha's mental state to consider. Having a stranger caring for her might add to her trauma. She's still confused about everything. Who's going to attend to her during the flight?"

The smaller woman coughed.

"Pardon me, doc, but maybe yah could be a makin' the trip with the youngun'."

Lonnie was momentarily speechless.

Good grief! Either this one is psycho or...or what?

Yemaya chuckled, her pale blue eyes twinkling.

"My partner can be very *country* sometimes, but she's working on it."

Dakota slapped her arm.

"Behave now. I be...I mean I...well dang,...so I be country. Ain't no law agin' it."

Yemaya and Lonnie couldn't help but laugh.

"No, there ain't," Lonnie replied. "I'd love to accompany Sasha, but I have obligations to my other patients. Plus, I'd have to check my passport, make arrangements for a visa. Two days really isn't enough time to do much of anything."

"Normally, that's true. However, since you'd be a guest in my country, the visa isn't a problem. My business manager already talked with your government officials. They've agreed to expedite your paperwork. Your administrator said it wasn't a problem if you agreed. I assured him your position will be filled by a competent doctor. Everyone will be well compensated during your absence, as will you."

Lonnie frowned. Apparently, there was more to this woman than just wealth.

"Seems you've removed about all my objections or obstacles."

"We've tried. I'd be very grateful if you did this."

"My main concern is Sasha. I'll need certain equipment and supplies if I decide to do this."

"Yah names it and it be yours."

"Yes, if you call my manager, he'll provide you with anything you need," Yemaya said, handing the doctor her business card.

"Sounds like I don't have a choice. I'll see you two on the flight."

"Unless something comes up, we'll be there."

"Yah kin bet yah booties, doc."

* * *

Intunecat knew instantly the moment Lilith entered his dark world, and marveled at her ability to negotiate the impenetrable blackness.

"I'm impressed," he said, his voice deep, but nothing like that of her ex, Dis.

"About what?"

"Few are able to find their way through the darkness. You seem comfortable in it."

Laughing, Lilith walked over to a large fluffy chair and sat down.

"I'm used to it. The Underworld is more than fire and brimstone."

"I can imagine, but even in its darkest corners it can't be completely devoid of light. Mine is the only such place."

"I don't need light to find my way anywhere. We both know the eyes see nothing here. It's the mind that sees all."

"Only a few."

"Perhaps, or perhaps you've lived here too long. The worlds are evolving. There are things out there we would never have imagined a few thousand years ago."

"I'm aware of the new darkness, my dear. Unlike the Twins, I haven't abandoned the mortal world." At the mention of the Twins, Lilith frowned. "Yes, I know the truth about them," he continued. "Your last great battle spilled over into our world. The spirits didn't appreciate that."

Handing her a glass of wine, the dark spirit sat down across from her.

"Those were terrible times for everyone," Lilith said. "but enough of this! Cammie said you may know something about the missing whores."

"I know of one named Sasha, if she is one of yours."

"Yes, where is she?"

"I'll show you."

From the blackness, a vision of the young woman in the hospital appeared. Beside her stood the two women she had met in her nightclub.

"What have Yemaya and Dakota to do with her?" asked Lilith, standing so she could move closer to the images.

"Sasha is one of Yemaya's people. These two women, however, are not who you think they are."

"Don't play games with me, Intunecat. I met them a few nights ago in my bar."

"I doubt it. The tall one is Mari. The other is her partner, Maopa. They are the ancestors of Yemaya and Dakota."

"Mari? Since when did the Earth Mother renew her interest in humanity?"

"Lilith, you surprise me. No one can mistake the likeness between Mari and her mortal offspring. Besides, you've met Yemaya. Mortals lust after her. She's very much like your young Cambion. Only Yemaya is an innocent. She isn't aware of her attraction."

"And her companion? Is she a victim of lust?"

"Unfortunately, no. If she were, Yemaya would be mine by now."

"You lust after a mortal?"

The Dark One shook his head and laughed.

"No. Her darkness is what interests me. Even she would be no match for my appetites."

"I'd never have taken you for a sexual creature."

"I said appetites, my dear. Unlike your ex, knowledge is more satisfying to me than sexual gratification...although I find the thought of the latter pleasing."

Lilith turned to stare at the spirit. His curious phrasing intrigued her, as did his beauty. Few males were actually beautiful. She couldn't help but compare it to Adam's boyishly handsome face.

Pale, with long golden locks of hair and azure blue eyes, Adam glowed with innocence and purity. Staying with him had eventually become too much of a burden. She didn't have the heart to corrupt the child in him. Also, his reluctance to defy the Twin's ban on the forbidden fruit had irritated her. An eternity with him would have bored her.

When Dis entered her life, she found him a better match. He seduced her with knowledge, showing her things she could never imagine. They explored their relationship from every conceivable angle. For thousands of years they enjoyed their affair, and the battle of wills for dominance. Sexually, neither could best the other. In time though, life stagnated. Lilith lost interest in Dis, and he lost interest in everything but sexual gratification.

Eventually, Lilith ended the relationship and moved into the world of humans, finding them and their evolution more interesting. Agra, who gained the rights to the whores, joined Lilith and was soon followed by fiery Kali, another demoness who had grown bored with life.

For ten thousand years, the three had been friends. At first, they indulged in all of the debauchery and sexual depravities imaginable, and some that weren't. In time their lust cooled. Their desires waned. The friendship remained.

Now, after all those millennia, here stood an intelligent, courtly, beautiful, dark and mysterious entity. She also suspected he was a virgin.

"Was it something I said?" asked Intunecat, interrupting her thoughts.

"No. Not really. I was just remembering a time long ago. Forgive my rudeness."

"Nothing to forgive, my dear. We all take those trips. I hate to interrupt yours but if your demonesses are anything like the spirits, they're growing impatient. Even time can't always teach patience."

"You're right, of course. Thank you, Intunecat."

"It was my pleasure. I hope you'll come again. I get few visitors."

"I'd like that."

Moving into the shadows of the darkness, Lilith disappeared, leaving the Dark One feeling more lonely than he had felt in his entire long existence, and more alive.

* * *

Catrina took a sip of coffee as she read the morning paper. A small article on the fifth page referred to a young Jane Doe discovered outside the local hospital. Other than referencing her as an assault victim, it said very little.

"Probably some asshole beating up on his girlfriend," she muttered disgustedly, throwing the paper in the trash and turning toward Ivan. "Has last night's business been taken care of?"

"Yeah, Breshni's cleaned up everything and disposed of it. There's nothing to connect her with you," replied Ivan, his eyes glancing at the discarded paper. "Anything of interest in the paper?"

"Nothing new. The President and Congress are spending money like it's their own personal bankroll. These Americans can be so stupid, sometimes. Thankfully, they have lots of money to spend."

"Well, if it weren't for stupidity and greed we'd be out of business," Ivan said. "In fact, our own people aren't much better. Look how easy it was to bribe our President's brother to look the other way in this venture."

"True. A shame the President isn't as greedy. We could send our product through Moldova instead of having to go around it. We could even acquire a few Carpis, although after last night I don't see anything special about them. My maid was a better lay. Still, it's amazing how a reputation can increase profits."

Ivan nodded.

"Yeah, let's hope it's just a reputation."

Catrina shrugged. "Makes no difference at the moment. I'm shutting down the overseas market temporarily. I've heard rumors someone's been asking about our European offices. Fill the last order and tell everyone to scatter until we contact them."

"What about the shipment of prostitutes we just sent to Saudi? It'll take two weeks for the freighter to get there."

"Contact the captain. Tell him to ditch the cargo. He'll know what to do."

"As you wish," said Ivan, reluctantly.

Looking up from her writing, Catrina sensed his hesitation. "Something you don't approve of?"

"No. I just think that's a little extreme. They're in international waters now. Once they reach their destination, no one's going to care, right?"

"That's not the point, but since you seem to be developing a conscience, get Breshni in here. He can make the call."

Once Ivan was gone, Catrina picked up the phone and dialed a number before leaning back in her chair.

"Rubinsky speaking," a gruff voice answered.

"Leonid, this is Catrina Drenkova."

"Good evening or should I say good morning, Ms. Drenkova. What can I do for you?"

"Well, first you can send a half dozen more girls to my client in Bosnia free of charge," Catrina stated coldly.

"Free? Why would I do that? Didn't they get the last shipment intact?"

"Intact? They were old women. He specifically said no older than eighteen, Rubinsky. The ones you sent gave him a lot of trouble and he's pissed. They killed one girl to set an example."

"If they treated their merchandise better, they'd last longer," Rubinsky replied calmly.

"Listen you asshole, if you can't do your job, I'll get someone who can. I deal in quality. We don't make mistakes like this. Now, do I get those replacements?"

"Satisfaction has always been my motto, Ms. Drenkova. Of course I'll send the replacements. I must insist, however, that you pay for the handling and shipping. After all, I have a large overhead, if you know what I mean."

"Yes, yes. One more thing. Someone in Moldova has been asking questions about our little enterprise. My sources believe the Lysannes are behind it. Have you heard anything?"

"Rumors. We need to stay away from that family. There's something unnatural about them. No one's willing to cross them. You'd think they were gods."

"Not gods, Rubinsky, just rich and powerful. I'm working on eliminating this problem. Ms. Lysanne escaped one accident. She won't be so lucky the next time."

"I like the way you think, Ms. Drenkova. The fewer problems, the better, eh?"

"And the more we both make. Now, I have other things to deal with. I expect delivery in two weeks. Oh, and Rubinsky, let the others know we're putting a temporary hold on things until this little matter is settled."

"What about the merchandise we're holding in storage?"

"How many are we talking about? And where is this merchandise?" asked Catrina, tapping her pencil on the arm of her chair.

"Somewhere between fifty and seventy I think. Most are spread out across Europe and a few Arab countries. There are nine in the States, not counting the six you just ordered. Are you sure you still want them delivered?"

"Yes. Get rid of the others. No witnesses, no bodies, Rubinsky. I'll talk with you in a few days." Spinning her chair around, she looked out the window at the loading dock. "Looks like I'm going to have to find my entertainment another way," she grumbled. "Guess that's why I have so many maids."

CHAPTER 2 3

THE FIRST MATE reluctantly knocked on the Captain's door. Torelli was known for his hot temper and wouldn't appreciate the interruption, especially since he was enjoying the evening entertaining a woman brought to him from below deck. Vicente suspected she was a stowaway but dared not question Captain Torelli.

"What is it?" yelled Torelli.

"Capitan, there is a call for you from one of Ms. Drenkova's employees. You aren't answering your phone. He said it was important."

"Tell him I'll call him back. I'm busy."

"I tried to, but he insisted. Quite vehemently."

The door was yanked open and it startled Vicente, causing him to jump back. Captain Torelli glared at his first mate as he buckled his belt and zipped up his pants.

"Get her out of here. Call Seaman Krokosy and have him return her to the hold," he ordered, nodding toward a woman on her knees by his desk. "And make sure she doesn't steal anything from my office."

Saluting, Vicente pushed an intercom button and ordered the seaman to the Captain's office. Stepping past the Captain he walked over to the woman and helped her to her feet. Seaman

Krokowsky met him at the door and took possession of the woman, pulling her roughly down the hall and out the hatch.

Cursing under this breath, Captain Torelli walked to his desk and sat down, picking up the phone.

"Captain Torelli, here...yes, I know who you are...the bitch's lapdog...I don't care what you tell her, I work for the shipping company, not for her. Listen, I have more important things to do than listen to your bullshit. What does Drenkova want?"

Vicente watched as the Captain's face grew redder and redder.

"You tell that woman I'm not her fucking servant. I transport her merchandise and that's it...I don't give a fuck how powerful she is. Your threats don't scare me. If she wants someone to clean up after her, she can do it when we're in port, after they're off my vessel. And Breshni? Tell the bitch this is the last package she'll ship on my freighter." Slamming the phone down, he motioned for Vicente to follow him. "Someone needs to kill that fucking cunt."

* * *

Yemaya dialed the hospital to talk with Dr. Sanders. The receptionist politely told her the doctor was in a conference with a patient's aunt and her partner but she'd be happy to take a message.

"No need. I'll call her later," replied Yemaya.

Dakota raised her eyebrows in a questioning gesture.

"It appears you and I are in conference with the good doctor."

Dakota shook her head and laughed.

"I wonder what would have happened if we'd just shown up."

"Mass confusion. I think we will leave them to deal with Sasha. Are you up for a ride?"

"Yep. Let's do it. I can't wait to meet Ms. Drenkova. As long as you behave."

Yemaya didn't answer.

The office of Eurasian Exports was located in a warehouse near the shipping docks at the harbor. As the taxi pulled up to the building, Ivan stepped outside the front door. Giving the cab a quick glance, he continued on. Had he waited to see who the occupants were, he'd have cancelled his trip.

"Promise me you won't lose your cool." Dakota watched Yemaya's face for signs of anger.

"I will not lose my cool."

"Somehow that doesn't make me feel better."

"Me either. Shall we go in?"

Entering the office, the two approached the receptionist, an older woman wearing glasses.

"Can I help you?" she inquired politely.

"We're here to see Ms. Drenkova," Dakota said.

"Do you have an appointment?"

"Not really, but she will see us," Yemaya said. "Tell her Ms. Devereaux and Ms. Lysanne are here."

"Very well. Please wait over there."

Picking up the phone, she dialed her boss's extension.

"Ms. Drenkova. There are two ladies here who wish to talk with you, a Ms. Devereaux and a Ms. Lysanne."

Putting her pen down, Catrina leaned back in her chair.

"I see. Send them in."

"Yes, ma'am."

So, thought Catrina. *At last we meet.*

Ms. Johnson opened the door, motioning the two women into the room.

"Welcome, Ms. Lysanne, Ms. Devereaux. Please have a seat," Catrina offered, gesturing to the two chairs in front of her desk. "What can I do for you?"

"Thank you. We will not take up much of your time."

"I have plenty of time," Catrina replied, folding her hands on her desk. "Especially for someone as well-known as you, Miss Lysanne. How can I help you?"

"I think it is more about how we can help you. Someone in your company may be using your facilities for illegal activity. I have information that human trafficking activity is being funneled through your warehouse complex. Without your knowledge, of course," Yemaya stated calmly.

"I see. Well, if this is true, I'll certainly take the necessary actions to put a stop to it. Would you mind telling me where you heard this? It's difficult to believe any of my employees would do such a thing," Catrina said, leaning back in her chair.

"I would not want to put them at risk. You understand."

"Of course. Just as I wouldn't want to falsely accuse anyone. I'm sure you understand my side. Perhaps you'll tell me why you came to me instead of going to the police. This is a serious accusation."

"A courtesy...from one business woman to another," Yemaya replied, coolly.

"Ah, then I'm in your debt. Could you at least tell me your interest in this? Not that it isn't a matter for all of us to be concerned about."

"Personal. A young friend of mine appears to have gotten caught up in this by accident and was almost killed. Fortunately, she was found and will recover."

Except for a slight downward turn of her lips, Catrina showed no emotion.

"She's very lucky...that she'll be alright, I mean. Does she remember what happened?"

"No, but it is only a matter of time before she does. At the moment, I have made arrangements to fly her home. It will be safer there."

"Hmmmm...No doubt you know what's best for her." Glancing at her watch, Catrina stood up quickly and walked around the desk. "I'm sorry to cut this short but I really should check into these accusations. If you'll leave a number and address where I can reach you, I'll let you know if any of them are true."

"Thank you, Ms. Drenkova. Unfortunately, we are in town for only a few days so an address serves no purpose. You can contact me on my cell phone."

Quickly writing the number on the back of her business card, Yemaya handed it to the woman.

"I'll be in touch," Catrina promised.

"We look forward to it. Have a nice day."

Yemaya ushered Dakota from the room and away from the building.

"Do you think it's wise telling her so much?" Dakota asked.

"She is more likely to make mistakes if she feels some pressure."

"I agree but we may have endangered Sasha."

"Sasha is safe. She will be back in Moldova within forty-eight hours. I am more concerned that others are being held around here. We need to find out."

"How are we going to do that? We can't stand here all day and night watching her."

"No, but I know someone who can."

Taking out her cell, she dialed her agent's number.

"Sonny, who can you get to stake out a place in Baltimore?"

"And hello to you too," he replied. "When do you want to start?"

"Now."

"Damn, Yemaya, why is everything always *now* with you? Anyone ever tell you it takes time to organize some things?"

"With what I pay, I doubt most people would say that. Who can you get?"

"Give me the facts. I'll have someone in thirty minutes. That's the best I can do."

"Good enough."

Yemaya gave him the information and hung up.

"Let's go," she said, taking Dakota by the arm.

"Where to?"

"Your place. Now, we wait."

* * *

Later that day, Yemaya and Dakota were curled up on the couch watching television when Yemaya's cell phone rang.

"Lysanne," she answered.

"Ms. Lysanne. My name's Willie. Sonny gave me your number and said to call you if I saw anything unusual at the waterfront."

"I take it you have."

"Oh yeah. Shortly after I arrived at the dock, a big goon showed up at Eurasian Exports. A guy named Breshni Vencheilli. He's been on Ms. Drenkova's payroll for about ten years. He doesn't have the brains of a pissant but he's as loyal as a dog."

"What about him?"

"Well, he was inside for about forty minutes and then came out. Next thing I know he's calling someone. A Captain Torelli. Telling him to ditch the merchandise. Apparently the captain took exception to the order and they had an argument. Breshni wasn't too happy."

"You heard this conversation?"

"With my very own ears, Ms. Lysanne. It's amazing what cell phone scanners can do now."

"Who is this Captain Torelli?"

"He operates a freighter registered in Greece but it's on its way to Saudi Arabia. It's been at sea for about a week and is due to arrive there in another two weeks."

"Is there any way we can intercept this vessel?"

"I'm sorry, Ms. Lysanne. That's way out of my league. It's in international waters. Any attempt to board would be considered piracy."

"Can you get in touch with Captain Torelli?"

"Sure. We captured his number when Breshni made the call. You want me to call this guy?"

"Yes. Tell him he is to do nothing, and I mean absolutely nothing with his cargo without your consent. Have him fax you a copy of his manifest."

"I'll give him the message, Ms. Lysanne, but I don't think he'll pay any attention to what I have to say."

"He will," Yemaya said coldly, struggling to suppress her rage. "Ms. Drenkova may be paying for the freight but she does not own the shipping company. Oh, and make sure the captain is informed that he will be held personally responsible for anything that happens to his cargo. And I don't mean by the authorities.

"If he has any doubts about what I can do, remind him of the Aegis incident. That captain and first mate are still serving time in Jilava, and everyone knows it's one of the worst prisons in Romania. Even Greece's effort to protect them from extradition failed once my agents visited the president.

"But before you call him, call my brother, Raidon Lysanne, and tell him exactly what you told me. He will get you the details and authorization needed to insure Torelli follows your orders."

"Will do," the private investigator said. Writing down the name and number, he told Yemaya he and his team would continue to monitor the docks and let her know if anything else developed.

After hanging up, Yemaya turned to Dakota and gave her the details of the conversation.

"You think they mean women?" Dakota asked. "Surely he wouldn't throw them overboard."

"From what Willie said, he seemed reluctant to. But he is obviously aware they are on board and he just might chance it."

"That's sick."

"Slave traders will do anything to avoid being caught. I think the women are safe for now. If something happens to them, the captain will be held accountable. Carpi accountable."

Not good! Dakota thought.

"What now?"

"I pay another visit to Ms. Drenkova. It is time to put her out of business."

Dakota felt the fury behind the calmly spoken words.

"We, Yemaya. We handle it."

"All right, we go see her. Then we can decide what to do."

* * *

"Back so soon," Ms. Johnson said cordially. "Ms. Drenkova is expecting you."

"Thank you," Dakota said.

Escorting them to Catrina's office, she opened the door and motioned them in.

"Please be seated," Catrina said. I've reviewed all my ledgers and found nothing suspicious. The shipping invoices show no discrepancies. Perhaps your sources are mistaken or have confused us with another company. It would be an understandable mistake," she suggested, amicably.

"Is there anything else you'd like to know?" she asked, attempting to appear helpful while at the same time dismissing the two women.

"There is no mistake. Perhaps you should ask Breshni," Yemaya suggested. Her voice was dangerously calm.

Catrina's eyes widened.

"What would Breshni know about this matter?"

"You tell me. Surely, since he is one of your most trusted employees, you must be aware he called Captain Torelli a few hours ago. Or did he take it upon himself to act on your behalf?"

"I resent your inference, Ms. Lysanne. I've tried my best to accommodate you and your silly accusations, but enough is enough. We have nothing else to discuss. Please leave," she ordered, reaching out to press the intercom button to summon her secretary.

Yemaya intercepted Catrina's hand before she could push the button and held it in a vice-like grip while she searched the woman's mind thoroughly and methodically. Within seconds she found enough information to make her recoil in disgust.

The woman epitomized the worst of humanity. For her, pleasure increased incrementally as the suffering of others rose. Yemaya could feel the *beast* inside her crawling from its cave. Catrina's victims were playthings, nothing more than distractions to appease a perverted lust and sadistic cravings. Sasha, however, had been different.

The woman took a sadistic pleasure in raping virgins. Then she discarded them like garbage. Images of the woman's "toys," the stealing of Sasha's virginity, the pain, sickened Yemaya. Catrina had ordered Breshni to revive the unconscious girl.

Rage fed the rising monster inside of Yemaya.

"You gave her to Breshni after you satisfied yourself, and then told him to dispose of her." Serpent-like, Yemaya uncoiled from her seat and leaned forward, her palms flattened on the desk as she released the hand. Her face was inches from Catrina's. Black, hatred-filled eyes narrowed ominously as they bored into Catrina's gray eyes. "You like to play games, Ms. Drenkova?" she whispered through clenched teeth, her voice cold and emotionless. "So do I. You like to inflict pain."

Reaching out with her right hand, she clasped the woman's chin with her fingertips.

Catrina felt as if her head was about to explode. Yemaya slowly ripped the memories from the woman's mind, one by one, gathering names and facts...caring nothing about the agony or damage left in the wake of her rampage. Layer by layer, she sliced away every thought, every minute detail of Catrina's past.

I thought you liked pain, the *beast* within Yemaya snarled. *That is your high when you torture your victims. Tell me, how does it feel to be raped? To have your thoughts stripped away and your mind opened wide like those young girls' legs? Exposed for my pleasure without your permission? You stole their virginity and their lives, Catrina. Was it worth your soul?*

Yemaya's thoughts continued to whisper cruelly as she caressed the older woman's cheek lovingly. *I can take you here and now, and you would not resist me. I can make you beg to be taken. Would you like that? Do you want to be my slave? To satisfy my every desire? My every whim?* she continued, her voice softening seductively.

At first Dakota wasn't sure what was happening but when she saw Catrina grab her head, her face contorted in pain, she realized the *beast* was in control of Yemaya and was now inside the woman's head.

"No!" she screamed, grabbing Yemaya's arm. "Stop it!"

Black eyes glowered at her menacingly. Shaking off Dakota's hand, *the beast* growled a warning. It would tolerate no interference with its thirst for revenge.

You see, Catrina, I can be gentle, or I can be brutal, it continued, dismissing the journalist. *You never learned to be gentle. Addictions are seductive, but there is a price to pay for pleasure. Perhaps if you beg me...maybe I would take pity on you...or not.* The *beast* enjoyed the fear growing inside of the woman.

Dakota was frantic. Yemaya was no longer in control of herself. The *beast* was intent on killing Catrina. If it succeeded, Yemaya would be lost forever.

"Please Yemaya," she begged, "you promised. You have to stop this. Don't let it kill her; you promised. Mari, Grandma, someone, please help her!" prayed Dakota, tears streaming down her cheeks.

"They can't help her," interrupted a low, silky voice. "She's consumed by her darkness."

"Who are you?" cried Dakota, looking around, expecting to see someone standing near them.

"Someone who heard your prayers. What would you give to save her?" whispered the voice.

"I'd die for her."

"Dying is easy. It's life that's hard. Would you give up your soul?"

"Yes. Yes, if that's what it takes."

"You answer too quickly. This isn't a game. The question is real, as are the terms. I'm asking you for your soul. In return I will save your lover."

Dakota hesitated, realizing exactly what had been asked of her.

"Good. You understand my question is real. What's your answer?"

"I'll give you anything you want," Dakota promised.

"Freely, when asked?"

"Freely."

"Then I will lead you to her. You must show her the way out."

Dakota felt herself being drawn into the battle between the *beast*, Catrina and Yemaya. As her mind slid past the memories, she felt the rage turn its attention toward her. Pain seared her brain like a knife cutting through flesh. Falling to her knees, she cried out, clutching her temples with her hands.

Yemaya, who was struggling to regain control, felt its momentarily distraction and Dakota's pain. Her anger grew. The battle had changed. It was no longer about her. If she didn't defeat this thing, not only would she be lost, but Dakota would die.

Lunging forward, she pushed the rage backward...again and again until she reached Dakota. Mentally, she wrapped herself around her lover's mind, shielding it from the assault. As she soothed away the pain, she fought her own demon.

Dakota could feel the pain subsiding. The effort was draining Yemaya's strength. Sensing her weakening, Dakota joined the battle. Still the rage resisted. Neither would yield. Suddenly, Dakota felt a mental nudge from something else.

Wavering slightly, the darkness retreated. Unwilling to accept defeat, it turned toward Catrina, striking out savagely in frustration.

Yemaya blocked as much of the force as she could. The *beast* screamed. Finally, slinking into the dark recesses of Yemaya's mind, it lay quiet, defeated but untamed. There would be another time, it promised, glaring angrily from its lair.

Dakota felt a sharp tug as she was jerked from Yemaya's mind.

"You have won. She won't remember your intervention or mine. The next time won't be so easy. Don't forget your promise," the voice reminded her and then vanished.

"Easy?" mumbled Dakota, exhausted.

Yemaya looked at Catrina and blinked. The woman was pale, dazed and sweating, but seemed unharmed.

"Is she okay?" Dakota asked.

"I think so."

"What now?"

"I wish I knew. Going back inside to see how this affected her is out of the question," she whispered, slumping into her chair, tiredly. "Let's get out of here. She should recover, shortly. Maybe all of this will scare her into changing."

"Wishful thinking. People like her don't scare. They adapt," Dakota said. "But this might buy us time to come up with a plan."

Catrina opened her eyes, confused. Her visitors were gone. Not quite sure what had just happened, she massaged her temples.

Damn headache. Might as well leave. I can't get much done feeling like this. Maybe a little distraction will ease the tension.

CHAPTER 24

ONCE HOME, CATRINA took a quick shower and crawled into bed. Closing her eyes, she tried to remember the conversation between her and the women that had visited her. At the moment, she couldn't even recall their names. Frustrated, she sent for Helena.

Reluctantly, the maid entered the woman's bedroom.

"Yes, ma'am. You wish my assistance?" Her voice quivered slightly.

"Your services, Helena, not your assistance. I have a headache. I need a little distraction. I'm sure you know what I mean." Catrina smirked, then winced.

"Ma'am, please! You should rest. You aren't well. I will get you aspirin; that will help, I'm sure," offered Helena, hoping to avoid a repeat of the night before.

"I don't want a fucking aspirin, you little cunt! I want you to eat pussy - my pussy. That will take care of the headache." The pain increased. "Now get on with it before I call Breshni and have him teach you obedience."

Catrina watched her maid undress. Anticipating the girl's hard, slick tongue stroking her vulva, she felt the wetness seeping down her legs. The headache grew worse.

"Fuck!"

Falling back against the pillows, she motioned for Helena to begin. When she felt the woman kneel between her legs, the pain in her temples spread to the back of her head, down her neck. A voice whispered somewhere deep in her brain.

Beware, Catrina! You've been warned, it murmured, softly.

"Get on with it!" she ordered, gritting her teeth. Helena separated the woman's lips with her thumbs. Swallowing, she took a deep breath and bent down.

Catrina screamed in agony, causing the maid to jump.

So be it. You still haven't learned your lesson about taking what isn't yours to have. There are many women who would endure your perversions willingly for a price. Forcing the unwilling is never an option. Had you only listened you could have had the world at your fingertips.

"Who are you?" Catrina demanded, tears streaming down her cheeks, her palms pressed harshly against her temples.

No one you know, my dear, but the condemned should know their executioner. I am Lilith, Queen of the demons, bride of Adam and lover of Satan. I'm the protector of whores. The one who has decided your fate in this world and the next. I promise you, the pain you feel now is nothing compared to the unbearable agony you'll suffer in the Underworld. Goodbye, Catrina, or should I say 'until we meet again?'

The voice disappeared, leaving a dark void in its place.

Drool trickled from her lips, down her chin and onto her neck. Gasping, Catrina rolled onto her side, drawing her knees to her stomach in a fetal position as she began rocking back and forth, groaning loudly. Her whole body shook, the tremors causing the bed to vibrate. Suddenly she opened her mouth as if to scream. No sound emerged except for a slight gurgling. Stiffening, Catrina's body spasmed. Then she lay still.

Frightened, Helena gathered her clothes and ran to the door screaming. The housekeeper and Breshni pushed past her and into the room. Their boss lay naked, sprawled on her bed, her lifeless eyes staring blankly at the ceiling. Blood dripped onto satin sheets from teeth still imbedded in her lower lip. Catrina Drenkova had been an attractive woman in life. In death, she looked old and haggard.

* * *

The last thing Breshni remembered was his boss lying in bed, and a strange voice whispering in his head, followed by intense pain and then darkness.

Slowly opening his eyes, he stared at the scene before him and blinked rapidly. Sweat beaded on his forehead and ran down his cheek, before dripping onto his bare chest. Confused, he looked around. Everything appeared alien, almost like a video game setting. Orange and red flames danced almost merrily in the distance while shadows moved stealthily along black paths between the fires. The sky was aflame with multi-colored clouds of silver, yellow and burnt umber.

Must be a dream. Shaking his head, he tried to flick the sweat away. When he failed, he started to reach up and wipe it, only to find his hands were tied to poles. His legs were also bound, forcing him into a spread-eagle position.

"You're awake," murmured a voice from behind.

Turning his head, Breshni saw a short, fat woman walking toward him. Skin the color of a bad sunburn, she wore no clothing. In her right hand was a small black bag.

Closing his eyes, Breshni tried to convince himself this was all a dream. No woman could be that ugly, he thought. Red hair sprang in frizzy tufts from her scalp and stood straight out like a porcupine. Heavy jowls, a large bulbous nose and crooked

156

teeth were bad enough but the beady brown eyes glinted with an unholy gleam.

"Actually, I'm quite good-looking...on the inside," she said. "You'll come to see that in time."

Breshni swallowed nervously. "Who are you?"

"I am what you have always been," she replied, giving him a toothy grin.

Not one to understand riddles, Breshni grunted his frustration.

"I see you are one of those stupid ones," continued the woman. "Well, I'll enlighten you. My friend, you are the worst of humanity...no conscience, no brains, no nothing except the need to satisfy your lust. Your whole life was spent abusing and raping women and children. You served your mistress well, doing whatever she told you to do like a pitiful lap dog."

Standing in front of him, she examined his naked body and smiled. Putting the bag on the ground, she reached for his penis, pulled on it and laughed when it fell limp.

"You don't find me as pleasing as those young girls? Too bad. I might have gone easier."

"Wha...what are you go...going to do?" Breshni stammered, struggling to break free.

"Why, Breshni, you're afraid of me." The woman giggled. The sound frightened the human more than her appearance. "Fear is a wonderful stimulant. To answer your question, I will do to you what you have done to others. You are going to know the horror and the pain of being fucked unmercifully and unwillingly. You see, I am the demoness Ramiera, and like you, I'm a rapist. Only I do to the souls of men what they have done to women. And I do it better."

Reaching into her bag, Ramiera pulled out a huge black dildo with bright red veins pulsing through it. Stroking it lovingly, she beamed happily at her captive and then began rubbing it against his groin.

"Remember how you used to do this to your victims? They begged you to stop but you laughed. Their pain and suffering was your pleasure. Now, yours will be mine. Their few moments of humiliation seemed like a lifetime to them. Your humiliation and suffering will be an eternity, as will my pleasure."

Breshni could feel the panic building as she continued to stroke him with her enormous toy. Feeling nauseous, he begged for mercy. Ramiera merely smiled. She'd waited a long time for his soul, and intended to enjoy every minute of his misery.

"I'm disappointed in you, Breshni. I thought you would be a lot braver. You were such a man when you were alive. At least when it came to anyone weaker than you. Why, I haven't even begun enjoying you and you beg like the whores you fucked unmercifully."

Stepping behind him, she pressed the dildo against his butt, making sure it was aligned with his anus. Breshni tensed, squeezing his cheeks tightly together and twisted back and forth. Cackling loudly, Ramiera pushed harder, enjoying the rapist's futile efforts to escape.

"Yes, that's what I like. It's intoxicating, isn't it? The feeling of power over someone. Remember that feeling? Remember, Breshni? Give it to me! Make me feel what you felt. You are now my woman, my whore."

Thrusting the toy deep, the demoness laughed joyously as screams of pain penetrated the bowels of the Underworld.

A few demons stopped to listen and smiled. Another soul was being initiated into the realm.

* * *

Exhausted, Yemaya and Dakota went to bed early. Neither had much to say.

Mari, Maopa and Intunecat watched the two sleeping women.

"Tonight they'll rest...no dreams...no interruptions," said Mari.

"That be best," agreed Maopa.

"Then I'll be gone," Intunecat said.

"One moment, Intunecat. Thank you, again, for helping Yemaya."

"I did little. Lilith was her real savior."

"Technically, but I suspect you had a lot to do with that, too."

"The demoness has a mind of her own. I doubt if anyone has much influence over her."

"Perhaps you are right, perhaps not."

"Believe what you will," chuckled Intunecat. "I accept no credit for what isn't mine. Until the next time."

"Until then. Oh. Intunecat..." continued Mari.

"Yes?"

"When you see Lilith again, please give her our thanks and tell her there is an issue I wish to discuss with her. Some souls cannot be bargained for."

Laughing, the Dark One smiled.

"As you wish."

"Thank you," said Mari.

The dark spirit merely tipped his head before disappearing.

"Well, darlin' maybe we need tah take ourselves a break. Hows 'bout we gather up some fixin's and go have a picnic?"

Smiling, Mari took Maopa's hand, and they vanished.

CHAPTER 25

THE NEWSPAPER LAY face up on the tray as the waiter pushed the cart into the hotel room. Uncovering the plates, he bowed to the two women and left.

Dakota was first to notice the headline.

Shipping Tycoon Dead at 55

Ms. Catrina Drenkova, owner and operator of the international shipping company Eurasian Exports, was discovered dead in her bedroom around 4 p.m. yesterday evening. Her housekeeper said a maid discovered Ms. Drenkova lying in bed unconscious.

Paramedics and the police were summoned to the scene. Efforts to revive the export tycoon failed, and her body was taken to Mercy Hospital for an autopsy. Dr. Carlson, the state coroner, has determined the cause of death was due to a massive aneurysm that ruptured, causing pressure on the brain. Death would have been instantaneous, according to the coroner.

Ms. Drenkova's receptionist told police her employer had left work early due to a migraine. Ms. Drenkova was a native of a small mid-European country called Moldova. It had been rumored that she was closely connected to several upper level members of the Moldovan Parliament. Drenkova was single and did not have any children.

"Do you think this was because of us?"

"I don't know," Yemaya said. "She could have had an aneurysm for a long time. Perhaps the strain triggered it."

Dakota didn't know what to say or think.

"Do you think I did this?" Yemaya asked, putting down her coffee cup.

"I don't know. You were so out of control...or rather that thing in you was."

"Maybe it would be better if we ended things now," offered Yemaya, stoically.

"No! That's not what I meant and you know it. I know you wouldn't break your promise to me. Whatever this darkness is inside you isn't you, Yemaya. Oh, I realize it's a part of you but it's only a small part."

She reached across the table and covered Yemaya's hand with her own. "The real you is the caring, loving, over-protective woman I'm with now. You're my life and my soul. You're not getting rid of me that easily."

Yemaya lowered her head and closed her eyes. A tear trickled down her right cheek.

"I felt something for a moment. It went after her," she confessed.

Dakota wrapped her arms around Yemaya and pulled her close.

"I know. We'll never know for sure. but I don't believe it was you. Trust me on this," Dakota murmured softly, gently rocking her back and forth.

Yemaya relaxed in her lover's warm embrace.

* * *

Cammie lay half-dozing on her bed when she felt a sleek body slip under the sheets. Opening one eye, she smiled at the dark-haired, lavender-eyed woman dressed in a white leather bra and thong. The contrast between her dark skin and the outfit was stunning.

"You look amazing," whispered the Cambion. "Nice outfit too."

"Thank you." Kali grinned, bathing in the warm, sensual energies emanating from the Cambion. "Although you don't seem to let me leave them on for long."

"Do you want me to?"

"You need to ask?"

Laughing, Cammie pulled the Destroyer onto her chest and kissed her. The next two days were theirs to do with as they pleased. Both knew exactly what that entailed.

After Lilith returned from her appointment with Intunecat, she had sensed their need and immediately ordered them out of the nightclub.

"You are putting out so much sexual energy, these mortals will be fornicating on the tables and floors," she declared. "With my luck, Dis will pop in and think we're having an orgy. I'd never live that down. Get out of here and don't come back for a couple of days."

They were both laughing like little girls as Kali grabbed the silver-haired demoness by the hand and pulled her out the door.

CHAPTER 26

FIVE WEEKS LATER Dakota found herself sitting between her mom and her grandmother at the sea aquarium. Yemaya had finished describing the facilities and had introduced one of their latest residents, an eight–foot-long tiger shark. She reappeared on stage in her blue and silver wetsuit and mask, climbed the platform and dove into the water.

The shark swam lazily around the tank, eyeing the woman.

"She's quite beautiful," Teetonka said, nudging Dakota with her elbow.

"The shark or the woman?"

"Both," her mother teased, wiggling both eyebrows.

Pashna nodded her head.

"I've never seen a live shark before. They really are quite magnificent. Nothing like television, although I did see Jaws a long time ago and swore I'd never go in the water again. Have you seen that movie, Daks?"

Dakota smiled. Tee and her grandmother could go on and on for hours.

"Shush. Watch the show."

As Yemaya sank to the bottom, the shark flicked its tail, sending the long sleek body rushing toward the Illusionist.

Yemaya remained motionless until it was within arm's length and then reached out and pushed off the shark's snout. The momentum propelled her several feet away. Surfacing, Yemaya took a quick breath and descended once more. The shark circled lazily around her.

Like a torpedo, it charged, mouth wide open. Once again Yemaya pushed her away. This time the shark's body turned, momentarily blocking the audience's view of the Illusionist. The fish twisted in a final attempt to grab the meal. When it swam off, the Illusionist was gone.

The audience gasped.

"She's been eaten!" yelled a voice from the back of the room.

"Where'd she go?" Tee whispered.

"I don't know," Dakota replied, leaning forward in her seat. "I haven't figured out any of her tricks yet, and she won't tell me how she does them."

The audience grew uneasy as the shark continued to circle. It was impossible for Yemaya to hide anywhere in the tank, let alone remain underwater for so long. Even Dakota, who had seen several of her shows, began to worry.

"Come on, sweetie," she murmured.

Two masked attendants, who had been standing at the base of the steps, rushed up to the platform and visually searched the water. After a few minutes, one raised her hands and shrugged. The two walked slowly down the steps.

The attendant who had shrugged announced, "Ladies and gentlemen, I don't know what to say...Ms. Lysanne has vanished!"

The audience was silent.

"Oh, I would not exactly say that," the other attendant said, pulling off her mask.

Everyone gasped. Before them stood the Illusionist dressed in an attendant's costume. Smiling, she bowed when the crowd stood and cheered.

"Thank you ladies and gentlemen. Fortunately, this performance went better than the last one here. Stay happy and healthy." Waving again, she bowed once more, accepting the applause.

Breathing a sigh of relief, Dakota turned to her mom to say something when a camera flash caught her attention. She glanced around to see who was taking pictures.

Not again!

Several aisles back stood a large, familiar-looking man. As the lights came on, he looked directly at her. She recognized him as the one who had left Catrina's office when they pulled up in the taxi.

"What is it, Daks?" Tee asked, noticing her daughter tensing.

Ivan felt the journalist's gaze. Smiling, he saluted her as he slipped the camera into his pocket and pulled out a small white envelope.

A final glance at the Illusionist showed that she, too, was aware of his presence. Making eye contact with Yemaya, he held her gaze for several seconds and then turned away. Motioning to an usher, he handed him the envelope and pointed to Dakota.

Although he would never fully understand what had happened to his boss, he knew that these two women were involved. With Catrina dead, he could go home now. Maybe even see his wife again, if she would have him.

From Sasha's memories, Yemaya recognized Ivan as the man who had guarded her for Catrina, but had also carried the young Carpi to the hospital. The last deed was the only reason he still lived.

Sasha was safe in Moldova. Mari and Maopa, in the guise of Yemaya and Dakota, had accompanied her and the doctor on the flight.

* * *

The night before their departure from Baltimore, Agra informed Dakota and Yemaya that she was going to the Middle East to recover the missing whores who had by now been removed from the freighter, Belinda among them. She also talked the women into joining the Sisterhood.

Tragically, the women warehoused in other countries were murdered as soon as word of Catrina's death became known. Agra promised the whores' families that she would do everything in her power to find and punish those responsible.

Lilith returned two weeks before Yemaya's performance, along with the rescued whores. She was surprised to find forty-three tickets to the event waiting, along with bus fare for the whores and airfare for Lilith, Kali, Agra and Cammie.

Now, a healthy contingent of sisters sat in the audience of The Illusionist's show.

"Do you think she suspects anything?" whispered Agra during an intermission, keeping her voice low.

"Perhaps. She won't say anything. She's one of those rare mortals who accept the impossible as probable."

"And her darkness?"

Lilith shrugged.

"It is a part of her. If it weren't for Dakota, she'd eventually lose that battle."

"Why did you help her?"

"It served my needs. There was a price to pay."

"You mean Dakota's soul?" Agra laughed. "Since when did you ever charge a soul for your services?"

Lilith grinned, mischievously.

"There's always a first time."

"Do you plan on collecting?"

"Do I look like a collection company? I have more important things to do at the moment."

"Well, have you told Dakota you aren't going to? Surely she has a right to know."

"In time. She needs to think about her actions for awhile. Besides, I may need her services at some future date. It's a good bartering tool."

"Now you're being evil," Agra teased.

Raising an eyebrow, Lilith gave her demoness friend a haughty look.

"And your point is?"

Before Agra could reply, Kali leaned over Cammie's lap and glared at the two demonesses.

"Would you two hush?"

Lilith was about to comment when she felt another presence in the room. Looking around, she noticed a handsome, dark-haired man sitting several rows to her left. Nudging Agra with her elbow, she nodded her head in his direction.

"You've got to be kidding me," whispered Agra.

"You know Dis. Always the attention getter."

"Yeah...but really! This is a bit much, don't you think? And why is he here anyway?"

"It's not for the entertainment. He's up to something."

"You think he's after Yemaya?"

"No, he knows he'll never have her."

"Could he have heard about your deal with Dakota?"

"Probably, but he knows he can't collect on it without my permission."

"Dis is the Underlord. He can claim any debt his demons or minions barter for."

"Really! Would you return your whores to him if he decided he wanted them back?"

"Hell, no!" Agra exclaimed, causing several people to look in their direction.

"There you go. Trust me. Dis wouldn't dare challenge me for her. I have too many followers of my own. The Underworld wouldn't withstand such a schism."

"I can't believe you would do such a thing over one mortal."

"Oh, I wouldn't. But I would on principle. What is mine, stays mine. Besides, Dakota and I never really finalized the deal. I simply asked if she was willing. She's under no obligation to anyone but me, and I'll release her from it if he tries to interfere."

"Would you two be quiet? What kind of example are you setting for our whores?" reprimanded Kali.

Shaking their heads, the two demonesses leaned back in their chairs and relaxed. Lilith glanced one more time at the man and chuckled.

Really, Dis! Elvis?

Turning his head to look at her, Dis gave a smug grin and winked. Even he enjoyed a good show, and who better to impersonate than one of the most idolized mortals in human history.

* * *

"Daks?" repeated Tee, squeezing her daughter's arm to get her attention.

"Oh...sorry, mother. It's nothing. I just recognized someone," Dakota replied, taking the envelope the usher had given her. Opening it, she glanced at the enclosed photo. Under the picture of a dead man was scribbled the name 'Breshni.'

Dakota looked again at where the man had been standing. He was gone.

"Is something wrong?"

"No. Everything's fine."

Yemaya smiled warmly at the journalist and winked before thanking the audience. Waving to everyone, she threw a small smoke bomb at her feet and vanished.

"Well, Daks," Pashna said, putting her arm affectionately around her granddaughter. "This was quite a show. If she's as good a lover as an Illusionist, I'll be expecting babies very soon."

They both looked at the elderly woman as if she was crazy.

"Grams!"

"Geez, mom," Tee exclaimed. "If you can figure out how that's going to happen, let me know. We'll be rich."

"Go ahead and laugh, but the spirits can do anything if they want," Pashna warned, shaking her head knowingly. "Shoot, if she's a real magician, she can too. You mark my words."

"Well, I have lots of questions I'd like answered," Tee said. "Like, how does she do all those things? And I especially want to know if she's going to make an honest woman of my daughter."

"Mother!" Dakota turned beet red.

When Teetonka saw her daughter's flushed face, she laughed even harder. Pashna just shook her head. Dakota groaned. It was going to be a very long night.

CHAPTER 2 7

YEMAYA AND DAKOTA returned to Moldova two weeks later.

"I'm going to sleep for a week," declared Dakota, burrowing further beneath the sheets to escape the cool breeze blowing through the open window.

Smiling at the green eyes and ruffled hair peeking out from under the blankets next to her, Yemaya shook her head.

"You look like a little kid."

"Hey, it's cold in here. How come it was so warm earlier and now it's freezing outside?"

"This is the perfect weather. Warm days for play...cool nights for sleeping...and love."

"Oh? I like that."

"Me too," Yemaya replied, lowering her voice to the husky, seductive tone she knew Dakota couldn't resist.

"Why, Yemaya. I thought you were an all work and no play sort of gal."

"Oh, I definitely play."

"Let the games begin," Dakota said.

Straddling Yemaya, she leaned down, her breasts swaying slightly. Grabbing each hand, she raised Yemaya's arms over her head, holding them in place while she stretched out, laying half on and half off the other woman.

"Keep your hands there." With her left hand, she slowly unbuttoned Yemaya's blouse. "You want to see what skills I've learned?" she whispered against Yemaya's ear, her warm breath caressing the lobe. Yemaya nodded her head slowly. "Well, then the least I can do is oblige."

Running her lips down Yemaya's neck, she stopped to nibble at the pulse beating wildly at the base. Her hand roamed slowly down the exposed arms until it finally settled on Yemaya's right breast. Shifting slightly, she used her knees to push Yemaya's legs apart.

Yemaya groaned.

The tip of her tongue moved gently back and forth across Yemaya's lips. Opening her mouth slightly, she nipped at the lower lip. Her hand continued stroking Yemaya's stomach and breasts. Her hips pressed against the strong thigh beneath her.

"Do you want to know what I'm going to do to you?"

Yemaya swallowed and nodded, her stomach clenching from the building tension.

"Well, first I'm going to touch you..." Dakota's hand moved slowly down Yemaya's body. "And when I'm done..."

* * *

Several miles away, a streetlamp flickered on and off as wind gusts buffeted the loose wires connected to a nearby transformer. A young, dark haired woman dressed in tight slacks and a skimpy sequined top glanced nervously at the occupant of a car that had just pulled up to the curb.

After a short verbal exchange, she nodded, glanced up and down the empty street, and then climbed in. There was no one to witness the prostitute's disappearance into the darkness, or to hear the two men questioning her about the Sisterhood.

End of Part I

LILITH

Part II

The Beginnings

CHAPTER 1

THERE WERE NO memories of the past. Nothing to tell her about herself or her previous life. She only knew *now*...and the unfamiliar sounds disturbing a dreamless sleep and the darkness. Opening her eyes, she sat up and looked around, searching for anything she could recognize. Her surroundings were strangely familiar.

She had a name, and she knew it. It wasn't much but it was comforting. Slowly, rising to her feet, she turned and gazed about looking for something that might trigger a memory. There was nothing. It was like she had never existed before this moment. Then came the realization. She hadn't!

This was the first day of her existence and before her, had she known it, lay a world only a few days older. One created specifically for her and one other.

* * *

The meadow was breathtaking, covered in a lush carpet of grass with flowers of every imaginable size and color scattered randomly as far as the eye could see. Trees grew in multiple groves, each perfectly positioned to give the best aesthetic appeal. From their dense foliage the sounds of singing birds floated melodiously through the air, giving the entire landscape a pleasing tranquility. In the distance, a lake extended to the horizon and beyond. Its emerald green waters lapped gently at the shoreline creating a soft rhythmic slapping noise.

The sound of splashing water caught her attention. She leaned slightly forward, shielding her eyes with her right hand against the mild glare. A large object moved smoothly through the water, creating small ripples. Unable to resist an overwhelming desire to see what it was, she walked hesitantly forward until she was near enough to make out the animal.

It emerged from below the surface and stood shaking the water from its smooth skin. A fine coat of golden hair glistened in the sun giving the creature a radiant glow. Long blonde hair clung damply to its head and, as she stared in awe, dark blue eyes widened in amazement when it became aware of her presence. She had caught it by surprise.

Strange, she thought, watching as it strolled casually in her direction. *I know him. I know the names of all of these things around me, and yet I know I have never seen any of them before. How can that be?* She shrugged, accepting that she would know what she needed to when the time was right. In the meantime, she would discover as much as possible about this creature...this...*man*.

He was beautiful...more beautiful than anything in the garden. Tall and muscular, but with a slender physique, his curly golden locks hung loosely about his shoulders.

"Who are you? I've never seen you here before," he said, his eyes roaming curiously up and down her body.

"Have you been here long?" she replied, avoiding his question.

He seemed hesitant to answer.

"No. At least not that I know of. I'm not sure. I feel like I've only just arrived. And you?"

"The same. This is all new to me, and yet it's as if I've been here forever."

"Yes. That's how I feel, too. I know the plants and the animals. I know I'm Adam."

"It appears we have much in common. I am Lilith."

"Lilith. That's a beautiful name."

"Thank you. Have you seen anyone else around here?"

"No. Have you?"

Lilith shook her head no.

"Then we should look around."

"Yes. First, I'd like to bathe. Do you mind waiting?"

Adam laughed. Lilith smiled as she waded into the warm emerald green water. Glancing at its surface, she saw her reflection for the first time. The fiery red hair, blue-gray eyes and golden skin slightly darker than Adam's surprised her. She hadn't thought about her own appearance, but expected it to be similar to his. *Another mystery.*

Adam sat and watched Lilith, intrigued that her shape differed from his. Of particular interest were the round objects protruding from her front and the lack of a small appendage between her legs. Several times he had glanced at his own and then back at her. He decided she didn't have one.

His own shrank and grew at random intervals, making him uncomfortable at times. The strange behavior was a nuisance. Sighing, he stood and brushed the grass from his legs and buttocks and helped her up the slippery bank. Later he would think about these differences. *Another mystery,* he thought.

For days they wandered looking for others like themselves, and found no one. A few creatures resembled them, walking upright or jumping from tree to tree, but the dark hair covering their bodies and their strange noises assured both Lilith and Adam they weren't related.

"Maybe they are like us but speak a different language," posed Adam, watching the animals playing with a stick and rolling around in the grass. Occasionally one would emit a high-pitched laugh and curl back its lips to show large teeth.

"I don't think so," Lilith said. "You and I could communicate from the very beginning."

"Perhaps they can only talk with each other like we do. They don't understand us just as we don't understand them."

"It seems reasonable."

Switching his gaze to the woman beside him, Adam felt himself grow stiff and reached toward the limb to push it down.

"Does that bother you?" Lilith asked.

"Sometimes. I think it means I'm happy. I seem to have no control over what it does at times."

"That certainly would explain the odd behavior. You must be happy a lot."

"Only when I look at or think about you. You are pleasant to look at."

"Strange," she said, glancing at it again and then at herself. "I find you pleasing too, but I have nothing to show for it."

"Nothing?"

Feeling an overwhelming sense of disappointment, he scuffed a foot along the ground.

"Well, nothing we can see. I get a strange feeling here." Lilith put her hand between her thighs. "But..." shrugging, she didn't finish the sentence.

"Oh."

The sadness in his voice made her uncomfortable.

"There's one more thing," she offered hesitantly, wanting to cheer him up.

"What?" he asked eagerly.

"These."

Lilith pointed at the small nubs protruding from the two orbs on her chest.

"These little things get hard and stick out, just like that," she said, pointing to his hardened limb.

"Really? I never noticed. Is it painful?" Gently poking at one with a fingertip, he noticed it was rather firm.

"Sometimes. If I rub them gently, it eases the pain."

"Oh. Do you think we're supposed to rub these things to ease the discomfort? I've never tried, but it might help."

"Why not try it and see?"

Adam did find relief, but it was only temporary.

One day, Lilith and Adam were sitting by the lake watching birds paddling near the bank. Both had been contemplating their dilemma, wanting to find a solution. Finally, tossing a small pebble into the water, Adam turned to her hesitantly.

"Lilith? I've been thinking about these differences between you and me."

"So have I. It's obvious you have this *thing* between your legs for a reason and I don't. We've discovered we like rubbing ourselves and enjoy stroking each other. Perhaps your limb was meant to give us both some type of pleasure. If you stroke me with it—"

"My thoughts exactly! Would you like to find out?"

"I think I would."

Lying down on the lush carpet of grass, they slowly and tentatively ran their hands up and down each other's bodies, shy but determined to continue their experiment. Soon, flushed by unfamiliar passions, Adam rolled Lilith onto her back and nudged her knees apart.

"What are you doing?" she demanded, pushing him away.

"I...uh...what I felt I needed to," he replied, confused by her rejection.

"Need? You feel the need to climb on me?"

"Well, not exactly. I thought you wanted me to rub myself against you."

"I don't see what that has to do with you pressing me to the earth and climbing on me in such a manner. Surely you don't expect me to enjoy that?"

Shrugging, Adam couldn't think of a reasonable reply. "Do you not feel pleasure from what we have been doing?"

"Yes, but what has that to do with you lying on me? It's like I am less important than you. We shall lie side by side as equals."

Adam frowned. This wasn't going exactly like he thought it would.

"Why?"

"Because that's how it should be."

"I don't see how it would work. And what does equality have to do with this? That's ridiculous! It makes more sense for me to lie on you. Since I'll be stroking you, I need to push downward."

"Ridiculous? It's just as easy for me to position myself over you. Besides, you're heavier. You'd crush me."

"I wouldn't hurt you," he argued. "Now, enough of this! We're wasting time."

Gently pushing her down, Adam once again tried to mount her.

Lilith didn't know if she was more furious at his renewed effort to climb on her or his dismissal of her feelings. Shoving him away, she jumped up and glared down at him, arms crossed defiantly.

"I'll not be treated like this. Either I have the top or we lie side by side as equals."

Adam rose to his feet and stood in front of her, legs apart, posturing with his hands on his hips.

"You're being unreasonable. Position is unimportant."

"If it's so unimportant, you take the bottom"

"Me? I've agreed we're equals. Why do you keep pursuing something so trivial?"

Lilith stamped her foot.

"I tell you what. You take the bottom first. Then I'll take the bottom."

"You really don't expect me to lie beneath you now when you have just said it's an inferior position? That means I would be less than you."

"Ah. I see. The truth comes out. You expect me to take the bottom but you're not willing to. I was right. You think you're superior to me."

"Lilith, you're beginning to anger me!"

"And am I supposed to quiver in fear from this anger of yours?"

Adam sighed, shaking his head.

"Be reasonable, Lilith! Look at me! I'm bigger than you. I have more muscles. I can run faster, swim farther and I'm a lot stronger. I was made this way for a reason."

"And that would be?"

"Well...ummm...to be on top, of course," he mumbled.

Throwing up her hands, Lilith turned and stormed off.

"Where are you going?"

"Away."

"Away? Where?" he demanded, running after her.

"Anywhere...away from you...from this. I won't live with someone who believes I'm inferior."

Imitating her behavior, he threw both arms in the air.

"Oh, all right! We can discuss this when you're in a better mood."

Lilith was about to reply when a voice stopped both of them.

"Why do you argue?" it whispered softly.

Looking around, neither could locate the source.

"Who are you?" demanded Adam, stepping protectively in front of Lilith. Giving him a disgusted look, she pushed him aside and stepped forward to stand next to him.

"Don't stand in front of me like that," she admonished, cutting him an angry glance.

A deep laughter was quickly followed by the appearance of a large man with dark red skin. Bowing slightly to Lilith, he turned toward Adam. Smiling, he spread his arms out, palms up in benevolent manner.

"No one you would know. I'm the keeper of my Twin's kingdom and guardian of his creations. This place is one of them...as are the two of you. Now, answer me. Why do you argue?"

"She is being obstinate!" grumbled Adam, nodding at Lilith. "We merely wish to explore these strange urges we're having. She refuses to cooperate."

"Me! I simply refuse to lie beneath you. I will be treated as an equal," declared Lilith, shoving Adam away from her.

"There! You see? Stubborn!"

"Yes. I see."

"I thought you would. You're like me. Naturally, you would understand my point of view."

"Naturally," the red giant said with a chuckle. "But I'm afraid I don't agree with you. She has a valid point. Why do you not take the bottom, Adam? Her compromise sounds reasonable."

"Because I should be on top...at least the first time."

"Why?"

"Because...I am...I mean it makes more sense."

"To whom?"

"To me, of course."

"And what of Lilith's thoughts and feelings?"

"If she will only do as I say, she'll find I'm right."

Before either Lilith or the stranger could reply, another voice intruded.

"What are you doing here?" it roared angrily, causing the ground to vibrate.

"Why, trying to settle a quarrel, brother. It appears there's trouble in Paradise."

"That doesn't concern you!"

"You wound me. Everything you do concerns me. Who else is there to look after your interests while you tinker with your hobbies?"

"I don't tinker! And I have warned you to stay away from this particular place."

"As I said, I was merely looking after your interests. How long were you going to let this argument continue?"

"That's not your concern. Since when did you ever bother with anything other than satisfying your loins, Dis?"

"Really, brother! You misjudge me. I came to resolve an argument. Nothing more."

Dis laughed, knowing his brother was right. He could care less what his Twin was up to, but from the moment he noticed Lilith, he desired her. If he could create a rift between Adam and Lilith, he could entice her away from her would-be mate.

Already, she was showing signs of immense intelligence and rebellion...not to mention boredom. The three were a dangerous combination in a perfect world, something his Twin hadn't factored into this new life form.

"There's no need for your intervention. Leave now. Lilith is intelligent. She'll see Adam's logic in time."

"Her logic is valid. Were they not created from the same dust? Does that not make her his equal?"

"This isn't the time to discuss it. Be gone from here!" ordered the Voice.

"Excuse me, brother, I'm not yours to order about. You're neither my master nor my creator. The female is at a disadvantage and needs an advocate. I am now assuming the role of her protector," declared Dis, crossing his massive arms. "She is more than capable of dealing with him, but she stands no chance against you."

Thunder rumbled in the distance. As lightning flashed across the skies, Lilith and Adam cowered. They had never experienced such fury.

"Dis! I won't tell you again! Leave this place!" boomed the Voice. "I won't be challenged on this matter."

"And I won't be ordered about as if I were your servant."

Lilith and Adam listened with interest to the exchange. Adam was confused and a little frightened. Lilith, however, was amused by the battle of wills. She felt a kindred spirit in the red giant.

"Stop this!" she demanded, stepping bravely forward. "I don't care who you are. I won't obey you or him!" she proclaimed, pointing at Adam.

"We'll discuss this later, child," admonished the Voice tenderly, its tone softening to a whisper.

"My name is Lilith, not child! And, no! We will not! Either you tell Adam that I am his equal or I'll leave this place."

When the Voice didn't answer, Lilith looked to Dis for help. Smiling broadly, he bowed slightly and took her hand.

"She's made her wishes clear, brother. Now, you must make yours."

"She is a child. They are both children, too young to understand the importance of this experiment. Leave us and I'll settle this dispute once and for all."

At that moment Lilith knew that if Dis left, the Voice would force her to obey Adam. Unwilling to concede, she looked at the red-skinned man beseechingly.

"Don't worry, my dear," Dis assured her, patting her hand. "I'm sorry, brother. When you first described this experiment to me, you said you created Adam and Lilith with free wills to see how they would evolve. I warned you it wouldn't work, having made the same mistake with my minions. You've clearly achieved more than you expected or they have evolved faster than you thought. There's no turning back. She's made her choice. I will make sure she achieves it."

Before the Voice could reply, they vanished, leaving behind a bewildered Adam, alone and dumbfounded.

"Where did she go?" he asked, turning in a circle like a confused child.

The skies exploded in brilliant flashes of lightning. The thunder grew louder, shaking the earth beneath his feet. Frightened, he sank to his knees and covered his head with his arms.

"I will not be defied in such a way!" roared the Voice and then quieted. "Don't be afraid, Adam. Nothing will harm you."

"Will she come back?" asked Adam, feeling very alone.

"Yes. Contrary to what my Twin has said, she has no choice. I will return her to you very soon. Rest now."

Adam nodded gratefully. Already he missed Lilith. If he had known all of this was going to happen, he would have willingly let her have the top.

CHAPTER 2

LILITH WALKED AROUND the chamber fingering the various objects on display. She had never seen anything like them and was curious about their origins and meanings.

"What are these? And what purpose do they serve?"

Sniffing one, she picked it up and licked it.

"This is awful!" she said, wrinkling her nose in disgust.

"Merely decorations," replied Dis, taking the small statue from her hand and putting it back on the table. Leading her to a chair, he motioned for her to sit. Cautiously, not knowing what to expect, she lowered herself on the thing and, finding it extremely comfortable, relaxed.

"This is comfortable. What is it?"

"A chair."

"It's easier on the body than sitting on the ground."

"That's why it was invented."

"Invented?"

"Yes. It was created it for a specific purpose...comfort."

"And that?" she asked pointing to the big round bed.

"Sleeping and entertainment."

"I see. What does entertainment mean?"

Dis laughed softly.

"It's better to show you what that means than explain it."

Lilith accepted the explanation without comment.

"Why can't I see the trees and animals?"

"You're in my home," Dis answered patiently.

"Home?"

"Yes. The place I live. Paradise was your home. This is mine. These things around us make it more pleasing."

"Watching the animals playing and listening to the birds is pleasing. Why do you need to create something? Wouldn't it be easier to just live without...these?" she asked pointing to the walls.

"Easier, yes, but not as much fun. Walls provide privacy."

"Privacy?"

"No one can see us."

"Who is there to see us besides Adam and that voice? Who was that, anyway?"

"My dear, there are entire worlds out there. Places and things you could never imagine. As for the voice, that's my Twin."

"What is a Twin and why could we not see him?"

"He's a recluse. He rarely leaves his home. Twin means he was created at the same time as I, and from the same material."

"You mean like Adam and I?"

"No...I mean...Well, in a way, but you and Adam are not twins."

"I don't understand."

"It's difficult to explain. There are a lot of new experiences awaiting you, Lilith. With your permission, I'd like to show them to you."

"Why?"

"Why?" Dis repeated, confused.

"Why do you want to do this?"

"Because I wish to please you."

"Why?"

Frowning, Dis realized Lilith was not only intelligent but intuitive, more so than even he had imagined. Although she was an innocent, there was no doubt she was smart enough to be suspicious of his motives. He liked that.

"You intrigue me. Besides, who else do you know who will show you these things? Certainly not Adam."

"True. Adam is content to stay where he is. Who are you? And what do you have to gain from helping me?"

Dis stared at the woman for several seconds and then burst into a loud booming laughter.

"An inquiring mind, I see. Forgive my rudeness. I'm not used to being unknown. I am Dis. My Twin and I oversee the inhabitants of the Over and Under worlds. He, however, hates making personal appearances, so I tend to take care of more important issues."

"Like Adam and me."

"Exactly."

"I see. You two don't get along very well. Why should I trust you any more than him?"

"I never said you should. I merely offered to show you around, although the one thing I can promise is to treat you as my equal. You can have the top as often as you like," he promised, giving her an amused look.

"And again what do you get in return?"

Dis shrugged.

"Your innocence. The pleasure of your company. I can teach you about those feelings of yours. Stay with me. I promise you an eternity of satisfying experiences."

"We'll see. What about your brother? Will he not object?"

"He objects to everything I do. What is one more thing?"

A loud knock on the door interrupted their conversation.

"Enter!" Dis commanded.

A small disfigured red creature shuffled into the room. Tiny horns protruded from its oversized head. Wrinkled skin, bony elbows and knees made it look peculiar. Lilith watched as it hopped awkwardly toward Dis and knelt at his feet.

"What is it, Cumo?"

"Master, your brother sent three of his servants for the female," Cumo replied, nervously wringing its hands and casting Lilith a furtive glance.

"Send them in. This should be interesting."

Within minutes, three males dressed in white flowing gowns trimmed in gold entered the room. Glancing momentarily at the woman, they dismissed her as unimportant to the conversation and turned to speak with Dis.

"Thank you for giving us an audience so promptly, Underlord."

"I always have time for my brother's most honorable messengers. What can I do for you?"

Bowing his head slightly, the tallest male gave Lilith a disapproving look before continuing.

"We have come for her," he said, pointing at Lilith.

"Then your journey is wasted. She's made her decision and chooses to stay here, as your master is well aware. Give him my apology and my regards."

"We have orders. He's displeased by her disobedience. I insist she return with us."

"You insist?" Dis asked with cold menace in his voice. "Have you forgotten your manners, Gabriel? You're here at my benevolence. Your master is my brother, not my keeper."

Gabriel lowered his eyes submissively, unable to meet the fury in the Underlord's blazing red eyes.

"Don't mistake my good manners for softness. Do you understand me?"

"Forgive me. I meant no disrespect."

"Good. She stays with me by choice. Is that not right, my dear?"

Lilith nodded but refused to stand. "I won't return to Adam."

"He is your mate, child. You were created to be together," Gabriel said, addressing her for the first time.

"We were made from the same dust and yet everyone but Dis treats me as inferior."

"In time you will—"

"What is time? I don't know that word nor care what it means. Adam is no more, nor less, than I, yet he believes he's better."

"He doesn't mean to," Gabriel said, spreading his hands in an imploring manner. "I regret that I've misjudged you. You're an intelligent female. Surely you see this is a simple misunderstanding. I'm sure it can be resolved."

"I will not return."

"Lilith, the decision is not yours to make. Our Master has instructed us to bring you back to Paradise."

"Your Master may be yours to obey. He isn't mine." Lilith glanced at Dis. The slight nod of his head was enough to give her the confidence to continue.

"I have no memory of my origin and no recollection of having pledged my allegiance to him."

"We must insist."

"If you force me to return, I promise you I'll do everything in my power to make Adam's life miserable. I'll destroy him. He and I will never join. He will never know one moment of peace or happiness. Your Master will grow weary listening to my screeching, and Adam's pleadings. Tell Adam I'm sorry for causing him pain. And tell your Master he made a mistake. His experiment is a failure."

Gabriel gave her an indignant look.

"Our Master never makes mistakes."

When he took a menacing step toward her, Dis stepped between the Archangel and his guest.

"Enough, Gabriel!" Dis bellowed. "You are trying my patience. Lilith has given you her answer. Give my brother my regards. Now, Cumo will escort you out of my home and the Underworld."

"This isn't over, Dis. No one defies our Master. His word is supreme and you know it!"

Dis stiffened, his whole body tensing in anger at both the implied threat and the show of disrespect. Stalking over to the three angels, he positioned himself in front of the senior angel and leaned down to make eye contact. Fire raged uncontrollably from his crimson eyes.

"You *dare* address me in such a manner in my home, and in front of my guest?" he hissed. "Do I again have to remind you who I am and what I can do?"

Gabriel shook his head no and took a step back, more afraid than he had ever been in his life. His unquestioning loyalty to his master didn't prevent him from fearing Dis. As Twins, it was possible their powers were equal, making the demon a force not to be taken lightly.

"Good! You would be wise to remember your place, Gabe...and it is not here. Now, get out!"

Bowing slightly, the three hurried from the room.

"Who are they?" Lilith asked, watching Cumo escort them away.

"Angels."

"I've caused more trouble, it seems."

Dis laughed.

"We've never agreed on anything. He resents my carefree life and the...ummm...partaking of pleasures it offers. I've never understood how he can stay in seclusion, hidden behind closed doors, tinkering with his projects as if they were the only things of importance. Where's the fun in that?"

"Tinkering?"

"Experimenting. He wants a perfect world. You and Adam are his latest attempt."

"Is something wrong with his world?"

"He thinks so. Mine isn't perfect, but it's fun and exciting. And the sex is great."

"Sex?"

"Forgive me. I forgot you're new to all of this. I'll explain that later. You need to decide if you want me as your mentor... teacher. Do you wish to begin your journey?"

"As equals?"

"As equals," Dis promised, taking her hand and kissing it lightly.

"Then yes. I'm eager to see what you have to offer."

"Good." Dis grinned, pleased with himself. "Let's begin. First, though, there are a few changes I need to make to protect you from my brother's followers. They can be quite persistent and devious at times."

Dis knew he needed to transform Lilith into a demon, and quickly. His Twin didn't take rejection well. He would send his forces to retrieve her, unless she was no longer a suitable mate for Adam. Minutes later, he took Lilith's hand and led her to a mirror.

Reaching up, she tentatively touched the black hair. Leaning closer, she stared into sparkling blue/black eyes and smiled. Lilith liked how she looked. The transformation was complete. For a new demon, vanity was a good emotion to start out with.

CHAPTER 3

AS AN ANCIENT spirit, Intunecat was aware of Lilith's pre-existence to Eve, but had only heard rumors about why she had left Paradise. Now it made sense.

"So you were the cause of the Great Battle," he said, matter-of-factly. "I heard it was because Dis angered his Twin. I suspect there's no real love lost between them."

"They have an affection for each other. I think both have mellowed over the ages. Anyway, I doubt I was the real reason for the battle." Lilith smiled. "More like the final straw. I've been told they never got along. Dis enjoys life too much. He's the proverbial child in a toy shop; there's no such thing as hands off.

"Unfortunately, his brother is quite the opposite. He believes in rules. A place for everything and everything in its place. He gets frustrated with disorder. It's a shame. He had such great plans for humanity."

"So I've heard. Mortals aren't so bad...at least some of them. They serve our needs quite well."

"True. I think Dis' brother was disappointed with all his failures. I was simply the final straw."

"Perhaps. I can imagine you were worth fighting for then and still are now."

Smiling at the compliment, the demoness let her gaze glide over the Dark One. Like Adam, he was extremely beautiful. Unlike him, though, Intunecat was worldly. Only the last few hundred millennia had brought him a semblance of companionship. He could leave the Darkness and roam both the spirit and mortal worlds, but only for short periods. Born into darkness, the Light was painful to him.

"Are you going to tell me about the Great Battle?" he asked. "Some of it spilled over into our world. We were afraid it would destroy all of us."

"The Battle. Many friends were lost on both sides. Unfortunately, those most deserving of oblivion survived," Lilith said, her voice tinged with sadness.

"Isn't that the way of things?"

"So it seems. There was a time when demons and angels were one. Oh, they fought, they disagreed but never with animosity. It was never personal. Now, angels and demons are consumed with so much hatred they're willing to destroy everything to achieve their goals. Instead of evolving into something greater, we've devolved. It will destroy everyone."

"I don't think that will ever happen," Intunecat said. "Especially if there are others like you. Tell me about the Battle."

Leaning back in her chair, Lilith gazed into the darkness, remembering a time long ago.

"He was an excellent teacher. Dis, that is. He taught me about life, and love, and in the end...lust and selfishness. At first I thought he was magnificent, large and muscular, glowing red skin and an insatiable appetite. The perfect male. In time I realized his feelings were superficial...controlled more by his loins than his heart. There was nothing he wouldn't do to get what he wanted, and back then he wanted me.

The Twin did send his Army. Dis gathered his Legions to protect me. I thought it was because he loved me. His real reason was to protect his property. He never gives possessions up willingly."

"And yet here you are," interjected Intunecat, interrupting her narration.

"I said, willingly." She laughed, her black eyes glinting with humor. "The battle raged for thousands of years until our forces were beaten back to the gates of the Underworld. We would have lost everything if Kali hadn't switched her allegiance to us. She was the Twin's most powerful warrior."

"Kali. The same Kali who protects the whores?"

"The very same. She was unique among the angels. She could project beams of light so bright and radiant, they scorched everything in their path. Even Dis could be burned."

"I never realized she was an angel."

"Few know, or remember. When she first came to me and offered us her services, I thought it was a trick...a way to infiltrate our Legions. I asked her why she would switch sides, after all those centuries. And why I should trust her. Do you know what she said?"

Intunecat shook his head.

Memories of the moment Kali entered her world flashed through Lilith's mind. She told Intunecat about the golden-haired, blue-eyed woman who appeared, uninvited, at her home in the Underworld. Her mind flashed back to the moment Kali appeared in her chamber.

* * *

"Cumo said you wished to talk with me?"

Kali nodded.

"Why me and not Dis?" Lilith asked, tipping her head slightly.

"He wouldn't understand."

"What is there to understand? You serve his brother. That says it all."

"Not all," murmured Kali, her head bowed.

"Care to explain what you mean or am I supposed to guess?"

"My Master once told me that the most important thing for an angel was to be true to one's self. It was the only way we could be assured of achieving perfection. I've thought about that for a long time and I realize I'm fighting for a cause I no longer believe in.

"Before I became a warrior I was a messenger between the Overworld and the Underworld. My life was simple. I was happy. When I pledged my loyalty to my master, he told me I had the potential to be great if I had the desire, but I wasn't ambitious like others. I willingly served both of the Twins as long as it didn't conflict with my oath to my Master. I can no longer honor that oath."

"Why not?"

"Before and above all things, I am first a woman. I won't force another to do something she does not wish to do."

"This is rather sudden."

"Sudden? I've spent a millennium agonizing over this, and no matter what I choose I will be damned."

Lilith knew she was right. Once the Twin learned of her doubts, he'd remove her from her duties, though he'd never cast her from the Overworld. She would be too dangerous as an enemy. More important, Dis' brother truly loved his followers. The pain of losing even one angel would devastate him.

"Your master would understand. He has a tremendous capacity for forgiveness. Why should I believe you?"

"Because I'm here. And angels don't lie. My only consolation is that I am, in a way, obeying my master. To be true to myself, I have to honor your decision of free choice. Afterward, I will return to my master for my punishment."

* * *

Lilith had never met such a tormented soul. Kali was not only betraying her master, she was betraying her own family and everything she held sacred. The demoness couldn't imagine what it felt like to make such an enormous sacrifice.

The image of Kali standing before her, torn between her loyalty to her master and what she knew to be right, still brought tears to Lilith's eyes. Shaking her head to banish the emerging emotions, she looked into Intunecat's dark eyes, her own reflecting a long felt sorrow.

"You can't imagine the sadness in her voice when she told me this," Lilith whispered. "The anguish."

"I heard that Kali has always been an honorable demoness. It must have been a great burden for her."

"More than any of us will ever know."

"Why did she change her allegiance?"

"She was true to herself."

True to herself, Lilith thought, remembering how that one moment in time had changed the future for both demons and angels.

"That was the moment I knew I wanted her on our side. It was one of the best decisions I ever made. She rallied the demons and minions, and we marched through the gates of the Underworld to confront the enemy with new vigor. We had the will to continue the battle for thousands of years if necessary... perhaps even longer."

"Why didn't you?"

"I grew weary of the battle and the losses. Both sides paid a terrible price. I offered to return to Adam if it would end the conflict."

"And you returned to him?"

"No. He felt it wasn't in his best interests. I was too independent and it frightened him." Lilith laughed, remembering the panic on Adam's face when she stepped into Paradise and told him she had returned. At first he didn't recognize her. The dark hair and eyes were so different from the red hair and blue-gray eyes of the woman he had known.

After talking with Lilith, he knew life would be Hell if she stayed. "He told the Twin he preferred loneliness to my companionship. There wasn't anything the Twin could say after that. I left Paradise."

"That's it? Just like that, the end of the story?"

"Hardly. More like the beginning. Kali had changed. She was no longer innocent. Still, she returned to the Overworld as she had promised. The Twin forgave her, but banished her from his kingdom. He didn't have a choice. She would never have been happy among the angels. I believe it was an act of love. He was happy that she had followed her conscience. I sometimes wonder if things would have been different had he been that understanding with me."

"We'll never know, but dwelling on what might have been serves no purpose."

"I know. Anyway, poor Adam was alone for a long time. The Twin took pity on him and created a new woman. This time he used one of Adam's ribs rather than the original dust. I think he believed it would somehow make her different...maybe not so independent or at least less forceful," smirked Lilith. "It's hard to believe anyone, especially someone as intelligent as the Twin, would think a sentient being could remain unchanged forever."

"Especially a woman."

"Poor Adam. He really wasn't a bad person. It certainly wasn't his fault what happened afterward."

"You mean the Adam and Eve saga. She enticed him to eat the fruit. Then they were kicked out of Paradise."

"That's the sanitized version."

Raising both eyebrows, the dark spirit cocked his head slightly, making eye contact with the demoness.

Lilith grinned.

"Eve was created to be the dutiful wife, and she was. The Twins called a temporary truce. Out of gratitude for her help, Dis gave Kali command over his Legions. Had it not been for the Child..."

Lilith's words faded. The Child...her child and Dis'. She was beautiful, with glowing red skin, and emerald green eyes. Her long red hair and slender build were her only resemblance to her mother, the human image of her mother. Everything else she inherited from her father...only she was worse. Where Dis used deceit for his own selfish purposes, she used it for malicious reasons. Everything she did was to inflict misery. Among the Underworld inhabitants the Child's presence meant trouble. Tolerated by the demons and minions because of her sire, she was mostly ignored.

"Did I lose you?" Intunecat asked quietly, interrupting her musings. He had watched the fleeting expressions passing across her face.

"I was thinking of my child," Lilith said, her voice almost a whisper.

"You had a child?"

Intunecat was stunned. He'd never have guessed her to be the motherly type.

"Once. She was...unexpected. Dis and I didn't think it possible to bear children so we didn't take any precautions.

When I realized my body was changing, I didn't know what was happening. How could I? I was created, not conceived."

Strange! I haven't thought about her in a long time.

Lilith suddenly felt uneasy.

"Do you mind if we continue this another time?" she asked, not wishing to pursue this subject.

"Of course not, my dear."

"Thank you. Now, as much as I've enjoyed my visit, it's time for me to get back to the Club. Kali and Agra have a party planned for Cammie. You're welcome to join us."

"Enter a den filled with females? I'll take a raincheck. It's bad enough I'm outnumbered in the spirit world let alone a bar filled with intoxicated humans and beautiful demonesses." Intunecat shook his head.

"Probably a wise decision."

Standing, Lilith patted his arm affectionately and walked into the darkness. Intunecat looked down at the spot she had touched, running his fingers across the area. It tingled pleasantly. He enjoyed the warmth of her touch.

CHAPTER 4

"HOW WAS THE visit?" Agra stopped her work to look at Lilith who had just materialized in the bar.

"Fine."

"Want to talk about it?" Agra asked, sensing Lilith was upset.

"There isn't much to talk about."

"Meaning there is but now's not the time. So what's up... and don't start the 'I don't want to talk about it' crap. Did Intunecat say or do something to piss you off?"

"Good grief, no! He's the perfect gentleman." Lilith laughed. "We talked. It brought back memories best forgotten."

"Ahhh. Let me guess...your origin and the good old days," Agra replied intuitively.

"What made you jump to that conclusion?"

"It's the only thing that puts you in your most pensive mood...and besides...Intunecat's ancient. He's probably curious about you. So...let me guess. You've been thinking about the Child, right?"

"We've been together too long."

"Naw...but I know the look. For all the trouble she caused, she was still your child."

"Yes, she was."

* * *

She had a name...or at least there was a time when she did. Even Lilith and Dis refused to call her by her real name, but she didn't care. There was a strange prestige in being called the Child. Most of the demons and minions pretended she didn't exist. Others acknowledged her, believing they would gain special recognition from her mother and father. Stupidity wasn't in short supply in the Underworld.

From the moment of conception, she was aware of the world beyond the womb. By the time she was born, she understood life in the Underworld. Dis and Lilith demanded complete obedience. That didn't stop demons and minions from forming secret alliances to create mischief. Those were the ones she focused her attention on. Power was a numbers game. If the Child developed a large enough following, she would take her rightful place as Underlord.

* * *

"Do you want to talk about it?" Agra asked quietly, interrupting Lilith's thoughts.

"What's there to say?"

Agra shrugged.

"Maybe the truth. No one ever knew what really happened between the two of you...and Dis was conspicuously absent for a long time afterward. Some say she was the cause of the rift between you and the Underlord."

Lilith snorted. "Only the ignorant. She may have played a small part, but we had already grown apart. Dis doesn't know the meaning of monogamous, and I don't have the patience to live an eternity with someone who thinks sex is the most important thing in life."

"Yeah, so I found out." Agra said.

"I can imagine. You sure didn't stay married to him very long."

Agra gave her friend a mischievous grin.

"It was one of the best things that ever happened to me. After a few hundred years, he begged me to leave him. Promised me half his kingdom. His half...not yours."

"That must have been something."

"Oh...you can't imagine. When I told him I only wanted domain over the whores, he was so relieved he released me from my fealty oath."

"Dis nulled your vow?"

"Yep. I'm a free spirit. And so is anyone else I choose to emancipate, not that I do that very often."

"No wonder he leaves you alone. Few demons ever achieve such freedom."

"Now enough of me. What really happened between you and the Child?"

The pain in Lilith's eyes was heart-wrenching. Agra picked up a glass and began polishing it, giving her friend a moment to compose herself.

"I'm not sure where to begin," murmured Lilith. "She was, I don't know...someone who should never have been born. A hybrid between two totally different species. I blame myself for what happened.

Anyway, when I found out I was pregnant, I wasn't sure what to think. Hell, I didn't even know what it meant. Dis explained it to me. The entire concept seemed...alien. I think she sensed my confusion, my reluctance, even before she was born. There were times when I felt as if she were calling to me...begging me to love her...to want her...and I pretended I didn't hear. I told myself it was my imagination. After all, she wasn't even born yet. How could she feel or know what I was thinking?"

I knew! came a reply, uninvited, and totally unexpected.

Shaking her head, Lilith frowned at the intrusion.

Child? It's been a long time!

Yes it has, Mother, but then you've tried your best to forget me, haven't you?

Forget? No, I could never forget you. You're still a part of me.

Then why do I feel forgotten?

Lilith couldn't answer that. Perhaps there wasn't an answer or perhaps the Child was right. She certainly had tried not to think about her daughter, avoiding anything that reminded her of the child she had abandoned before she was ever born. *I'm sorry,* Lilith replied.

Am I never to be forgiven, Mother?

There was no pleading, no sorrow in her question. It was asked calmly and unemotionally as if they were discussing the weather or something more mundane. But behind the pretended dispassion were thousands of years of a haunting loneliness, and millions of lost souls who had died because of her personal vendetta.

Lilith still remembered her daughter's face. She was beautiful. How could she be anything else? Dis was the perfect male, large, muscular and irresistibly handsome. His dark red skin glowed. The reddish brown eyes and elliptical pupils were mesmerizing. He was a sexual predator who could sense every female's wants and needs, and fulfill them. The consummate charmer, few could deny him once he started his seduction...and that was the problem. Dis grew bored with his conquests.

Lilith lasted the longest, staying with him for over 10,000 years. Although he never grew tired of her, she grew bored with their relationship. Their decision to part was mutual, though he retained a strong affection for her. She was the one person he came the closest to actually loving.

"Am I interrupting something?"

For a moment, Lilith looked confused as she stared blankly at Agra. Her daughter's sudden mental intrusion had caught her by surprise.

"Sorry. Where was I?"

"You were wondering if the Child sensed your reluctance to have her."

Lilith nodded. "At birth she was already able to walk. Within months she could talk."

"Wow!"

"At first Dis was smug about her achievements, but he quickly lost interest. When she was ten, she roamed the Underworld getting into all sorts of mischief. Perhaps if I had paid more attention, things might have turned out differently."

Or not!

Other than a slight frown, Lilith gave no indication she heard the comment.

"It's a little late to second guess things."

"I know. Anyway, somewhere along the line, she heard the story of Adam and me, or at least some perverted version of it, and decided to punish him on my behalf. Can you imagine? She hated him because of some stupid rumor. My child wanted to defend my honor when there was nothing to defend."

I was just a child, Mother. I knew a lot about the world, but nothing about feelings.

"What in the world did she hear?"

"Mostly bullshit. Had she been more mature she'd have known it for what it was. Then again, had I been wiser, I'd have seen what she was becoming and intervened."

"You surely don't blame yourself for your lack of knowledge."

"No. I feel no guilt about what I didn't know. Maybe I should, but I know there was no way for me to understand what a child was. That doesn't stop me from wishing I had though. Many demons were still angry about the Great Battle, and blamed me for their losses. Everyone lost friends."

"And they used her to punish you."

"Yes. They told her Adam tried to force himself on me. That he was abusive. Then they said the Twin kicked me out of Paradise. The stories were so ridiculous I never took them seriously. I guess I expected my daughter to know better, too. She was so bright."

"But still a child."

"I know. Remember, I was created fully cognizant of everything around me. I had no childhood, no infancy. There was no reason to believe her to be any different."

But I was different! I was a half-breed...the cross between a human and a demon. You should have known better, the voice said.

Why? I wasn't human at the time, and in my own way, I am the real half-breed. More so than you. I was completely human before Dis made me a demon. Contrary to what you think, you were conceived from two demons.

You have never been pure demon, Mother. Even Father, as powerful as he is, could never completely alter his brother's creation. Within you there will always lie the essence of humanity.

Maybe. I've never really thought about it. As far as I'm concerned I'm a demon and will always be one. I have no desire to be anything else.

The Child's laughter felt like a gentle breeze.

Lilith smiled.

Uh huh! So that's why you spend so much time with humans! Forgive me for not believing you.

Okay. Maybe there are times. It's no excuse but I never knew what it was to be carried in the womb. To be loved or protected. I simply...was."

You had Father to teach you.

Pfft! Have you ever heard him explain anything dealing with women? He hasn't a clue what we're about. Hell, he still thinks male demons determine the sex of their offspring. That hasn't happened in over a million years.

He is rather naïve about some things, but it's part of his charm.

A charm that's very superficial.

And effective!

True.

The light banter eased some of the tension Lilith was feeling. When she nodded her head, Agra stared at her suspiciously.

"Is there something you're not telling me?"

The demoness shook her head.

"No. Just thinking. It must —"

Before she could finish her thought, Kali walked in carrying two cases of beer. Behind her was a young man pushing a dolly with several boxes stacked on top of each other. From his puppy dog expression he was clearly smitten with the bartender. Rolling her eyes, Kali motioned for him to put the liquor cases in the corner.

"I've doubled our order. If we get any more customers, we're going to need a bigger bar. Umm...I'm not interrupting anything, am I?" she asked, glancing from Agra to Lilith

"Not really. We're just talking about the good old days," Agra replied.

"Uh huh. Like I believe that. Well, in case either of you are interested, I'm not going to be here tomorrow. Cammie and I are going on a date."

"Date? You two have been fornicating for months. I have to leave the pad just to get some peace and quiet. Don't tell me you haven't gone out together yet!"

"Hey, it's not like we just met. We have to see if we're compatible."

"Oh, I see. Test drive the car before you buy it, eh?"

Kali grinned, her lavender eyes sparkling.

"But of course! And I have to say this car purrrrrsss quite nicely."

"Geez, Kali. I hope Cammie doesn't hear you talking about her like that."

"Talking about me like what?" asked Cammie, strolling up to the bar.

"Hey, Cam," Lilith said, grinning. "Kali tells us you purrrr nicely."

Cammie looked at Agra and winked.

"PPPPUUURRRRR!"

Giving Kali a quick kiss, Cammie slapped her on the butt and then left, waving bye to everyone as she dragged the Destroyer behind her.

"I've never seen her so happy," Lilith said.

"Yeah...and Cammie, from the way she's acting."

"What about you?"

"Me? What do I have to do with them?" Agra asked, looking confused.

"Well, you and Kali have been together for a long time."

"She's my best friend...not my lover. That was over eons ago."

"No regrets?"

"Nope. I'm happy for them. They make a cute couple... and they deserve to be happy."

"Well, we'd better get busy. It's almost time to open up."

"Uh huh. Don't think you're getting off the hook that easily. We'll finish this discussion later," threatened Agra, good-naturedly. Glancing at the young man standing quietly in the corner, she motioned with her head for him to scram. The disappointed expression on his face was priceless

I think you are as lonely as I am! said the Child.

What makes you say that? I have my friends, human and demon. I come and go wherever I wish.

That has nothing to do with loneliness. When was the last time you had someone to hold, to love...someone you really cared deeply about?

I care deeply about Kali and Agra...even your father, in an odd sort of way.

I'm not talking about friendship, Mother, and you know it.

What I know is you're going somewhere that is none of your business! snapped Lilith.

You're right, of course! It's none of my business. I'm sorry.

Silence followed for several minutes while Lilith calmed down.

Why did you do it? Lilith asked, changing the subject.

She could almost feel the mental shrug.

I was angry...angry at you and Father. I wanted Adam to be my father. He would have loved me. At least that's what I thought. Then you would have.

Lilith couldn't stop the tear from trickling slowly down her cheek. Bowing her head, she tried to imagine what it must have been like for her daughter, knowing neither of her parents felt anything for her.

Maybe. I'm not so sure. It wasn't an emotion I was familiar with, and staying with him would not have guaranteed our love. At least, not in the beginning. But you wouldn't have known that.

No. All I knew was what I was told and what I felt from the moment I was conceived.

Who told you these stories about Adam and me? Why didn't you come to me for the truth? It would have saved all of us a lot of pain.

Does it matter? Many of them are gone. Others...well, it happened a long time ago. Besides, what would you do to them now?

The Child was right. What good would it do to seek out those who had poisoned her daughter's mind. She was more responsible than anyone else.

Nothing. Stirring up old memories and hatreds serve no purpose. The past can't be changed. At least tell me what you heard.

For several minutes, Lilith felt nothing. Then came a soft mental sigh.

You know about the resentment over the Great Battle. You were blamed for the rift between the worlds by everyone.

Dis and I believed they'd get over it.

You were wrong. The hatred festered until the opportunity for revenge presented itself. That was me. You and Father ignored me as if I didn't exist. No one paid attention to my comings and goings in the Underworld. I was aware of the furtive glances cast toward me. I thought it was jealousy because I was the child of the Overlord and his whore.

Lilith cringed at the description but knew it was accurate enough, although she and Dis eventually married.

Sorry. Later came the rumors about you and Father and Adam. They confirmed what I heard. That you were why Dis and the Twin fought, but Adam was the real cause. Had he not abused you, Dis would never have come to your defense, and you and he would never have joined."

Abused me? Adam was never abusive!"

Just the thought made Lilith bristle. Adam may have been many things but he never mistreated or said an unkind word to her or about her. His only fault was his failure to recognize her as equal. Even then, she didn't blame him entirely. The Twin could have resolved the dispute by simply declaring them so.

Whether he was or wasn't didn't matter. They said he was arrogant and self-centered. He made you serve him...and expected you to service his needs. Father rescued you and offered his protection. When Gabriel couldn't take you back, Adam became angry. He ranted and raved about you being his and goaded Gabriel. The Twin was so infuriated by Father's defiance, he sent his Army to the gates of the Underworld with an ultimatum...and against the Legion's advice, Father ordered his followers into battle. I believed them.

That's ridiculous! How could you believe such trash...and even if it was true, what did it have to do with you?

Nothing. But in my mind, everything. No child likes to hear her mother or father being talked about like that.

Do you still think that?

The laughter held little joy.

No! I've had a lot of time to think. It was all very confusing back then.

Yes, I can see that.

I'm glad. Knowing you understand makes my exile more bearable.

210

It wasn't until a warm drop landed on her hand that Lilith realized she was crying. Staring at the tear, she touched it with her fingertips.

Don't cry for me, Mother. I've grown used to the isolation. It's given me an opportunity to explore my feelings. I don't blame you or Father. I understand your reasons. Exile was a fitting punishment for the chaos I created.

Maybe it was then...or maybe Dis and I should have been more compassionate. It must have been awful to be banished to that place. I can't imagine what it's like to see everything but never be seen...to no longer feel a touch or to share thoughts...to be alive and yet to know you have no substance.

Awful? In the beginning, and for thousands of years afterward, I swore vengeance. I thought I would go insane, but I didn't. I accepted what I had done...and learned how wrong I was. Your punishment was just. I'm comfortable with myself, now.

And if you could return to this world, would you still be?

I believe so. Whether I'd be happy is another matter. But we both know it is a moot point. As you and Father said in the beginning, once the deed was done, there was no undoing it, even if you wanted to.

Times have changed. We're more knowledgeable than then. I'll talk with Dis. You've borne the burden of our neglect long enough.

For a fleeting moment Lilith thought she felt a dark satisfaction emanating from the Child but it came and went so quickly she wasn't sure. Frowning, she wondered if she had imagined the darkness.

You still doubt me! the sad whisper was almost more than Lilith could bear. *Until you are confident about your own decisions, Mother, don't dwell on my loneliness. Like I said,*

I'm comfortable with myself, especially now that I have you to talk to. My world is brighter.

Lilith decided to ignore her doubts temporarily.

How did you manage that?

I'm really not sure. I've been able to see and hear everything in your worlds, but not what anyone thinks. The first time I became aware of your thoughts was when you were talking with the Dark One.

That was the first time I thought about you in a long time. I understand. At least this part of the barrier is broken. I am thankful for that.

Looking at her watch, Lilith realized she was going to be late for work.

We'll talk later, she said, reluctantly.

When the Child didn't respond, the demoness realized she was alone.

CHAPTER 5

PUTTING DOWN THE phone, Dakota turned to Yemaya and gave her a thumbs up.

"He said he liked the rough draft and wants me to come in to discuss publishing the story about my mom's tribe. I'm supposed to meet him next week."

"That is terrific!" Yemaya said, giving her lover a warm hug. "I am going to know a famous author, now."

"Famous? Look who's talking. Say, how about we head on over to Lilith's place and celebrate?"

"That sounds like a plan. Hopefully she has found something out about the missing women in Europe."

"You're still thinking about the people that killed those girls?"

"It is one of my primary concerns. Agra got her whores back. They were lucky. The others were not. Putting an end to the sex-trade industry is one of my primary goals."

"Mine too. I'm still amazed that I like Agra and Kali so much, I mean considering what they are."

"Maybe there is a lesson in all of this."

"Yeah. The first being not to get too close to Cammie," smirked Dakota, remembering how she had made a fool of herself over the Cambion. "Let's hope she's like the measles...a good dose and I'm immune."

"Are you still bothered by that?"

"Wouldn't you be? I told her I was interested in BDSM and a threesome, for Christ's sake! Me! In a threesome and doing S and M? Not on your life!"

"I notice bondage was not in your objections," teased Yemaya.

"Weellll...I wouldn't object to mild restraints...or handcuffing you to the bed, not that it would do me much good. You'd just escape from them."

"Why would I do something so stupid?" Raising one eyebrow archly, Yemaya picked up the car keys and headed for the door. "Promise me you will be gentle."

"Paleeeze."

The parking lot was filled with cars and motorcycles when they arrived.

"Looks like it's going to be crowded."

Nodding, Yemaya took Dakota's arm and walked her to the door. Several women were standing in line. A large woman with tattoos on both arms was checking IDs. Looking up, she motioned for them to go on in, causing one of the girls in line to grumble.

"Ya got something ya want to say to me?" challenged the bouncer, standing up to glare at the complainer.

"Yeah. How come they get to go ahead of us? We been waitin' in line for twenty minutes."

"Aww...now ain't that just too damn bad! But seein' as you don't like how I do my job, maybe I should just piss you off a little more and send you on your way. We don't like troublemakers, little girl. Are you a troublemaker?"

The girl swallowed and looked down at her feet.

"Umm...no. I was just thinkin' out loud, that's all."

"Next time...think quietly."

Overhearing the conversation, Dakota looked at Yemaya and grimaced.

"I wouldn't want to piss her off."

"Me neither," agreed Yemaya, motioning her toward the bar. "What would you like to drink?"

"The usual."

Kali and Agra moved up and down the small enclosure mixing drinks and serving beer to the women crowded around the bar. As Yemaya waited patiently in line, she felt a cool hand take her elbow and gently pull her backward.

"They'll bring it to you. Come sit at my table."

Yemaya couldn't mistake the club owner's low throaty voice.

Turning, she smiled appreciatively at the dark demoness dressed in a cranberry red tank top and black leather slacks. Three-inch heels gave her a slight height advantage over Yemaya.

Seeing the two women together, Dakota couldn't help but notice their similarities. Tall and sleek, with long dark hair, both exuded sensual auras.

"They make quite a pair," whispered a voice, causing the journalist to shiver as a warm breath tickled her ear.

"Cammie! How are you?"

"Great! How are you doing?"

Cammie watched Dakota closely for signs of discomfort. Noticing a slight flush creeping into her cheeks, she pulled the journalist aside.

"Listen, don't think about it. There's nothing to be embarrassed about."

"Easy for you to say."

"Well, if it makes you feel any better, Kali and I are an item now, and it seems to reduce the effect I have on people. I don't have nearly the following I used to. You're safe for now."

"That's a relief. I'd hate to put Yemaya through another episode like the last."

Cammie smiled slightly.

"She can handle it. Here they come. We'll pretend nothing ever happened."

Yemaya's explanation about the Cambion had made it easier to understand what happened. Tonight, however, was different. Dakota was attracted to Cammie, but it wasn't overwhelming.

Cammie laughed and led her to a table in a darkened corner. Yemaya and Lilith joined them. Agra followed carrying their drinks.

"Hey, Cammie, Dakota. Hi, Yemaya. That was a great show last month; thank you for the tickets. Our whores loved it."

"It was my pleasure."

"Well, drinks are on the house...boss' orders."

Placing them on the table, she winked at Lilith and left.

"Are you sure you own this place?" teased Dakota.

"Sometimes I wonder. The longer I'm here, the fewer decisions I get to make...except for paying bills. I definitely get to take care of those."

"One of the benefits of being the boss," Cammie said. "What are you two going to do now that the tour is over?"

"Take a break. Dakota and I need some quality time together."

"Yeah, lately our attempts at relaxation end in some sort of crisis," Dakota added.

"I know what you mean. One of these days I'm going to disappear and let Agra and Kali take over for a few months," said Lilith.

"Right." Cammie rolled her eyes dramatically. Lilith shook her head in disgust.

"I can't even get respect from my clientele."

In an unusual gesture of affection, Yemaya patted the demoness' hand sympathetically.

"Trust me. I know the feeling," she said, glancing toward Dakota.

"What?" Dakota asked, giving her an innocent smile. "How'd I get drawn into this?"

Yemaya leaned over and gave her a quick kiss.

"I'll make it up to you...later."

Dakota shivered.

"Ummm...I think I need to pee!" she blurted out and then turned bright red. Jumping up, she dashed toward the bathroom.

"She's a gem," Cammie said, smiling at the rapidly retreating figure.

"Yes, she is."

Before Lilith could say anything, she saw Agra take out her cell phone. When she slammed the phone on the counter, the club owner decided to see what was up.

"Excuse me. I need to talk to Agra."

Yemaya and Cammie nodded understandingly. Agra's unusual display of temper had also caught them by surprise, considering the barkeeper's normally happy demeanor.

"I hope it is not bad news," Yemaya said, feeling the hair on her neck and arms standing up. The air in the club pulsed with an unknown but very noticeable energy...at least to the Illusionist.

"Oh, you can be sure it's worse than that. It takes a lot for her to act like that, especially here. If she's that angry, something big is up. I think I'll wander over and see if I can calm her down a bit. That's another advantage of being a Cambion. We can soothe the savage beast, so to speak."

Walking quickly to the bar, Cammie passed Dakota, who was wiping her hands on her pant legs.

"Hey. Are you feeling better?" Yemaya asked.

"Yeah. Sooo...what's up? Where'd everyone go?"

"To check on Agra. She received a phone call from somebody and looked very unhappy. Apparently something is up."

"It can't be good if Agra's upset."

"I suspect it has something to do with their whores."

CHAPTER 6

MARGO WASN'T THRILLED about having to take a month off from work, but she didn't dare defy her bosses. The infection wasn't directly related to her sexual activities, but she could pass the bacteria on to one of her clients. The doctor gave her a prescription for antibiotics and told her to lay low for a few weeks. Once she was cleared, he'd notify Agra.

Working under the protection of the Sisterhood came with benefits, health coverage, and guaranteed pay. Of course, the whores had to obey the rules. If they didn't, they were given their savings and sent on their way.

Bored from inactivity, Margo decided to meet up with a couple of friends for a late night coffee. She was trying to convince them to leave their pimp. Marcy and Sylvie's boss was brutal when his girls didn't meet his monetary quota.

Freddy was a smooth talking man with no regard for women. They were meant to service men without complaint, nothing more. If it took getting physical with the bitches, he had enforcers more than willing to keep them in line.

Margo was taking a shortcut home from her rendezvous when she saw a young girl lying in the shadows. Checking the area to make sure it was safe, she hurried over and knelt next to the body. If she hadn't recognized Candy's clothing, she wasn't sure she would have known the woman's identity. Her badly bruised body was left in an alley. Pulling out her cell phone, Margo dialed a number while stroking the injured woman's hair.

"It's okay, baby," she murmured, keeping her voice low so she wouldn't attract attention. "Hello? Miss Agra, this is Margo. I need your help."

Quickly outlining the situation, she listened to her boss' instructions, unconsciously nodding her head.

"Okay...but hurry up, please. If Freddy or his goons show up, I'm dead. He don't like no interference with his hoes... Yes ma'am... Thirty minutes...Ok, but I'm gonna try and get her out of sight just in case. This guy is trouble. No one crosses Freddy. I'm scared, Ms. Agra, hurry please."

Hanging up, she looked around nervously. Candy moaned softly. Nervously, Margo put her hand across her lips.

"Hush, baby. Miss Agra's comin' to help."

Margo dragged the woman into the shadows and waited.

CHAPTER 7

LILITH MOTIONED FOR Agra to join her in her office. She could feel waves of violent energy emanating from the angry demoness. "What's up?"

"It's Margo. She may be in trouble. I need to get to her, fast."

"Then go! I'll cover for you."

"Thanks."

"Take Kali. You may need her."

Lilith knew Agra could handle almost anything on her own, but Kali's presence would keep her calm. It wouldn't take much to send Agra on a rampage. Then there would literally be hell to pay.

The last time the demoness had lost control was 1908. Kali and Agra were traveling through Europe and Russia, searching for a new city in which to relocate. In those days it was necessary to move every twenty or thirty years. Appearing young forever in a mortal world created problems.

They had just departed London for Siberia when they received word from a minion that some of their whores were killed in an accident in New York City.

* * *

Agra was fond of the NYC Sisterhood, and especially Marylou, its oldest prostitute. At 52, she was too old to hook. When Kali discovered her sleeping in a small cubbyhole under an alley staircase, she offered her a place to stay at a rented boarding house on 47th Street. Too tired and disillusioned by life to argue, Marylou had agreed. For her, it meant warmth and safety. After Kali introduced her to Agra, she was assigned a small room in the attic and given a few menial tasks to see if she fit in with the rest of the "sisters."

Soon the demonesses discovered the old whore had a knack for settling petty disputes among the women. She was a natural leader. The girls liked and listened to her.

The Sisterhood grew, attracting more than sixty members. Marylou became Madame and ruled the stable with a gentle fist. Another ten years passed. The whores settled into an almost normal existence.

In 1907, the day came the demonesses always dreaded. Agra was in her office when there was a knock on the door.

"Come in," she said, smiling fondly at the elderly Madame. Leaning heavily on her cane, Marylou shuffled slowly into the room and plopped down on the thickly padded chair near the small fire that always burned.

"Are you real busy, Ms. Agra?"

"No. I always have time for you."

Agra could tell by her fidgeting that Marylou was uncomfortable.

"Have you looked in a mirror lately?"

"No, I don't have much use for them. Should I?"

"Not really. It wouldn't help anyway," sighed the elderly woman. "I've known you and Ms. Kali for almost seventeen years, Ms. Agra, and it's been the best part of my life so don't go thinkin' I'm tryin' to get rid of you two. It's just that...well...some of the older whores are whisperin' about how you don't look a day older than when they first met you."

"I see. And you think this is going to be a problem?"

"It already is. There's talk among the younger whores that you ain't normal. I don't know why that should make a difference. They got better lives now than before. Mind you, the old girls don't care none, but you know how people are...especially youngun's. They ask questions and want answers."

"What do you suggest?"

"Ain't my business to suggest, Ms. Agra. I'm just lettin' you know there's talk. One day, someone's gonna say something to the wrong people and there's gonna be trouble for you. I don't like thinkin' about that."

"I'll talk with Kali and get back to you. Thanks, Marylou."

Nodding her head, the faithful old Madame heaved herself from the chair and walked tiredly from the room, closing the door softly behind her.

A few days later, the two demonesses called her back into their office. On Agra's desk was a stack of papers and a large brown envelope.

"Thank you for coming," Agra said, motioning for Marylou to sit down. Kali handed her the documents and asked her to read them. The two sat silently as their Madame slowly read each paper and placed it in a neat pile on the table next to her. When she was done, she looked first at Kali and then at Agra. Tears trickled down her cheeks and dripped onto the two shaking hands clasped on her lap.

"I don't know what to say," she choked out, her voice barely above a whisper.

"There's nothing to say. Kali and I have decided it's time to move on. We want you to take over ownership of the Sisterhood. All the funds have been transferred into your name, as well as the deed to the property. If there are any problems in the future our attorney will handle things. You have final say in anything pertaining to the Sisterhood or the property. You've run the stables for a long time, Marylou. We know you'll take care of our whores."

"Where will you be goin'? Surely, you'll come back and visit now and then."

"If you ever need us, we'll be here. Now, Kali needs to go over some final instructions. Tonight will be our last night here."

"So soon! What do I tell the girls?"

"Whatever you want. They'll accept anything you say, but please let them know we'll miss them...especially the older ones."

"I will," Marylou said sadly.

The next few hours were spent going over financial details. Once satisfied that Marylou understood everything, they bid her goodnight, not goodbye.

The next day, their rooms were vacant. Nothing was left behind to indicate that they ever existed except for a small golden amulet with Marylou's name engraved on the back. An oval-shaped, blood-red stone with a black center that resembled a cat's eye was embedded in the middle. When Marylou touched the gem with her finger, she felt a tingle and jerked away, startled.

Don't be afraid, my old friend, whispered Agra's voice in her mind. *If ever you need us, just touch the stone. We will come.*

Marylou smiled. She always believed Kali and Agra were special. Now she knew the truth. They were guardian angels.

Kali and Agra chuckled at the irony.

After leaving NYC, the two demonesses took an ocean liner to Europe. The summer of 1908 found them in a hotel in

Eastern Europe. Kali was trying to convince Agra to settle in London when the air around them was suddenly disturbed by an unusual energy. Within seconds, a tiny, dark red minion popped into their room and scurried nervously toward them on all fours. Head bowed, it whimpered pitifully, fearing retribution for the uninvited intrusion.

"Bezsuth!" The stunted minion cringed. "What are you doing here?" Kali asked in a quieter voice, not wanting to scare the little minion any more than it already was. Stroking the smooth, bald head, she tenderly scratched behind the small horns on its wrinkled forehead.

"So sorry, so sorry!" wailed Bezsuth. "Please forgive, Mistresses...please forgive. Bezsuth not want intrude...not want intrude."

"It's okay. What's up?" soothed Kali, glancing at Agra with raised eyebrows. The other demoness shook her head and shrugged.

"She dead...she dead...soul gone...soul gone."

Kali frowned and reached down to lift the minion's chin to look into his dark brown eyes.

"Who's dead? What are you talking about?"

When Bezsuth cringed, Kali softened her grip and patted his head affectionately.

"It's okay. I'm not mad at you. Tell us who you mean."

"The whore...the whore...she dead...she dead."

"What whore?"

"Your whore...your whore, Mistress...Marlou...Marlou."

Both Agra and Kali stiffened.

"How?" growled Agra and then softened her voice. "What happened?"

Slewing a glance at her, the minion quickly looked away, not wanting to make eye contact with the powerful demoness.

"She die in accident...in accident...train crash...train crash...many, many whores die...many, many."

"Why didn't the amulet let us know? It's connected to her essence."

"He take it...he take it."

"He? He who? What are you talking about, Bezsuth? Just tell us what you know."

"Sanarixs...Sanarixs...he want souls...want many, many souls...know whores easy...easy... no one care."

"Sanarixs? Since when did that creep care for souls. He only enjoys decaying flesh."

"He want power, Mistress, power. Ever since Sabnock leave he grow braver...braver. He take their essence...all of them. He take whores' essence... and amulet...and amulet. Say you no do nothing...say you weak...weak from years with the humans."

Agra slowly stood up, her body rigid with anger.

"Where are my whores' souls?" she hissed, coldly. At that moment, Kali knew her friend was barely in control of her temper but, considering the circumstances, she was not inclined to interfere.

"He eat them...eat them...say you no do nothing...no do nothing."

"Does Dis know this?"

"No...no...I tell you first...you first...you always kind to me...kind to me...me pay back...pay back, Mistress."

"Thank you, Bezsuth. You can go now. I'll deal with Sanarixs."

Before either Kali or the minion could respond, Agra was gone.

"Oh shit!" Kali exclaimed, looking at the terrified minion crouched next to her. "Don't worry. She's not mad at you, but I'd better check this—"

Before she could finish, the earth trembled and then shook violently. Running to the window, Kali noticed a large plume of smoke billowing up in the distance. The cloud soared skyward as if a huge bomb had been dropped. People in the streets screamed and dropped to the ground, covering their heads with their arms.

"Fuck! Gotta go, Bezsuth. Return to the Underworld and get Dis. I may need him," she ordered and then vanished.

Kali reappeared on a hillside overlooking the Tunguska Valley in Russia. Around her was such complete devastation she would have sworn the apocalypse had occurred had she not known Agra was involved. On the valley floor stood her friend, legs spread apart with hands on her hips as if posing for a statue. At her feet lay the crumpled figure of a large male demon, one arm held high in the air in an attempt to ward off his assailant.

"Where are their souls?" Agra screamed. Bolts of energy bounced all around them, setting small patches of earth on fire.

"I...I don't know!" stammered Sanarixs. "I only deal with decay. You know that!" His voice held that whiny tone that the demoness detested.

"One last time, Sanarixs! If you don't tell me where their souls are, I promise you, you'll know pain such as no demon has ever experienced. I'll give you to Bhuta and let her feed from your essence every day. She'll suck your life force slowly and painfully, leaving only enough for you to survive. When you recover, she'll do it over and over from now to eternity...and that will only be the beginning of your misery."

"Please, Agra..."

A rumbling, followed by the appearance of Dis and Bezsuth interrupted his pleading.

"Dis!" cried the fallen demon. "She's mad! Do something!"

The Underlord ignored Sanarixs and turned to Agra, demanding an explanation.

"He has stolen my whores' souls. I want them back!"

"All of this over whores? There are plenty of them out there for the taking."

"They aren't his to take!"

"So what? What difference does a few lost souls mean? It's not like they're an endangered species. Look at all of this destruction, Agra. Have you lost your mind?"

"No! I have a right—"

"You have no rights to their souls!" stormed Dis, his voice rising with his anger. "They were given to you only as humans to do with as you wish. Their souls still belong to me. You've overstepped yourself!"

Sanarixs smirked slyly. Now that Dis was here, he had no doubt he would escape the demoness' wrath. Seeing the look, Agra stiffened and glared at the insolent demon.

"Enough of this!" ordered Dis. "Curb that temper, Agra or I will."

"I won't leave without their souls!"

"You'll do as I say!"

"I think not, Underlord!" she hissed, her eyes blazing a brilliant red. "You forget. I'm no longer yours to command. You granted me freedom."

"Obviously, poor judgment on my part."

"Or a wise move," she countered.

Dis sighed. She was right. At the time it was the only way he could get her to divorce him. As ruler of the Underworld, his word was law but not necessarily enforceable without the help of others. Unfortunately, the female demons were more powerful than the males, giving them immense influence.

Females! he thought.

"I suggest you give Agra what she wants," advised Lilith, appearing next to her.

"As do I," added Kali, joining the two women.

Dis snorted. It didn't bode well for him whenever his exes and their friends banded together in a common cause. Turning to look at Sanarixs, his eyes blazed angrily.

"Now look what you've done, you idiot! Give her the damn souls before they do something extreme! I don't have time for this crap!" he said and disappeared.

It was Agra's turn to smirk. Swallowing nervously, Sanarixs nodded. If the Underlord was afraid of these females, he was in trouble. Bending his head and clutching his stomach he regurgitated six small golden spheres. They floated upward. Reaching out his hand, he pushed them toward Kali. After examining each globe, she nodded to Agra and placed them in her friend's outstretched hand.

"You may go," Agra said. "But not unpunished!"

Snapping her fingers, she smiled wickedly as Sanarixs vanished.

"What did you do?" Lilith asked.

"Since he loves the taste and smell of decaying flesh so much, I removed his taste buds and his sense of smell. What he enjoys most, he will no longer enjoy at all."

The three women laughed.

"What are you going to do with the souls?" asked Kali.

Turning to Beszuth, who was crouched behind Lilith, she motioned him forward.

"Beszuth, you have done me a great service this day. I'm in your debt." Agra knelt to make eye contact with the small minion.

"No debt, mistress...no debt," he replied, smiling for the first time.

"Yes, there is. Now I must ask you to do me a great favor."

"Anything...anything..."

Taking his small hand, she placed five of the spheres on his palm.

"Keep these safe. They are precious to me. I will consider it an honor if you accept them and the trust I place in you."

Beszuth beamed with joy and straightened up until he was standing on two feet. It was an awkward position for him. He had spent most of his existence scrambling around on all fours.

"Thank you, mistress...thank you. Is great honor...great honor. I protect with my life...my life."

"I know you will, my friend," she said, stroking his knobby head.

"And the last soul?" Kali asked, pointing to the remaining globe on Agra's palm.

"This is Marylou."

Opening her mouth, Agra placed the last small globe on her tongue and swallowed.

"I'll keep her safe until I can talk with the Twin. She deserves better than what we have to offer. Hopefully he will give her a second chance at life."

"Good luck!" replied Lilith.

"Oh, I think I have something better than luck," Agra replied, looking at Kali. "I have her...and we both know how he feels about her."

"Good point!"

Kali grinned.

The three stared at the devastation around them. For a moment, Agra felt guilty at the lives lost from the explosion when she hurled Sanarixs' body to the earth. She had tried to pick an uninhabited area but hadn't realized the power behind her anger.

"This is going to be hard to explain," Kali said, shaking her head unconsciously.

Agra shrugged. It was worth it to have retrieved the soul of the one human she truly loved.

"The humans will come up with something. They always do."

And they did. Years later, scientists determined a meteorite had struck the Tunguska Valley on June 30, 1908. The destruction to the area and for several kilometers around it was the equivalent of an atom bomb exploding, leaving nothing alive. Fortunately, very few people died in the explosion.

CHAPTER 8

YEMAYA FROWNED WHEN she saw Kali and Agra leaving the club. Cammie followed them outside. Bertha, the bouncer, joined Lilith behind the bar and started taking orders while the club owner mixed the drinks. It was obvious the large woman wasn't comfortable playing barmaid.

"Something is wrong," she told Dakota, nodding toward them. "I think I will see if Lilith needs help."

Before Dakota could reply, Cammie returned looking slightly perturbed.

"Maybe you should see if you can learn something from Cammie."

"Will do," Dakota said.

Lilith handed Bertha the mixed drinks and had started on the next order when she felt the Illusionist's presence.

"Can I help you with anything?" asked Yemaya.

"Unless you know how to mix drinks, I doubt it," she replied, good-naturedly.

"Well, as a matter of fact, I do. It comes in handy when entertaining. Move over and tell me what you need."

Raising both eyebrows in surprise, the demoness stepped aside to let her pass. Smiling, Yemaya listened to the order, picked up a bottle of rum, spun it around and quickly poured two drinks. Adding coke to one and tonic to the other, she passed them to Lilith and then proceeded to prepare the next drink.

Seeing the customers were now in good hands, Bertha sighed and headed back to her stool by the door, grateful to be away from the noisy crowd.

"You really are a magician," teased Lilith once the backlog of orders was cleared.

"Illusionist," corrected Yemaya, enjoying the moment.

Dakota watched in amazement as Yemaya poured liquor into glasses, added the various mixes and spun the bottles like a baton before setting them on the shelves.

Damn, she's good! she thought before switching her attention to Cammie.

"Anything I can do?"

"No. One of Agra's whores is in trouble. Kali went with her."

"And you don't like it."

"Not really."

"You think something could happen to them?"

"Nowadays, anything's possible. Demons aren't the immortals they once thought they were."

"Surely they know that."

"Oh, they know...but Agra loves her whores. She loses control sometimes. Even Kali has a hard time calming her down."

"Well, I get the impression they make a formidable team. Since there's nothing we can do, maybe we should help Lilith?"

Watching the two women making and passing out drinks was watching grace in motion. They were so in sync with each other that the line at the bar shrank to just a few women standing around gossiping.

"They don't need our help. Besides, it's a good opportunity for them to get to know each other...and for you and me to talk."

Dakota wasn't sure she liked the sound of the last part.

"I just want to make sure you're okay with what Yemaya told you about me. I know you were embarrassed."

"To say the least."

"Do you feel anything now?"

The journalist was surprised that she didn't.

"No, I don't! What happened?"

"I'm not sure. Kali and I have been spending a lot of time together. It's the first time I've ever been in a real relationship. It seems to have taken the edge off my gift. At least that's what I think. I'm not sure if I miss the attention or not!"

"I can imagine. Well, I can't feel the attraction anymore, but I'm not complaining. Yemaya's attention is all I need."

CHAPTER 9

MARGO HUDDLED IN the alley waiting for her boss. Whenever the woman lying beside her moaned, she'd lean down, stroke her hair and whisper soothingly, trying to calm her down. Nervously, she pressed her back against the wall. Silhouettes of people moved up and down the streets. When a blue Toyota Sequoia pulled into the alley, blocking the entrance, she knew her time had run out. Freddy's enforcers had arrived.

"What have we here?" asked a thin white man, walking up to Margo and nudging her with his foot. His two companions snickered. "Hey, Stumpy, looks like we have another whore here. When's the last time you had one from the Sisterhood?" he sneered.

"Never, boss. Everyone knows them whores are hands off," said a tall, stocky man with a lumpy complexion. He was quickly slapped across his unintelligent face. "Hey, what was that for, Lenny?" he whimpered.

"There's no such thing as hands off for whores, you idiot. Take this one down the alley and teach her to mind her own business. It'll be a good message for those bitches running her stable. Nico, put Candy in the car. Make sure she stays alive. He wants to make an example of her."

"Aw, boss. Why can't Stumpy do it? I'd like a little fun with this bitch," whined Nico, a skinny man with a sallow complexion and greasy hair. "I'm tired of fuckin' the same old stuff."

"Do what I tell you, stupid. You can have her when he's done with her. Until then, make sure no one sees you."

"Sure boss," grumbled Nico. "You'd better not be infected with any diseases," he growled, looking at Margo, then turning to Stumpy. "I catch something from her after you've fucked her and I'll kill yah!"

"Aw, man. You know I don't do no diseased whores. She's from the Sisterhood. They keep their girls clean."

"Please, Mister..." begged Margo, grabbing Lenny's pant leg. "I ain't done nothing! Let me go. I won't say anything."

"Jesus, bitch. Don't touch me!" yelled Lenny, kicking her hand away. "My boys here are gonna make sure of it."

Motioning to his bodyguard to take her away, he pulled out a cigarette and lit it, ignoring the whimpers from the whore as she was dragged deeper into the alley. Nico leaned down and picked up Candy's limp body, carried her to the SUV and dumped her on the floor behind the back seat.

Tossing his half-smoked cigarette on the pavement, Lenny stepped on it and peered into the shadows. He wanted to send a message to the Sisterhood, but letting Stumpy fuck the whore was taking too much time. A loud "oof" made him straighten up.

"Hey! Hurry up!" he yelled.

When his man didn't answer, he cursed and signaled for Nico to go get Stumpy.

"Stupid bastard! How long does it take to fuck a whore?" he growled, pulling out another cigarette.

"Maybe he couldn't get it up," Nico suggested, trying to make out the images in the dark alley. "You know why he's called Stumpy?"

"Yeah. Looking at his size you'd think he'd at least have a big fuckin' dick," snickered Lenny. "Go get him and let's get out of here."

"What about the whore?"

"If you have to fuck her, hurry up! Then kill her!"

Lenny decided it would be better not to leave a witness around. It could create a turf war if she blabbed to the bitches she worked for.

Disappearing into the alley, Nico pulled a folding knife from his pocket and opened it.

"Stumpy, where you at, man?"

The sound of a dull thud made him chuckle.

"Bout time you finished with her. Boss says we gotta hurry. You better have saved some of that pussy for me."

When Stumpy didn't answer, Nico frowned, fingering his knife blade nervously.

"Stumpy, you there?" he asked uneasily, and waited for his eyes to adjust to the darkness. After a few seconds he saw two shadowy figures walking toward him. Their shape told him they were women. He relaxed.

"Who are you?"

"Your worst nightmare," murmured a female voice.

Nico didn't frighten easily. As one of Freddy's top enforcers, he was used to dealing with women. They were weak.

An invisible hand grabbed him by the throat and squeezed tightly, cutting off any chance of calling out. Helpless, Nico swung the knife back and forth trying to slash his attacker.

"Don't make it any worse. I'd hate to kill you too quickly."

Nico's eyes bulged. The pressure around his neck increased. Giving a painful rasp, he tried to speak.

"What's the matter, Nico? You've held plenty of people like this. Mostly women. Surely you've wondered how it felt?"

Nearby stood two women. Both were tall and slender. One was slightly shorter. Glowing red eyes blazed with an unholy anger. Dropping the knife, he crossed himself and muttered a prayer for redemption.

"I assure you, no god will help you."

"This scum isn't worth wasting our time on," said the other woman.

"Hey!" yelled a male voice from the alley entrance. "What the hell is taking you so long?"

"Tell him to come here!" The grip on his neck eased enough to allow him to comply. Coughing and gagging, he thought about warning Lenny but immediately changed his mind when the freaky-looking orange haired woman stepped closer.

"I wouldn't."

Nico nodded.

"Bo...Boss," he rasped. "Get back here!"

"Stop playing games, Nico. You and Stumpy get your asses out here."

"Ummm..."

"Tell him Stumpy fell and hurt himself."

"Stumpy fell. He's hurt!" Nico yelled.

"Shit! Do I have to do everything?" Lenny muttered, throwing his third cigarette down.

Lenny hated getting his hands dirty. If Stumpy was down, it would take the two of them to get him to the car. Shaking his head, he trudged into the darkness, moving slowly so his eyes could adjust to the low light. He was only a few feet from his goons when he noticed the two women. Looking at Nico, he motioned toward them.

"Who the hell are they?"

238

"I don't know," gasped Nico, rubbing his throat and swallowing painfully.

Shaking his head, Lenny turned to look at them. His eyes moved up and down their lithe figures. Smiling his appreciation, he put his hands in his pockets and licked his lips, rocking slightly forward and backward on his feet.

"What can I do for you good-lookin' ladies?"

Agra stiffened. Kali's anger was barely under control. She touched her friend's arm lightly.

"Let me," she murmured and then turned to give Lenny the same appraisal he had just given them. "There's nothing you can do for us, but we can do something for you."

Lenny's thug was about to comment when he felt the grip tighten lightly around his neck. A warning. Shut up or die! Nico wasn't ready to sacrifice himself for his boss.

"Well, two reasonable women. Personally, I hate fucking in such a crude place, but for you it would be worth getting a little dirty," Lenny replied.

"I don't do animals," Kali replied, stepping close to him.

"Ah...a woman with spirit. I like that. Taming you is going to be fun."

Reaching out to stroke her cheek, he cried out when he felt his fingers burning. Instinctively, he jerked his hand back and and shook it. "What the —"

"Hell?" finished the woman, her eyes flashing a bright red. "You're about to find out."

"Who are you? Who are they?" he demanded, looking at Nico for answers.

"Oh. Forgive my rudeness. This is Agra, my friend, and I'm Kali. You know, those bitches who own the Sisterhood. The ones you want to teach a lesson to."

"Oh, uh, well, apparently there's a misunderstanding here. How about we let bygones be bygones, eh?" he asked, giving her a boyish grin.

"Oh, I think not," hissed Kali. "Instead, you tell me where I can find your boss and I'll make your death less painful."

Lenny laughed. "Sure. Whatever you say," he responded, sarcastically. *Stupid bitch!* he thought.

"Bitch, maybe. Stupid, no."

"Huh?"

"Listen, bitch, I'm ti—"

Lenny felt his throat grabbed. Fingers pressed against the veins in his neck. A sharp pain in his chest made him look down. He was sure he had been stabbed but didn't see a knife. The grip on his throat tightened

Agra, who had been standing quietly a few feet away, stepped in front of him, making eye contact.

"Where is Freddy?"

"At...at...323 Fifteenth," he gasped, turning red as the pressure increased. Temples pounding, he clawed at the invisible hand. His nails tore the skin on his neck. Blood sprayed from his right jugular. Eyes bulging, he stared in horror when he realized he had severed the vein.

"Don't worry. You won't feel any more pain," Agra said. "At least not in this life."

Slumping to the pavement, Lenny's body twitched, then lay still. The demoness turned to Nico.

"You want to live?"

Nodding yes, he was relieved to feel the grip on his neck ease.

"Good. Do as I say and we might spare you, understand?"

Again he nodded, swallowing painfully.

"Take your whore and Margo to the hospital. Make sure they're treated for their injuries...and pray neither die. Then you can haul this piece of shit to Freddy's place. Tell him we'll be paying him a visit. Soon."

"Ye...Yes, ma'am."

"And Nico, if anything happens to my other whores, you're dead. Your life depends on their welfare. Now, go!"

Gently lifting Margo to her feet, Nico escorted her to the SUV and then came back for Lenny. The two women had disappeared. Looking at Stumpy's body, he decided to leave it alone.

Nico heaved Lenny's body over one shoulder and staggered to the trunk, sweat pouring down his face. Then he lifted Candy onto the back seat. Glancing at the rearview mirror as he drove away, he gasped. Two fiery red eyes stared angrily back at him.

CHAPTER 10

KALI AND AGRA returned to the nightclub. Agra had calmed down once she knew Margo and Candy were going to be cared for. When they saw Lilith and Yemaya working behind the bar, they couldn't resist teasing them.

"Hey! Barkeep!" yelled Kali. "Two beers and hurry up!"

"Yeah! How come two thirsty women can't get a cold beer in this place?"

"Did you hear something?" asked Yemaya, looking at Lilith.

"No. Why?"

"I thought I did. Must be my imagination."

"It's the job. Sometimes you think you hear strange noises. Take my word for it, it's nothing more than static."

"Did you hear that, Kali? We've just been relegated to nothing!" exclaimed Agra.

"I'm crushed. And to think we actually worked here once."

"Yeah. Guess we need to find new jobs."

"You know, Yemaya, you may be right. I'm hearing voices too," said Lilith.

"Really? Maybe they will go away if you ignore them."

"Good idea."

"Okay ladies. We get the point. Now get out of here and let us do our jobs," ordered Kali, shooing the two women away from the bar. "I hope you two haven't messed up my filing system."

"It's about time," Lilith said. "And no, we didn't. How about making us some drinks for holding down the place?"

"Sure, boss...and thanks," Kali said.

"Everything turn out ok?"

"For now. We have unfinished business, but it can wait..."

Agra quickly outlined what had happened. Lilith knew better than to ask what they had in mind.

"This Freddy sounds like he could use a little lesson. I need to talk with Dis about this. I'll let him know you're sending new arrivals. He'll love that," chuckled Lilith.

Waving goodbye to Yemaya, Dakota and Cammie, the demoness disappeared into her office and then vanished.

CHAPTER 11

THE GATES WERE impenetrable, except to those who belonged. No key, no force had been able to open them in tens of thousands of years, but they opened effortlessly at Lilith's approach, and closed swiftly behind her.

Several demons stopped to see who had arrived, then went about their business, secretly enjoying the knowledge that Dis was probably going to catch hell from his ex. It was comforting to know that his life wasn't all fun and games.

As she strolled toward the fiery castle rising majestically above the lower levels of the Underworld, Lilith stopped to chat here and there with a demon or minion, catching up on the latest gossip.

At the entrance of Dis' estate stood Cerberus, his three-headed guard dog. Lilith scratched his ears affectionately, amused at his puppy-like enthusiasm. She had always been fond of the giant beast. His ferocious reputation was well earned, but he was a softie around the demoness. She was one of the few who played *fetch the demini* with him, a game that terrified the smaller creatures that scurried through the Underworld. Knowing Cerberus would never hurt them, Lilith would grab one and throw it in the air, much to the delight of Dis' watchdog. Catching it in one mouth, he'd spit it out, then retrieve it with one of his other mouths. Lilith would pluck it away from him, shake the drool off the demini and send it scurrying into the darkness. One of Cerberus's heads would smile happily. The other two looked demonically expectant, hoping another demini would show up.

Dis watched his ex playing with his pet. Eyes gleaming bright reddish-brown, he laughed when two of the heads curled up their lips to grin while the third stuck out a tongue, giving her a quick lick. Cerberus rarely showed his playful side. Picking up his robe, Dis slipped it over his shoulders and tied the belt loosely around his waist. Lilith entered through the hall door just as he walked into his living room.

"Don't you ever knock?" he groused good-naturedly.

"Why? You know I'm here the moment the gates open."

"True, but it would be the polite thing to do."

Lilith snickered. "As if you ever cared about that."

Shaking his head, he smiled. Lilith knew him too well.

"So, what is it you think I have done now?" he asked, resorting to his usual placating demeanor.

"What makes you say that?"

"You never come here unless you think I've done something."

Lilith smirked. He was right. Over the millennia her journeys to his fiery domain were rare.

"I guess there's no reason for me to pretend otherwise."

The Underlord laughed and motioned for her to sit. Walking to a small refrigerator, he opened the door and pulled out two chilled bottles of cola.

"Humans would be appalled to know we drink this stuff," he said, holding up the small plastic bottles, "or that we have ice." Handing her one, he tapped his against hers in a toast. "What can I do for you? If it's about those whores, I don't know anything."

"So you say."

"Surely you of all people don't doubt me. I'll gladly arrange a tour of my dungeons if you'd like to see for yourself."

"No. I believe you. Lying to me would only make things worse for you, but that's not why I'm here."

"So, what is it this time?"

"Our child."

Dis frowned. "Your child. I disowned her the day she was banished." The Child was a closed topic. "Unless you wish to talk about other things, I have guests to entertain."

"They can wait...and you can either hear me out, or I go into your bedroom and tell everyone in there that the party is over. I really don't think you want that."

Dis' laughter was like the deep rumble of a waterfall.

"No, I definitely don't want that. They're already terrified of you. If I didn't care so much for you, Lily, I'd banish you from this place."

"You'd try. Now, about our daughter..."

Sighing, Dis adjusted his robe and leaned back in his chair, crossing his legs. Bare-footed, he reached down to flick a piece of yarn off a polished cloven hoof.

"You still haven't given yourself feet. How come?"

Raising one hoof in the air, he turned it back and forth, admiring its smooth, glossy shape.

"Why should I? I find them interesting. Besides, ordinary feet are boring, don't you think?"

Lilith had to agree. Even she enjoyed the aesthetics of them, not to mention the unusual clicking noise they made when he walked. Hooves were unique to him and a few demons carrying his bloodline.

"Anyway, why bring her up after all this time," he asked. "She's where she belongs. You agreed to the terms of her banishment. What was done can't be undone."

246

"I don't believe that, especially now."

"And what's so different about now?"

"She and I talk."

"Talk?" he asked, straightening in his chair, showing the more serious side of his nature. "Talk how?"

"I don't know how."

"When did this start?"

"Not long ago."

"How do you know it's her?"

"How could I not know? She's my child, Dis."

"Well, she's up to something then. Trouble. Don't go getting all sentimental and motherly, now. She should never have been conceived."

"But she was. She's our daughter...my daughter. I didn't know what to do with her when she was born, but you did. Instead, you took her from me and gave her away."

"For your own good and hers. It was the right thing to do," growled Dis, angrily. The vessels in his neck pulsed visibly, a sure sign he was barely controlling his temper.

"You're right," agreed Lilith. "We had no choice back then. But this is now and we've changed. All of us."

"Not all, my dear. You may forgive her, but I won't. She forfeited any consideration when she broke the rules and betrayed us. The Great Battle was painful for everyone but we reconciled our differences with my brother. Angels and demons were just starting to get along again. Then she broke the truce."

"She was only a child, Dis."

Rising to his feet, Dis walked onto the balcony overlooking the Underworld. Before him burned the eternal fires of Hell, their flames dancing gracefully between the buildings as far as the eye could see. He enjoyed their flickering colors in much the same way humans found trees and forests pleasing.

"A child, yes, but she was our child...my child. She knew the rules. Besides, her actions were not those of a child. The chaos she caused was inexcusable. Look!" he commanded, motioning toward the scene in front of him. "Once we lived in peace with my brother's people. Maybe he and they didn't approve of our ways, but there was no animosity after the Truce was agreed upon. We had put our differences aside. As beautiful as this land is, it lacks the color we once had when we were as one."

"I know. I helped write the Truce."

"All the more reason why this discussion shouldn't even be taking place. You know the price we still pay for her indiscretion. Had she not pissed off my brother, we would have harmony here. Humans would live blissful lives and my Twin and I would be having silly arguments over his latest experiments. She got what she deserved."

"And what about us?"

Dis frowned.

"Us?"

"Yes. Are we blameless?"

"If you were asking me that about the Great Battle, I'd say no. In this, however, I say yes."

"Then you're a fool. Listen, Dis, I'm not defending her actions. What she did was horrible. Every living thing suffers because of it. There's no going back, but you and I, we took no interest in her when she was born. We abandoned her, and then expected her to follow our rules unquestioningly. Did you know it was your own demons who poisoned her mind?"

Dis shrugged. "I suspected as much."

"And you did nothing to punish them?"

"It would have served no purpose. By the time I found out who else was involved, the Child was in the Netherworld, the

Truce was broken and we needed every demon we had to balance the odds. It was a matter of survival."

"You banish your own daughter to an eternity of loneliness and yet do nothing to those who betrayed you?"

"Our daughter," corrected Dis unconsciously. "Like I said, I needed them. We had already lost too many. I owed it to my people to protect those that were left. Now, I really am growing tired of this discussion. What is it you want of me, Lily?"

"I want her freed."

"Impossible. The Netherworld was a one way ticket then, and it still is. Nothing has changed. Once she passed through that door, she no longer existed."

"If that were true, she couldn't communicate with me."

"Exactly! You're imagining those chats. For some reason, you're feeling guilty about the past."

"Don't be an ass! She's as real as you and I."

Knowing it was useless to argue with his ex, Dis decided on a different approach.

"OK. Let's say you're right. What am I supposed to do?"

"Tell me how to release her?"

"There's no way!"

"There is. When she was banished, you said she wouldn't be able to talk to anyone. She talks to me, now. If you're wrong about that, you're wrong about everything else."

"Lily, if I knew I'd tell you just to get you off my back. If you figure it out, let me know. In fact, all my resources are at your disposal. Consider it my contribution to your theory. Now, do you mind if I get back to my guests? They've waited long enough for the party to begin."

Lilith realized Dis had reached the limits of his patience. She had gotten what she wanted...his permission to free the Child. Without it, even if she found a solution, there would be no place for their daughter to live.

"Thank you, Dis. One more thing, if you don't mind."

Sighing, the red giant rolled his eyes and looked at her distrustfully.

"Quit that!" admonished Lilith. "You can be such a baby! Agra sent you a soul she wants given special attention."

"Really. She hasn't participated in that practice for over a thousand years, although Sanarixs came close. What's so special about this one?"

"He tried to kill one of her whores."

"And for that she's out of retirement? She's getting soft."

Lilith shrugged.

Dis pondered the request. "Well, the least I can do is accommodate her. It's good to see she still has it in her. I'll let the Erinyes have him. They have a special knack for punishing the dead."

The demoness smiled. These three sisters had perfected the art of torture. As the demonesses of vengeance, they were even feared by the inhabitants of the Underworld. Whips were their favorite tools, although they had many devices at their disposal. Eternity with them wasn't necessarily the worst thing, but it came close.

"That'll work! She'll be pleased."

"Think nothing of it. For you, almost anything, Lily. Are you sure you don't want to join me? It would be like old times."

"Orgies don't interest me anymore."

"I'm sorry to hear that. Forgive my manners for not escorting you out, but my guests are waiting. You understand."

Leaning down, he kissed her gently on the cheek, removed his robe and walked away, his hooves clicking lightly on the hard floors. Lilith watched him disappear into the bedroom. She still admired his physique. He was magnificent.

* * *

Yes, he is! Even though he's my Father, I can't deny his attractiveness, observed the Child, breaking into her thoughts.

There's nothing wrong in appreciating beauty. Do you see and hear everything I see or think? Lilith thought.

Not everything. Most of the time I can see and hear you and them—all of them—but I can't touch anyone. It's like looking at the world through a two-way mirror...so close but untouchable. And, of course, after this much time, no one knows I ever existed...well, almost no one. You and Father think about me occasionally. Humans are more difficult to hear, demons the easiest. I've found trying to listen to everyone confusing. Hearing billions of thoughts is overwhelming, even for me. I only focus on those I think important.

It sounds very lonely!

Lonely? I've always been alone, but I realize I was too harsh on you. You had no idea what pregnancy was, let alone raising a child. I could feel your misery. Father didn't want to deal with a child. It would have interfered with your relationship. When he arranged for demons to care for me, and you accepted his decision, I was hurt.

There was nothing Lilith could say.

Anyway, believing Adam was behind everything that happened to you, and hearing how much he loved Eve, well...I hated him for being happy.

Adam wouldn't have known how to care for you any more than I did. At least Dis knew what was happening, interjected Lilith.

I know. Poor Adam! He didn't deserve my hatred, but it was Eve I wronged the most. Eve...innocent, naïve, trusting... the perfect wife...the perfect victim.

She wasn't a victim. I'd never have left her with him if she hadn't been the perfect mate or if he had misused her. She was happy. As much as I disliked his attitude toward me, I never wanted Adam to suffer. Her innocence protected them. They were safe from the sorrows I experienced in the Great Battle...the losses both sides suffered. We knew pain. Eve didn't, and that's how I wanted it.

I know, but the stories. Those whispers. I thought I wasn't meant to hear them. Later, I found out it was all a ploy...a way to manipulate me into serving vindictive little minds. It was a subtle campaign to poison my mind.

Why didn't you tell me? I'd have stopped the gossip.

Tell you! You barely knew I existed or cared once Father turned me over to his nursemaids.

* * *

The Child was right. When Dis carried the infant from her bed, Lilith was relieved. The crying made her uncomfortable. His assurance that the child would be properly cared for was enough. Lilith never even asked who would foster her.

They weren't so bad. The whispers, though. They called you Adam's whore. I knew it wasn't true, but I did believe he humiliated you, then cast you from Paradise. And for the Twin to allow it was unforgivable. He was untouchable. Adam wasn't.

So you corrupted Eve. What did you think you would gain?

Satisfaction!

And were you satisfied?

At the time, I was ecstatic. It didn't last. My success was bittersweet. The other demons laughed at me. It was quite a revelation to suddenly realize I had been used and then banished to the Netherworld.

And yet you still refuse to tell me who they are.

252

Like I said before, it serves no purpose after all this time.

For what they did, they deserve some sort of punishment.

It was I who did the deed.

You were young. They knew better.

So did I. I just didn't care.

That's not the point and you know it.

The Child didn't wish to argue with her mother, particularly over those who had deceived her. There would come a time for retribution.

I suppose. They made sure I overhead their gossip. I noticed their secretive looks but didn't think much about them. As the daughter of you and the Underlord, I never suspected anyone would dare lie to me. They played on my ego by telling me I had the potential to be as powerful as Father...maybe more so because I had the blood of both Father and the Twin. I believed them. They nicknamed me the Demon Child. I thought it was a compliment.

Dis and I heard the nickname. We thought it was a reference about us, or because you were up to no good.

Well, there's that. I did manage to make a few lives a little more exciting.

Lilith felt the smirk. She and Dis had received several complaints about her. Besides, demons were always complaining about something.

So we heard.

I can imagine. Actually, I intended it that way. I thought if I created enough trouble, you would take an interest. I even trespassed into Paradise a few times hoping someone would tell you. That's when I first saw Adam. He was very handsome.

Yes, he was.

Eve was there, too. She was constantly waiting on him as if he were a lord. The whole situation was disgusting. You'd never have done that. Even Father knew better.

Dis would have grown bored with a woman who never challenged him.

True. Anyway, corrupting Eve was easier than I thought...

A knock on Lilith's office door interrupted them.

"Come on in, Kali."

Can we continue this later? Lilith asked.

I'm not going anywhere.

Kali walked in looking somewhat flustered and a little sheepish.

"Hey boss. Just reminding you I need the night off. Cammie wants to take me somewhere."

"You two are really serious about each other, aren't you?"

"I've waited a thousand years for her to realize I love her. I guess she's finally starting to believe it's real."

"About time. Go and have some fun. Besides, I've hired a couple of extra girls. The place has grown so much we need the help. It'll give all of us a little breathing room."

"Anyone we know?"

"If you mean Yemaya and Dakota, the answer is no."

Kali looked disappointed. Once she had realized Cammie wasn't interested in Dakota, she decided she liked the human.

"Damn. They'd be good for business and they fit right in."

"In your dreams. Those two have enough to do without getting involved with a bunch of demons and whores."

"Well, a girl can hope. Who are these girls?"

"Jouvart and Mudada."

Kali choked as if she'd inhaled something awful.

"Shit! Why those two? The last thing we need are demons who specialize in sexuality and lewd behavior," she said, sounding thoroughly disgusted.

"Oh, please. This from the Destroyer! You've mellowed. They probably have too."

"Lilith! Have you watched any television lately? Or picked up a magazine? They're worse than ever! Half the planet is fornicating. The other half is bitching about it, as if they were any better. We both know they're all closet fuckers."

"Really, Kali. You can't blame Jouvart or Mudada for that. Besides, they've promised to behave at the club...and I seriously doubt they want to piss you or Agra off."

"Well, since you've already hired them, there's nothing I can do. Jouvart will certainly be popular with the girls. The demoness of sexuality should fit right in. As for Mudada, her lewd jokes might be entertaining."

Lilith chuckled. Mudada knew more jokes than anyone she had ever met. Most were popular among demons, but she doubted the clientele at the bar would be as impressed. They didn't have the same sense of humor as the Underworld inhabitants.

"We'll see. if you're taking the night off, go. I'm sure Cammie is getting impatient."

"Yeah. Call me if there's a problem."

When Kali left, Lilith decided to rest before opening for the evening. Although sleep wasn't necessary for the demoness, she enjoyed the sensation. Sometimes she would dream, but never like humans. There were never clear images. Just moving colors accompanied by music...beautiful, soothing music, wonderfully relaxing. Perhaps that was why her dreams were so special.

CHAPTER 12

FREDDY WAS PISSED. Two of his enforcers were dead. One of his whores was taken away, and all Nico could say was that the Sisterhood's two main bitches were responsible.

"How could those bitches take out two of my best enforcers?" he demanded, pacing up and down the room. "And where were you? How come you're still alive?"

"They told me to take Candy and the other whore to the hospital. I guess that's why." Nico didn't tell Freddy about the invisible hands.

"And you just gathered them up without a word and did it, eh? You let two fuckin' bitches tell you what to do? Why shouldn't I kill you for that?"

Shaking his head, Freddy snapped his fingers at two men standing by the door. "Get him out of here...and call the rest of the guys in. I want them here by nine. We're paying the Sisterhood a little visit tonight. It's about time they realize they can't fuck with me or my whores without paying a price."

"What do you want me to do with him?" asked one of his bodyguards.

"Shoot him!"

Nico felt his bladder explode, releasing its entire contents. The stain spread between his legs, down his pants and puddled on the floor. All he could do was stare at it, humiliated.

"Jesus Christ!" exclaimed Freddy. "What the Hell did they do to you? You were one of my best men."

"Sorry, boss," mumbled Nico, too embarrassed to even plead for his life.

"Get out of here and get cleaned up. Until I find out exactly what happened out there, you've got a reprieve."

Turning his back, he walked away. Something wasn't right and he knew it. Nico wasn't the type to run. Whatever had frightened him...Freddy shook his head. It had to be bad news.

CHAPTER 1 3

"**SOOOO. SHE GAVE** you the night off, eh?" Cammie slowly unbuttoned her blouse.

"Of course. Lilith is a softie, at least when it comes to love."

"Love. I thought I'd grown tired of the word. It sounds so different when you say it."

"It is different," whispered Kali, stepping close to the Cambion and nudging her hands aside. Pushing the last two buttons through their holes, she slipped the garment off Cammie's shoulders and pressed her lips against her neck. "It took a thousand years before I could even get you to look at me."

"I'm slow," teased Cammie.

Running her nails across smooth skin, Kali noticed the marks left behind and smiled. Cammie's skin was velvety soft and sensitive.

Kali was an experienced lover. She sensed her partners' needs, and was quite capable of satisfying them. Asmodai had been her biggest challenge. The demon of lust, he was insatiable...until Kali finished with him. After spending almost a year with him, demanding every minute of every day that he satisfy, he had suddenly disappeared. A decade passed before he reappeared in the Underworld. Then he avoided the dark demoness.

Now Kali was the insatiable one, only this time it was for Cammie. She wanted to touch and taste her in every possible way. To consume her until the Cambion begged her to stop... not that such a thing would ever happen. Cammie was born for sex.

She was a Cambion, the offspring of an Incubus and Succubus, demons who seduced men and women while they slept. By nature the two species hated each other, although no one ever knew why. The history of the succubi and incubi was almost as old as Dis and the Twin.

Why Cammie's mother and father ever mated was beyond imagination and neither parent cared to discuss it. In fact, they had done everything they could to avoid each other after Cammie arrived...as well as her. Maybe they sensed she was different, possessing something unique, apart from her species, the ability to love and the gift of being loved. She had always thought the latter was a curse. Things had changed since Kali. This love was real.

"What are you thinking about?" whispered Cammie.

"You. I've waited so long for you," Kali said.

"I know."

The sadness in her voice made Kali want to cry. "Sounds like we have a lot of time to make up for. How about we get to it?" she teased, wiggling her eyebrows lewdly.

"Works for me." Rolling the dark demoness onto her back, Cammie ripped the tee shirt away from Kali's chest and pulled it from beneath her. Tossing it across the room, she grinned.

"Hey. That's my favorite shirt!"

"I'll replace it."

Unbuttoning Kali's dark jeans, she slithered down the bed and yanked them off, almost pulling the demoness with them.

"Damn, woman! Are you in that much of a hurry?"

"Are you complaining?"

"No."

Cammie let her tongue move up her lover's leg, across her hip and along her stomach. Leaning back she stared into Kali's eyes and watched them morph from lavender to hot, flaming red. Her own turned the same brilliant, burning color. It was said that fire smoldered in the souls of all demons, but when they loved, it burned hotter than the hottest flames of Hell.

"I want you to feel what I feel," whispered Cammie, flicking her fiery tongue across Kali's left breast. Circling her tongue slowly around the nipple, she watched the skin turn dark red. Tiny flames followed the path of her tongue, setting the surface on fire. When Kali groaned, Cammie blew gently over the scorched skin, soothing it with a cool breeze.

"How...how do you do that?" gasped Kali.

Cammie grinned. "It's a succubus thing. You've never felt this before?"

"No."

"Is it too much?"

Kali shook her head.

"Nooo. It's...nice."

"Nice?"

Kali swallowed and nodded.

"Let's see if I can make it more than...nice."

Shifting to the side, she ran her fingers lightly over Kali's ribs and then leaned down to flick her tongue along the trail her fingers left. Again the flames ignited. The skin rippled. Kali's eyes widened nervously.

"You...you...wouldn't," she gasped as fingers worked their way between her legs.

"Oh, but I would."

Stroking the hair just above the lips, she created a small flame and then pulled her fingers away. The fire followed them upward and then retreated. Cammie played with it as if stroking a harp. The rise and fall of the flames created fluctuating temperatures around the entire area. The caresses grew more intense. Cammie leaned down and nuzzled Kali's neck, nipping at the skin playfully.

The seduction had begun. It was the first time the Destroyer had ever been defeated in battle...and she willingly surrendered to the victor.

CHAPTER 14

THE TWO SUVs slowed as they passed in front of Lilith's Den. Outside a line of women waited patiently to be screened and admitted to the nightclub. Circling the block, the lead vehicle parked near a dimly lit corner. The second pulled up behind it. Eight men climbed from the cars and huddled against the building.

"What time is Freddy getting here?" asked one of them, keeping his voice low.

"When he gets here," snapped another.

"What's your problem?" demanded the first, bristling at the man's tone.

"Ignore him. He's just pissed because he screwed up earlier. Freddy should have shot his ass," growled a third.

Nico would have slugged the man if a dark Jeep hadn't pulled up next to the first car.

"Any problems here?" Freddy asked, glaring at the group.

"No, boss."

"Good. One more screw up and I'll have all of you shot. Now shut up and listen. Cooley, you take three guys and go the hospital. Get Candy and that interfering bitch. Take them to my place. I'll tend to them later."

"Sure, boss."

"Oh, and Cooley, if they give you trouble, do whatever it takes to shut them up. Get it?"

Cooley grinned, rubbing his crotch. Signaling for three of the men to follow him, he climbed into the lead SUV and drove off.

"What about us?" mumbled Nico.

"We're paying a little visit to Lilith's Den. Come on!"

As they neared the nightclub, Freddy signaled for two men to watch the back door. The others followed him. Pushing past the line, he forced his way through the door.

"Hey man!" complained one women. "This is women only!"

"Shut up, bitch!" snarled Freddy, palming the gun handle protruding from his pants. "Or I'll make you."

Throwing up her hands, she backed away.

"I ain't looking for trouble, mister."

"Smart move." Freddy continued inside followed by his goons.

Seeing the gun, Bertie pushed a button on the wall and then stood to block the entrance to the main room.

"No men allowed," she growled, unimpressed.

"I'm sure tonight you'll make an exception," Freddy warned, once again displaying his weapon.

"No exceptions. No men."

Patting the wooden handle of his gun, he smiled knowingly. "I'd suggest you rethink that."

Crossing her arms, Bertie stood her ground.

"Okay. I've rethought it."

"I thought you would."

"The sign says 'no men', so it's no men. Now get out!"

Freddy wasn't used to women standing up to him. Pulling out the gun, he pointed it at Bertie's head.

"I don't take lip from no fucking broad...especially a fat slob like you!"

The woman blinked and stiffened. Taking a step forward, she pushed up the sleeve on her right arm.

"That's okay, Bertie," said a quiet voice from behind. "Let the gentlemen in. I'll handle this."

"You sure, boss? I don't mind removing these vermin."

Lilith laughed, knowing Bertie could do just that. "I'm sure."

Stepping aside, the bouncer motioned them past. Freddy smirked.

"Another time," Bertie promised, her voice low and threatening.

Freddy cringed when he saw the look in her eyes. He had made an enemy, a woman big enough to do damage if she got the chance. He'd have his men take care of her before another time arrived.

"Now, now, Bertie," admonished Lilith. "Mr. Perez is a guest here. We don't want him to feel unwanted."

"Sorry, boss."

Everyone knew she wasn't.

"What is it I can do for you, Mr. Perez?" Lilith asked, leading him through the room toward her table in the corner. Several women turned to stare at them and frowned.

"I thought men weren't allowed in here!" one yelled from across the room.

Lilith stopped to stare at her and then the other occupants. The grumbling stopped, although the low whispers were indicative of the discontent permeating the room. Motioning to the chairs, she signaled to Agra to bring drinks.

Freddy looked up at the tall, dark-haired woman with the black eyes. His gaze wandered slowly from her face, down her body, and then back up. Licking his lips crudely, he imagined what it would be like to fuck her.

"You wouldn't last two seconds."

"Huh?"

"Fucking me. You wouldn't last two seconds," she said, sitting down and crossing her long legs.

"How did—"

"That's all men like you ever think about."

Freddy didn't like women talking down to him, especially in front of his men.

"You want to play games, eh, Miss—"

"Lilith."

"Lilith. Well, Lily, I'm here to clear up a few things."

"Ah. I'm intrigued, Mr. Perez, but I don't believe you hear well. The name's Lilith. L...I...L...I...T...H. In case you can't spell. What is it you think needs clearing up?"

Ignoring her sarcasm, Freddy looked at his fingernails and stroked them slowly with his thumb.

"Oh, let's say an understanding. Keep your whores away from mine and we'll get along fine."

"*My* whores?"

"Don't play games with me. The Sisterhood."

Lilith laughed.

"Agra!" she called. "Would you come over here?"

Freddy watched the bartender swagger toward them. The orange hair with the purple tips made her look like a punk rocker.

"What's up, boss?"

"Agra, Mr. Perez here seems to think I'm the pimp for the Sisterhood."

"You?" Turning to the other barkeeper, a short plump woman, she called out. "Hey Mudy, this guy thinks the boss runs the Sisterhood."

Several women choked on their drinks. The sound of coughing filled the room. Others snickered and stared at

Freddy as if he had grown horns. Mudy gave him the finger and went back to making drinks.

Turning red, Freddy felt his anger growing.

"Look ladies, I'm trying to be nice."

Placing her palms on the table, Agra leaned down, her face inches from his. Her eyes flared fiery red.

"I own the Sisterhood...and I don't take threats well," she hissed, her hot breath fanning his cheek.

Freddy jerked back and reached up to touch his face. It felt hot and tender.

"Hey, my mistake. We can be reasonable. You stay on your turf and I'll stay on mine. That's all I'm saying."

"I'll tell you what, Mr. Perez. I'll think about it. In the meantime, call your goons back from the hospital before they end up like the two in the alley."

Startled, Freddy flinched.

"I...uh...I don't know what you mean."

"Oh, I'm sorry. Perhaps I'm mistaken. I thought you sent four of your men to the hospital to get Candy and my whore," snarled Agra, curling her upper lip slightly.

When he didn't respond, Agra straightened up and glared down at him. "I was jus...just making sure they were ok. That's...all."

"How nice. Then you don't mind calling your goons and having them drop the girls off here."

"Yeah. Sure."

Taking out his cell phone, he punched in a number, glancing at the bartender nervously.

"Cooley. Bring the whore to Lilith's Den."

"Both of them," ordered Agra.

"But Candy belongs to me."

"Not anymore. She's mine, now!"

"You can't—"

"What?" demanded the demoness, quietly threatening.

"Nothing. Cooley, bring them both here...No, I'm not kidding. Just do it."

Before he could hang up, Lilith reached over and took the phone from his hand. Smiling graciously, she put it to her lips.

"Oh...and Cooley, if you lay a finger on them, if you so much as look at them wrong, I will personally cut off your hands and your dick, and feed them to you."

The threat was said so calmly everyone who heard it knew the club owner was serious. Handing the phone back to Freddy, Lilith stood up and smiled.

"Now, Mr. Perez. You rudely pushed your way into my club, threatened my bouncer, who happens to be a very good friend of mine, and then threatened me. Members of the Sisterhood have been killed or injured. I don't take these things lightly.

"Cooley's about to have a terrible accident," she continued. "I especially don't take kindly to rapists. As for the two jerks at the back door, pick them up when you leave...they are currently indisposed."

Freddy started to interrupt when Lilith held up her hand.

"No. Not a word. Your reign is over. You have one week to get your business in order and leave town. One week. Not a day more. Agra will be by in a few days to collect your whores. They are under the protection of the Sisterhood."

Freddy wasn't sure what to do or think. Once he was out of there, he'd decide on his next move. For sure, he wasn't going to let this bitch order him about.

"Not very smart, Mr. Perez. I suggest you do as I say."

"Huh?"

Reaching over, she caressed his cheek lightly. The pleasant, cool trail left by her fingers turned warm and then burned, causing him to gasp. Jerking his head back, he covered his cheek with his palm, his eyes watering from the pain.

"What are you?"

Lilith looked at Agra, then back at him.

"What's the old cliché, Agra? His worst nightmare?"

"You got it, boss."

It wasn't exactly the truth. Freddy's worst nightmare wasn't happening in this life. He had an eternity of them ahead of him.

"It's time you left, Mr. Perez. This is a women-only bar."

Motioning for Bertie to come over, she watched her bouncer escort the three men from the club.

"I don't trust him," Agra said.

"Neither do I. Have Mudada watch him. If he tries anything, she can handle it, but make sure his soul is left intact. I want him to spend a long time repenting his sins."

Nodding, the bartender returned to the counter and whispered to Mudada. Wiping her hands, the plump demoness nodded and grinned. Grabbing her crotch in a lewd manner she made a slicing gesture across her lower body.

Lilith chuckled. Mudy would like nothing better than to cut Freddy's nuts off. The loss wouldn't affect his soul. *I could almost feel sorry for him*, she thought.

Why? asked the Child, intruding on her mother's thoughts. *He doesn't deserve anyone's sympathy.*

True. I did say almost.

You're growing more human in your old age.

Old age? Demons don't grow old.

Everything grows old. Many of our kind have disappeared. No one knows where they've gone.

Lilith had to agree. Thousands of other demons had vanished long after the Great Battle had ended.

Only time will tell.

Time, something demons never think about. I do. Do you think I've aged any, Mother?

I don't know.

I'd hate to think I still had the face and body of a child.

I can understand that. You were telling me about your plan before. How did you get Eve to cooperate with you?

Eve was naïve, but intelligent. She was also curious about everything except for one particular tree. I asked a demon why. He told me about the Tree of Knowledge and that the Twin declared it off limits to all of his creations.

He thought absolute knowledge would corrupt anyone. Even Dis and the demons believed this.

Every day I climbed the tree and wait for her to walk by. One day, she stopped and looked at the fruit so I whispered to her.

You talked to Eve?

Yes. I turned myself into a serpent so the Twin wouldn't notice.

When did you learn to shapeshift?

I'm my Father's daughter.

Lilith thought about the times Dis changed his appearance for his own reasons. He was especially fond of Elvis.

Exactly, said the Child. *She and I talked a lot. She said she was bored with her existence, and that's when I knew I had her. I told her about the Underworld and its inhabitants. She thirsted for knowledge. It was like an addiction and I was her fix. She asked about the demons...how many there were...how many angels. What I didn't know, I made up.*

Eventually, she wanted to know how I knew so much. I told her about the Tree of Knowledge. It was the beginning of the downfall of Paradise. I didn't think about the consequences of what I was doing.

You were a child.

I wasn't that young, Mother. Nor was I innocent. I wanted to teach Adam a lesson he'd never forget. That's why I told Eve he had eaten the apple.

CHAPTER 15

AS IF WATCHING a movie on fast forward, Lilith saw images flashing across her mind, some so quick they were nothing more than blurs. Others gave her glimpses of the Child's lonely existence. Suddenly the visions stopped and then moved slowly forward.

* * *

"What will Father say?" Eve asked.

"He won't know," replied the serpent, coiled loosely over a limb, her head within inches of Eve's face. "It won't hurt you, I promise. When Father created me, I was given a bite. So was Adam."

"But, why didn't I get one?"

"I can't tell you. Father made me promise."

"Tell me what? Why not give me a bite too?"

The serpent shifted her position slightly.

"To keep you innocent."

"I don't understand," Eve said, hurt at the thought that Father deliberately kept knowledge from her.

"I'm sure it was in your best interests. Father loves you. Lilith knew everything Adam knew, and look what happened. She was kicked out of Paradise for standing up to him."

"Lilith?"

"Adam's first wife."

Eve frowned.

"I'm his first wife."

"No, you're his second. Father made Lilith when he created Adam. They were equals."

"What happened to her?"

The serpent told her about her predecessor and how she was kicked out of Paradise for wanting to be treated as Adam's equal.

"That wasn't right. This means I'm only a substitute for her."

If ever there was a moment the Child would have stopped, it was when Eve's eyes teared up. Feeling guilty, she hesitated, but her hatred for Adam was strong. The serpent sighed dramatically.

"I shouldn't have said anything."

"No. Please. I suspected something wasn't right. I'm bored with our lovemaking, with my life. It's always the same."

"That's a shame. Sex can become boring if you only do it in one position. And besides, there's so much more to making love than just the physical union. I'm surprised Adam never told you."

"Maybe he was afraid I would want to be his equal, and no longer lie beneath him. I bet that's it."

"That was the reason he and Lilith argued. Eve, I know I gave Father my word that I'd never disclose the secret of the Tree but...well...I feel you've been misled. It's not right."

Eve looked down at the ground, shaking her head. "It's not your fault. Adam could have told me."

"He was probably afraid you'd want what he had."

"He's right, I would...I do, but I don't think he or Father will let me eat one of the fruits."

272

"You're probably right." A slight hesitation followed and then the serpent continued. "I'll grant you one bite."

"No. You're my friend. I won't do anything to get you in trouble."

"You won't. I promise."

"But Father...won't he know?"

"I'm the keeper of the Tree and the protector of the fruit. I'll conceal the bite with my body. Father will never know."

"I don't know," Eve said, wavering.

"Eve. You're my friend. It's only fair that you enjoy the same knowledge as Adam. I'll be fine."

Uncoiling its body, the serpent slithered across a limb and wrapped itself around a large golden fruit. Nudging it with its nose, it swung it toward Eve.

"Do it quickly, but don't pluck it from the Tree. Father will know a fruit is missing."

Eve nodded. Leaning close, she tentatively placed her teeth against the shiny skin. As they penetrated the fruit, she felt the sweet juice flowing into her mouth. It was heavenly. Unable to resist, she bit off a small chunk and then jumped back, expecting to hear the loud thunder of Father's anger, a sure sign he knew what she had done.

When nothing happened, she chewed a few times and swallowed. Almost immediately, she felt a warmth grow in her stomach and spread rapidly throughout her body. Strange images flashed through her mind. She closed her eyes, trying to understand what they meant. When she finally opened them, Paradise was forever changed.

"Why didn't he tell me?" she whispered, overwhelmed by the new information available to her.

"Do you really need to ask?"

"No," Eve replied, then hesitated. "Yes. Yes, I do. Thank you. You've given me a new reason to exist. I must confront Adam with what I know."

The serpent remained silent. The Child had accomplished what she wanted. Eve would do the rest.

Adam was lying near the lake when he noticed Eve walking rapidly in his direction. Standing up, he brushed the grass from his legs and buttocks and went to meet her.

"Hi."

"Why didn't you tell me?"

"Tell you what?"

"That you had eaten from the Tree of Knowledge."

"I've never eaten the fruit. It's forbidden."

"You're lying!"

"Lying? What is lying?"

"It means you haven't told me the truth. You know that! I want to know why!"

"I've always been truthful with you. Where did you get such an idea?"

"From the Tree. You and Father intentionally kept me from acquiring knowledge so I would never be your equal. That's why Lilith left you, isn't it?"

"Lilith? How do you know about her?" demanded Adam.

"The same way you learned about everything. From the Tree."

"Eve, I've never touched that Tree. Father would never allow it."

"I know he wants you to remain superior to me. All of this is nothing more than an illusion to keep you happy. I was made to keep you happy. Father never cared for me."

"Father loves you. You must believe me. I never ate the fruit."

"Prove it."

"How?"

"We'll go back to the Tree and you will take one bite."

"What is that going to prove?"

"It will prove you love me. If you don't, then I'll know it's because you already ate one."

Adam shook his head. "That makes no sense."

"It makes perfect sense. If you already ate the fruit, you know what it can do and don't need to do it again. If you haven't eaten it then you have no reason to refuse since you wouldn't know what to expect. I took a bite. You don't see or hear Father, do you? If it was really forbidden, he'd be here by now."

Adam couldn't argue with her logic.

"Why won't you believe me?" he asked, hurt by her distrust.

"Why should I? All these years you've led me around, teaching me things I should have known from the beginning...just like Lilith...just like you, Adam. I've done everything you've asked. I even lie beneath you when we make love. You've never reciprocated. Why?"

"It isn't necessary. You were happy with the way we did things."

"No, I wasn't. Now, I realize why. You were the happy one. You knew how Lilith felt about the position. If you loved me—"

"Father said——"

"Father was wrong!"

Adam gasped and looked around, expecting to be struck by a lightning bolt. When nothing happened, he frowned. Could Eve be right?

"What's the matter, Adam? Not so sure of yourself anymore?"

"I...I don't know."

"Prove you love me. Take a bite from the fruit."

275

Feeling trapped and unsure of himself without Father's support, Adam relented. Following Eve to the Tree of Knowledge, he noticed the small serpent wrapped around a fruit. As he leaned in for a better look, it moved away, exposing a large white blemish where a bite had been taken. Looking back at Eve, he hesitantly placed his teeth against the white pulp and bit down. When nothing happened, he tore the piece away, jumped back and swallowed. It was sweet and juicy. Adam smiled at Eve. True knowledge was intoxicating.

The sky darkened. Black clouds boiled across the horizon. Thunder rumbled. The heavens blazed with flashes of lightning.

Eve and Adam never noticed the small serpent slithering away.

* * *

It's amazing how easy it is to get someone to believe what they want to, said the Child.

Lilith reluctantly admired the ingenuity of her daughter. That someone so young could conceive such a plan was one thing...to carry it out so successfully against the Twin seemed inconceivable.

After listening to her story, she was more determined than ever to free her daughter from imprisonment, knowing that she and Dis bore responsibility for their demon child's actions.

CHAPTER 16

MUDADA FOLLOWED THE men from the club and watched as they walked to the back of the building. Minutes later they reappeared carrying the body of one of the goons guarding the back door. Throwing him in a dark SUV that had just pulled up, they disappeared again and came out carrying a second body. Tossing it on the first, they climbed into the vehicle and waited. A short time later, another car pulled up. A short, stocky man opened the rear door, helped two women out, and escorted them into the nightclub. When Bertie appeared, he handed the women off to her and then hurried back to the car. Both vehicles drove away, wheels spinning.

* * *

Walking over to a black Suzuki Intruder 1200, Mudada swung a leg over and started the bike. Flipping the kickstand up with her heel, she tapped it into first gear and gunned the motor. Releasing the clutch, she spun her rear tire and took off after her prey. She was going to enjoy this, she thought.

Freddy was furious. Not only had the bitches humiliated him in front of his own men, they had the audacity to take his whore. Word would spread to the other pimps in town. He'd be targeted for elimination. Weakness was an open invitation for a takeover. To save face he needed to get rid of the Sisterhood and their bosses. His first order of business, though, was to find Arnie the Arsonist.

If the bitch likes playing with fire, he thought, unconsciously rubbing his burnt cheek, *I'll show her a real one.*

"Where to, boss?" asked Nico.

"Find Arnie. I need his services."

"You ain't thinking about doing something stupid, are you?"

"You questioning me, now, Nico?"

"No boss. It's just that I know what them bitches can do. There's something not right about them…like they ain't human or something."

"Yeah, well, human or not, no one messes with me."

"Okay, but I don't like it!"

"I don't pay you to like it."

They found Arnie standing on a corner near his apartment smoking a cigarette. Opening the lid to his lighter, he flicked it on and then flipped the lid shut, extinguishing the flame. A cigarette lighter was magic to him. His own little flame that he could carry with him wherever he went. This particular lighter had been with him for several years. He had a special attachment to it. The date of the first building he set on fire was engraved on the side.

When Arnie saw the dark SUV pull up to the curb, he smiled.

"Hey Freddy. What's up?" he asked, leaning through the open window to stare at the men in the front seat. Glancing at the ones in the back seat, he noticed they were unconscious.

"Geez, guys, what happened to you?"

"Nothing that concerns you," growled Freddy, making sure he kept his face in the shadows so Arnie wouldn't see the burn on his cheek. "I got a job for you."

"Sure. Name it. Usual price, of course."

"Of course. Lilith's Den. On the west side. I want it gone by tomorrow night."

"Tomorrow? That's too quick. I need to check the place out. Find its weaknesses and the hours it's closed."

"It's a nightclub, for Christ's sake. They have the same hours as any bar. Just take some gas over there and torch the place."

"Shit, Freddy! I'm an artist! If you think it's so damn easy, do it yourself!"

Fuck! thought Freddy. *Guy's a damn fruitcake!*

Unfortunately, Arnie was the best arsonist in town. His success rate without getting fingered was impressive.

"Look, Arnie. Just do this! Hell, write your own ticket. I'll pay."

"I'll check it out, but I ain't making no promises."

"Fine. Do this for me and I'll add another grand to your price."

Flicking his lighter open and shut, Arnie smiled again.

"Consider it done."

Pushing away from the car, he walked away, playing with his lighter. No one noticed the motorcycle or its rider as it passed by them.

"Where to now?" Nico asked.

"My place. I'm throwing a party. Nothing like having a good alibi when you need it."

Nico didn't say anything. His gut told him this was a mistake. Once he dropped his boss off, he was going to disappear.

* * *

Arnie gathered up everything he needed from a small storage area in his apartment basement. Engrossed in putting together the tools of his trade, he didn't hear his front door open or the quiet footsteps moving toward him, until a board creaked.

Spinning around, he saw a short, heavy woman wearing a black motorcycle jacket and tight jeans...very tight jeans. Thighs bulged, causing the material to stretch and wrinkle. The woman was clearly packing.

"Damn, woman! How'd you get in here? And what do you want?" he demanded, unable to take his eyes off the huge bulge protruding down her left thigh.

When she giggled and grabbed her crotch, he shook his head.

She's fuckin nuts!

"Listen, You're in the wrong place. I don't do dykes and they definitely don't do me. Now, get out!"

Again she giggled and smiled. Crooked, yellow teeth made her look a little freaky, not to mention the wild look in her reddish-brown eyes.

"And I don't do men, sweetie," she said, winking. "At least not the way you mean."

"Then what the hell are you doing here?"

Laughing, the woman clapped her hands together gleefully. It was such a childish action, the arsonist was positive she had escaped from some nuthouse.

"Geez!" Arnie rolled his eyes. "Look! You have the wrong idea. Now are you leaving or do I throw you out?"

"Hee...hee...hee...I choose...ummmm...neither!" Peeking over his shoulder, she saw the can of acetone. "It makes a pretty flame, doesn't it?"

"What do you know about this stuff?"

"Oh...well...hee...hee...hee...I have something better...and it doesn't leave any traces like your stuff. The pretty firemen won't find a thing."

"Really?" he said skeptically. "Everything leaves something behind."

"Not everything. Wanna see?"

"Sure. Why not?" Humoring her was probably the best bet at the moment.

The woman grinned and nodded. Rubbing her hands together rapidly and closing her eyes, she mumbled a few words and then flipped her hands toward him, palms facing upward. Blue flames shot from her fingertips, incinerating Arnie within seconds.

"See!" she said, gleefully. "No trace!"

A distant scream made her laugh.

"Guess you don't like fire as much as you thought."

Slapping her hands together as if knocking off dust, she bent down and picked up a small object lying on the floor.

My own little fire maker!

Minutes later, Arnie's neighbors heard the roar of a motorcycle. It would be days before anyone thought about checking up on him.

* * *

Freddy was in his glory. Several acquaintances had showed up to the party despite the short notice. Booze flowed freely. His whores wandered around trying to drum up future business. Tonight, though, they had to put out for nothing. No one dared protest.

"Great party, Freddy!" yelled a short, balding man who saluted him with a bottle of beer.

"Thanks, Tony. Feel free to make use of one of the girls. It's on the house tonight."

"Will do!"

"Hey, bro!" interrupted a handsome black man, wearing a flashy blue suit and matching tie. "I hear you lost one of your hoes."

"Yeah. She decided to join up with another pimp. No big deal."

"You must be getting soft! Last I heard no one quits you!"

"Don't be stupid, Carlos! She was shit! Couldn't please the customers so I cut my losses. You know how it is!"

"I know what I heard," Carlos said with a smirk.

Freddy stiffened.

"What did you hear?"

"Nothing much. Street talk. Like those lady pimps at the Sisterhood had you pissing your pants."

"That's a fuckin' lie, and I'd be careful about repeating it," threatened Freddy, giving one of his bodyguards an angry glance.

"Whoa, man! No need you getting' that way with me. We're bros, remember?"

Freddy glared at the black man for a few seconds and then decided to cool it. He had enough enemies without alienating Carlos.

"Sorry, Carlos. It's cool."

"No problem. Just thought I'd let you know the talk on the street in case you need someone to cover your back. We bros got to stick together."

"I got it covered."

"There you go."

Slapping Carlos on the back, Freddie motioned to one of his younger servants to come over.

"Elliot, this is Carlos. Make sure he gets whatever he wants...you get my drift?"

* * *

Elliot was in his early 20s. By the way he dressed, it was obvious he was gay...and high on drugs. Smiling coyly at the dark Hispanic, he took his hand and pulled him toward a bedroom. He understood exactly what his boss meant and since Carlos was fairly handsome, in a dark way, he didn't object to the order.

The party was in full swing with half the men drunk while the others banged whores in the bedrooms or wherever else they could. Freddy was sitting on the couch joking with his drug supplier and feeling good. Looking at his watch, he was sure Arnie had completed his job by now. One of his men should be back soon to let him know the extent of the damage.

When the front door opened, a few occupants glanced up to see who else was arriving so late. Mouths dropped open as a slender, dark-haired woman strolled in and looked around as if searching for someone in particular. After making eye contact with Freddy, she smiled and strolled casually over to him, her hips swaying seductively.

Freddy couldn't help but whistle at the sleek figure in tight, low cut blue jeans and orange tank top. Round full breasts jutted perkily from beneath the thin cotton shirt. Exposed stomach muscles rippled as she moved slowly in his direction. Wavy, dark brown hair hung wildly around her face, emphasizing the brilliant green eyes.

"Mama mía," exclaimed Julio, his dealer. "Who is she?"

"I don't know," Freddy answered. "But I'm about to find out."

Rising to his feet he stood and waited for the woman to reach him. As his eyes wandered lewdly up and down her body, he could feel his penis harden against the tight chinos he was wearing. Unconsciously, he reached down to adjust himself but stopped when he noticed she was watching his actions. He quickly slipped his hand in his pocket and blushed slightly. She smiled knowingly but didn't say anything.

"You must be new around here. I'm Freddy, the owner of this place."

"Oui. Je suis nouvelle ici," she replied, drawing the words out slightly, her voice a husky whisper.

The room grew quiet. Everyone wanted to hear what the woman had to say.

Holding out her hand, she offered it to him.

"Je m'appelle Jouvart."

"Jouvart. An unusual name, but a nice one. What can I do for you, Jouvart?" Freddy asked, taking her fingers in his and bowing to kiss them. "I'm afraid I don't speak much French."

"It eez ok. I speak Engleesh. Some friends of mine...they tell me you are having a party, oui? They say women like me can come."

"Oh, you can come here anytime. Right boys?" he asked, looking at the others smugly.

Grunts and nods confirmed his offer.

Taking her by the arm, Freddy led her to the couch and motioned for her to sit, before hiking up his slacks and sitting down next to her. He couldn't stop admiring her looks or physique. She was stunning, and he wanted her badly...for himself.

"So tell me Jouvart, who sent you here?"

"No one send me, monsieur. I come on my own. Am I not a big girl?" she asked, giving him a coquettish look.

"Oh yeah. I'd say you were that."

You're a fuckin' goddess! he thought, running his tongue across his lips. *And before the night's over I'm going to be fuckin' you.*

Too engrossed in his own thoughts, Freddy didn't notice the slight stiffening of her body or the red sparks glowing faintly in her green eyes. All he could think of was slipping his dick inside of her and filling her with pimp juice. Shit, she'd be worth getting pregnant with her looks. He might even pay the bitch's medical bills, he thought.

Jouvart's growl was so low Freddy barely heard it.

"Something bothering you, lady?"

"Mais non, monsieur. You make me a leetle nervous is all. You are...how you say...such a beeg man...un grand homme...oui?"

"Bigger than you think. How about we go to my room and I'll show you size does matter?"

"As you weesh, monsieur. Tonight weel be a night we weel both remember."

Grinning at his companions, Freddy took the woman's hand and stood up. Saying his good-byes, he led her into his bedroom and shut the door behind him, making sure it was locked.

"I don't want anyone popping in while I'm entertaining you."

"But of course...and just how weel you do thees entertaining? You must show me what you like, Freddee."

Freddy rubbed himself, trying to alleviate the pain from his engorged penis, and hoped he didn't come too quickly. He was sure the bitch knew how to please a man.

"Take off your clothes."

"Ah, monsieur, that ees too easy. I theenk first you must remove yours. After all, it ees I who must please you, yes?"

"Well, yes."

"Then let me do my job, please," she offered, stepping in front of him and unbuttoning his shirt. Each button was taken gently between her fingers and pressed through the slot with care. The process was slow but it made Freddy grow so hard, he felt his erection being compressed painfully against his groin and thigh. The pressure on his testicles was excruciating. Unwilling to wait for Jouvart to finish with his shirt, he unbuckled his belt and unzipped his slacks. When his erection popped out, he felt an immediate relief and sighed.

"My, my. You are queek. But then most men are. Such a shame men don't appreciate foreplay. We women, we take hours to reach such a state of arousal."

"I can't wait hours," Freddy replied. "Get undressed."

"I think not! I didn't come here to be fucked by a pig," Jouvart hissed, suddenly losing her accent.

Startled, he grabbed her by the arms and shoved her onto the bed, where he straddled her.

"Listen bitch! You got me this way. Now you get to deal with it. There isn't a bitch alive who tells me when or where, you got it?"

Jouvart laughed as she stared at the angry man perched over her.

"Then you won't be so disappointed, monsieur."

Reaching up, she grabbed him by the jaw and pulled him down to her. Freddy relaxed, expecting to be kissed, but soon found himself on his back with her sitting across his thighs.

"Top or bottom. I don't care as long as I get to fuck you." he said.

"That is going to be your dying wish. Sadly, an unfulfilled one." Scraping her nails across his chest, blue flames trailed the scratches left behind. As the nerves below the skin reacted to the burns, Freddy screamed and tried to throw her off him.

"Poor Freddy. While you suffer, your friends will think you are having too much fun, if they even care."

"Who are you?"

Each stroke of the fingers scorched the skin, making him writhe and scream louder. A banging on the door caught his attention. When he started to call out, a hot fingertip was placed over his lips, searing them. Instinctively he licked them, trying to soothe the pain.

"Shhhhh! If you cry out I will have to kill you too quickly."

Freddy's eyes widened. This woman was like the two at the nightclub. She had to be one of them.

"Good. You understand! A little late, though. You should have listened to Lilith. Trying to burn down her club wasn't very nice."

"At least you're too late to stop that." Freddy smirked, trying to regain his composure.

"Poor Freddy. Did you really think we'd let Arnie do such a thing? Mudada assures me he has been taken care of."

"Mudada?"

"An old friend. No one you need concern yourself with."

Freddy swallowed nervously.

"What...what have you done to him?"

"Arnie played with fire. Now it plays with him. It is, how do you say, ironical, yes?"

This isn't real, he thought. *Someone probably spiked my drinks.*

"Oh no, this is very real. As is the pain. Your death will be real."

"Listen, I can pay you. I'm very rich. Just name a pri—"

"You've always bought everything you wanted or taken it. Tonight your money is useless. Agra, she is most unhappy you tried to kill her whore. She has requested I give you to the ones you killed. They will decide your fate. Most fitting, don't you think?"

Before Freddy could reply, Jouvart gripped his throat and squeezed lightly, her long nails pressing into the skin. Leaning close, her hot breath fanned his skin, scorching his face and singeing his eyebrows. The pressure around his neck prevented him from screaming. All he could do was lie there and feel the skin and muscles burning away. The fluid in his eyeballs boiled and still Jouvart wouldn't let him die.

Shielding the nerves to his brain just enough to prevent him from going into shock, she fed him images of what was happening. Flesh bubbled and peeled away from muscles. The muscles sizzled, turning black. Ashes fell onto the pillow. His eyeballs exploded. Only then did she free the nerves to feel...and Freddy died one of the most horrible deaths imaginable.

When his guests heard his final scream, they broke open the door and stared in horror at the body and incinerated skull. The woman was gone. No one thought enough of the pimp to call the police, nor did they want to be around to answer their questions. Besides, he wouldn't be missed. There were plenty more out there to take his place.

CHAPTER 17

THE VISIT WAS unexpected, but a pleasant surprise. Motioning for the demoness to sit, Intunecat brought her a glass of wine and then sat down across from her. Crossing his legs, he leaned back and smiled pleasantly.

"So, what brings you into the Darkness so soon? Not that I'm complaining. It's always a pleasure to see you."

"I wish I could say it's a social visit. Unfortunately this is more business than pleasure."

"Ah. Well, any visit from you is a pleasure, my dear. What can I do for you?"

Lilith quickly outlined to him her conversations with the Child. Intunecat listened without comment until she reached the point where Eve had been deceived into believing Adam had eaten fruit from the Tree of Knowledge.

"So, she led to the downfall of mankind, and its rebirth?"

"Yes. The Twin didn't know what he was getting into when he made women."

"Understandable. You're a rather unpredictable gender." The Dark One chuckled, then sipped his drink. "I'm curious. How did Eve get Adam to go against the dictates of the Twin?"

"She accused him of deception. Of course he denied everything. When she accused him of eating the fruit and not wanting her to have it..."

Lilith quickly outlined the entire story.

Intunecat laughed.

"It's hard to contradict that logic," she said.

"Impossible. And Adam, being Adam, didn't have a clue how to deal with a disgruntled Eve."

"He was damned if he did and damned if he didn't. No pun intended."

"Yes, literally. I've always wondered how the Great Battle came about. Another mystery solved. So what brings you here, now?"

"The Child. I want to free her."

"And you think she's repented her indiscretions and deserves a pardon?"

"She's suffered enough. She was just a child needing guidance and I failed her."

"She was never just a child, my dear. As your daughter and Dis', she was destined to be someone greater than either of you."

"I'm not so sure about that. It's true she has Dis' blood running through her veins, but it's not pure."

"That may be so, but she also carries the blood of the Twin's creation, too. She's the product of two very powerful entities, three if you count her uncle."

Lilith frowned. "The Twin? I never considered that."

"Contrary to what you may believe, Lilith, the Underlord may be able to change who you are, but not what you are. Even he could never remove the original dust from which you were created. But that's not important now. Why do you think I can help you release your daughter?"

"I'm not sure you can. I've been thinking about why she was able to contact me after all this time. The only thing different that I could come up with is my visit here. That's when she first intruded into my thoughts."

"It makes sense. My world is one of nothingness. If she wanted to communicate with you, this would be the best place. There's nothing to interfere with thoughts. Can you talk to her now?"

I'm here.

"Yes. She hears you."

"Can she hear me when you're not present?"

No. His world is impenetrable, as are his thoughts.

"No."

"Good. My world is my fortress. I'd hate to think there was a weakness. Listen, child..." said Intunecat, talking to her indirectly. "Look around. Tell me what you see."

Only darkness, except for you and Mother.

"She sees only the darkness and us."

"How did you and Dis get her into the Netherworld?"

"By opening a door. He said it was one way. Once it closed, it could never be reopened."

"That's probably true."

"I don't accept that. There must be a way."

"No...at least not through the door."

Intunecat put his fingertips together and leaned his chin on them, trying to think of another way to help the demoness. After a few minutes, he straightened up and looked directly at Lilith.

"I must talk to her directly."

"How? She can only communicate through me."

"There's a way, but the price is high."

"What is it?"

"I need access to your thoughts...to enter your mind. Only then can she and I talk."

Lilith didn't like the idea. To allow anyone to take control of her in such a way was unthinkable.

If you don't trust him, don't do it. I can wait until we find another way.

I trust him. I just don't like someone else inside my head.

I'd know if he did anything more than talk with me. Besides, I'd never allow him to see more than you want him to. Trust me, Mother. I'll protect your thoughts and memories against him...and I promise not to intrude into the areas beyond the boundaries you set.

"I still don't like it, but I have no choice."

"You always have a choice, Lilith," Intunecat said. "Be sure of this, though. Once we merge, you won't be able to change your mind."

"I'm sure. Let's do it quickly."

Intunecat knelt next to her and placed his right hand across her temple. With his left, he clasped her two hands and gripped them gently.

"Close your eyes."

Reluctantly, she obeyed him and immediately felt her barriers being eased aside. His entry was barely noticeable, more like the soft flutter of a butterfly.

Can you hear me?

Yes.

Good. Once again, Child, look around and tell me what you see.

Just the darkness and the two of you.

Are you sure? Examine the minutest areas for anomalies. I believe there is a way out. Take your time.

Intunecat waited patiently, giving her a chance to inspect her domain. He could feel Lilith growing restless. Even she could not control her own will if it rebelled against him.

Only a few more minutes.

Lilith could feel his attempts to soothe the part of her that resisted his intrusion. Her will calmed, granting him more time.

I think I see it! the Child sounded like...well...like a child who had made a great discovery.

What?

A crack. No, that's not it. It's too perfect. A...circle...an oval...but like a crack in glass.

Very good. Is it in the darkness or in the window from which you view the other realm?

There's no darkness here. I'm completely surrounded by other worlds. Well, except yours and the spirit world. I can't see into those places.

Okay. Look closely at the center of the circle. Tell me if it is different in any way.

Again he waited. Lilith's will remained calm, unwilling to give in to its own weaknesses.

It's different. Slightly distorted.

What do you see when you look through it?

A bedroom. I see a bedroom.

Do you recognize anything?

No.

Turning his thoughts to Lilith, he asked the same question. The demoness emerged from where she was resting and looked at the distortion.

That's Dis' room! Only he would have such a huge bed.

Is there a mirror in the room?

Of course! He likes to admire himself! Why?

That's the doorway you seek. The Child is another Alice.

Alice?

A human story. Alice Through the Looking Glass. That was her way home, too.

It's too easy, Lilith thought. *Why didn't Dis know this?*

He had no reason to. Rarely do we see the obvious. Speaking of which, your will has been patient enough.—

His exit from her thoughts was as gentle as his entry. Standing, he returned to his chair.

"Are you well?" he asked.

"I feel fine. Thank you for making it so painless."

"My pleasure. Now, as much as I'd like to keep you here longer, I'm sure you're anxious to reunite with your daughter. She'll need help to make the transition."

"I don't understand. If it was this simple—"

"Why didn't she? It wouldn't have done her any good. You and the Underlord banished her to the Netherworld. The banishment had to be nulled by both of you before she could be released."

"Dis granted me full rights to make the decision. He has no objection to this."

"Then you should have no problem bringing the Child through the mirror. I look forward to meeting her one day."

Standing, Lilith walked over and kissed Intunecat on the cheek.

"Thank you."

The blush creeping up his neck and around his ears made him feel awkward...in a pleasant way. Patting her hand, he smiled his most beautiful smile, pleased by her small gesture.

"As always, it was my pleasure."

Lilith stroked his hair once and then walked into the darkness. Once again, Intunecat felt a great sadness and loneliness.

Give her time, whispered a soft voice. *Mother has never been one to rush things.*

I know, he replied, aware that by merging with Lilith, he had given the Child access to his own thoughts. Hopefully, the bond would weaken and disappear.

I won't abuse your trust, Intunecat, but I wanted to thank you, myself. Without you, I wouldn't be going home.

Things have changed, Child. It's no longer the place you knew. Although I personally think humans are better off for what you've done, there are those who will disagree. Don't misunderstand me. You were wrong and others suffered, especially Adam and Eve.

That is my burden to bear. I only wish I could tell them how sorry I am.

They're long gone.

Intunecat?

What, Child?

All humans have souls. Why didn't they? Was the Twin so angry he wanted to punish them by not giving them one?

I don't have an answer for that. He clearly loved them very much. They were his children in a way. Perhaps he realized they would never be happy in Paradise once they gained knowledge from the tree. Setting them free was their only chance at happiness. It was also a death sentence. But enough of this for now. Come back one day and we can discuss this in more detail.

I will. Thank you.

Intunecat felt her slip away, and as she did he felt a similar loneliness to that her mother had left behind. Feeling an unusual need for companionship, he decided to visit Mari and Maopa. The Earth Mother and her peculiar partner would wonder why he was paying them a social visit. The thought amused him.

CHAPTER 18

THE MIRROR SHIMMERED like water rippling gently over a large lake. Lilith stepped away from it and watched to see what would happen next. As if in slow motion, a hand emerged, tentatively at first, followed by an arm and foot. Seconds later, the Child stepped from the mirror and blinked rapidly, trying to adjust her eyes to the light.

Just like that! Lilith thought. *So simple and yet none of us knew.*

Watching her daughter's expression, the demoness was stunned at how much the Child had changed.

You are beautiful!

When her daughter didn't answer, Lilith frowned. Something wasn't right. She could no longer feel the Child's presence in her mind. The emptiness was uncomfortable.

"Mother?"

"Yes."

"I can't feel you."

"I know."

The Child lifted her hands and stared at them. Running the fingers of her right hand up her forearm, she seemed to be concentrating on the texture of her skin.

"It's been a long time," she whispered.

Lilith knew what she meant. Her daughter hadn't seen herself since she was a child...by demon standards. She was a grown demoness, now. Reaching out, Lilith took her hand and turned her toward the mirror.

"Look."

The Child gazed into the mirror, mesmerized by the image staring back at her. Lilith towered over her by several inches. While her mother was tall with long, dark hair, she was short with waist length, wavy red hair. Lilith's skin glowed pale white. The Child's was a light rose color. Her brilliant green eyes met her mother's blue onyx eyes in their reflections.

"Your hair..."

Running her fingers across the top, Lilith noticed the small protrusions above and to the right and left of her forehead.

Horns, she thought.

Few from the Underworld had horns. Only those carrying the bloodline of the most ancient of demons had them and even then, the horns disappeared over time. The same would probably have happened to the Child's if she had not been imprisoned in the Netherworld. Then again, her sire was the eldest of the demons. As his direct descendent, it was possible she would keep them forever.

"I always wondered if I looked like you or Father. I hoped it would be you."

"Well, I'd say you don't look like either of us. You're your own self. Be thankful you didn't get his big feet," Lilith teased, glancing down at the small hooves.

The Child's eyes blazed happily. She smiled.

"I am. I like me," she said, tilting her head at a slight angle.

"Me too. You're beautiful."

"I get that from you."

Laughing, Lilith turned her daughter to face her.

"Let's hope that's all you inherited from me. I'm definitely glad you don't look like your Father. That would be awful!"

"How can you say such a thing?" interrupted a deep baritone voice.

Strolling into the room, Dis walked up to the Child, took her by the shoulders and turned her so he could examine her more closely. Seeing the small horns, he nodded approvingly, but didn't comment about them.

"I see you're grown up although you're tiny. My other offspring are big like me. You must get that from your mother. She said you'd changed...matured."

"Really, Father! I've been locked away for hundreds of thousands of years. You can't expect me to stay a child forever."

"Don't be impudent. In the Netherworld, anything is possible. You're the first to escape from it."

"I didn't escape. I was released."

"Escape... release...it's all the same. What are your plans? You must learn a discipline. It is one of the rules of the Underworld. All demons must have a trade. And no mischief...at least for a while. Demons have long memories."

"Dis! Give her time to adjust!"

"Adjust? She's my daughter. She doesn't need to adjust," he declared, looking first at Lilith and then at the Child. "Well, I see I'm going to get nowhere with your mother. We'll talk again when she isn't around."

"Leave her alone, Dis."

The Underlord shook his head and laughed.

"You're a bad example for my daughter, Lily. I hope she shows me more respect than you do."

Without saying another word, he left them.

"That's it? That's all he has to say to me after all this time?"

Shaking her head sadly, the Child was obviously disappointed. Lilith patted her arm.

"It's more than I expected. His appearance and desire to meet you after all this time says more than any words he may have spoken. By coming here, he has acknowledged you as his own. Don't expect much more. At least until he adjusts to your presence."

"I guess you're right."

"Listen, Child. Dis isn't like anyone you've ever known or ever will know. He has his own agenda. He feels things differently. Everything is an extreme to him, which makes him appear shallow. Don't let that fool you. Give him time."

"I don't have a choice, do I?"

"No."

"Mother?"

"What, Child?"

"Everyone calls me Child, or Demon Child. Did I ever have a name?"

Lilith gathered her into her arms and held her for several minutes, thinking back to the moment of her birth. She remembered the excruciating pain and the relief when it was over. The demon midwives had bundled the Child into a blanket and handed her to the Underlord. Without looking at her or Lilith, he had walked away.

"Yes. Caelene."

"Caelene. I like the sound of it. What does it mean?"

Lilith rested her head against her daughter's hair and felt one of the small horns press into her cheek.

"Child," she whispered.

"Child?"

"Yes. It means 'child'. At the time it seemed appropriate."

Laughter rang out through the Underworld. The minions and demons didn't recognize the new voice, but it sounded familiar.

CHAPTER 19

IT WAS HOT...very, very hot! Opening his eyes, all Freddy could see was the multi-colored orange, red and black landscape of flickering flames. Screams pierced the air like rolling thunder. Around him stood several women, all dressed like whores. He was sure he had never seen some of them before but he recognized a few of them.

"You should!" whispered a voice from behind him.

Blinking from the sweat burning his eyes, he tried to turn to see who was talking to him. It was then that he realized he couldn't move. His wrists and ankles were bound to poles on each side of his body, leaving him spread-eagled. Flexing his muscles, he tried in vain to break the bindings. Sweat poured from his brow and chest, pooling beneath him. Looking down, he saw that he was completely naked.

"This is a dream!" he muttered and then screamed as a searing pain shot across his back.

"You will talk when we say you can talk," said the same voice, now to his left.

Turning his head, he saw a tall, thin woman with beady black eyes standing a few feet away with a whip in her hand.

"Who are you?" he demanded, his voice hoarse from pain. The crack of a whip was followed immediately by more pain, causing him to suck in his breath and gasp.

"You will talk when we say you can talk," repeated the voice, this time on his right.

Freddy glanced in each direction and saw the same woman.

This is a nightmare! he thought, afraid to speak. He was surrounded by the same woman. *Must be twins.*

"Triplets!" responded a voice behind him.

About to speak, Freddy decided to remain silent.

"Good. You learn quickly, doesn't he, sisters?"

"Yes. That's too bad," replied the second.

"Definitely too bad," agreed the third.

As if responding to some unseen signal, the other women who were silently watching started circling him slowly, each one stopping in front of him for a few seconds so he had a clear view of her face. He immediately recognized two of them.

"Charlotte? Pammie?"

The whip sounded and the pain was instantaneous. Biting his lip, he tried not to scream.

"You will talk when we say you can talk," repeated the voice again.

Nodding, Freddy said nothing.

"These are the women you have murdered. They have names. It's good you remember them."

The pimp noticed that each of the triplets took turns speaking, rotating in the same direction every time.

"When you can name all of them, you will have passed the first of your trials."

"And one will be left. Do you understand?"

He nodded.

"You may speak!"

"Who are you?" gasped Freddy.

"We are the Erinyes sisters. Have you never heard of us?"

Shaking his head no, he wasn't sure if he was making a mistake by denying it.

"We punish the worst souls condemned to hell. You have been given to us for eternity."

"Or until you pass the two tasks set before you."

Freddy was about to ask about these tasks when he noticed one of the triplets flicking her whip.

"You may talk," she said.

"What tasks?" he asked nervously, glancing at the demons on each side of him. He knew the third was right behind him. The whores continued to circle silently.

"You must name each of the whores you murdered. Only then can you go to the final task."

"I've never seen all of these women, only a few of them."

"That's your problem. You either killed them or ordered their deaths."

"You will remember them in time."

"In a very long time."

"It's time to begin. Name these whores," the demoness to his left commanded.

Freddy watched the faces passing by and was able to name five before he missed. Those five disappeared. The whip cracked and he screamed.

"Name them again."

"I don't—"

The whip cracked.

"You will talk when we say you can talk."

The monotony of the sentence itself was enough to drive him crazy. He felt like screaming for them to shut up but knew better.

"Name them again."

Freddy tried and failed, tried and failed and each time he suffered the same punishment. Each of the triplets took turns with their whips, hitting the exact same spot on his back with an accuracy that foretold of eons of experience. Had he been human, he would have died a long time ago. Freddy realized he would suffer the unbearable pain for an eternity if he didn't guess their names.

Occasionally, the triplets would stop and talk among themselves, oblivious to his presence. Then they would resume their torture, methodically, stoically. On one occasion, when he was allowed to talk, he asked them what his final task would be, thinking if he guessed enough names, he'd eventually eliminate all of the whores.

"You must guess each of our names. Only then will your soul be transferred to the fires of hell. Only then will you know some peace...although I warn you, it will still be painful."

"But not like this. There you get periods of rest to contemplate how to redeem your soul," the second demoness said.

"In time you may get a reprieve from the Underlord and be allowed to serve him," added the third.

"I've never heard of you before. How can I know your names?" he asked, dejected at the thought of spending eternity under their reign.

"That is not our problem."

"Prayers will do you no good."

"But please us and we may give you a hint."

"How can I please you?" he asked, hope surfacing.

"You please us now."

"Yes, each failure gives us joy."

"But if I fail every time, I will never leave here," he cried hopelessly.

The triplets smiled their satisfaction. Freddy knew he was doomed.

CHAPTER 20

THEY HUDDLED IN a dark corner away from prying eyes and ears, whispering amongst themselves. The rumors were right. The Child had returned. Many demons had either forgotten her or pushed aside their feelings about her and moved on. Tens of thousands of years were too long for even the most hardened to want revenge. There were too many other distractions for them to focus on.

The weaker minions, however, were different. As the lowest of the low, they would never rise to positions of power and so they lived in constant fear of their own scheming. Zagam, Paymon and Dagon were three of those minions.

Zagam was a master of deceit, but most demons knew his tricks. Paymon was the master of ceremonies. Unfortunately, the Underworld rarely held any events requiring his services. Then there was Dagon, the baker. Why the Underworld even had a baker, no one knew.

"Do you think she'll remember us?" whispered Paymon, looking around nervously.

"I don't know. It's been a long time. Maybe she's forgotten or maybe she doesn't care anymore," said Dagon, his voice shaking slightly.

"You are fools," hissed Zagam. "How can she not remember? Would you forget the ones who had you locked away for hundreds of thousands of years?"

Neither demon answered.

"No!" replied another voice, startling the three conspirators. "No one would forget!"

"Child! It's good to see you!" Paymon said, looking to the others for support. Nodding vigorously, they smiled weakly at the petite red-haired demoness.

"Oh, I'm sure."

"You've changed," Dagon said.

"Time can do that," the Child replied, her voice cold and emotionless.

"Yes...yes. We heard what the Underlord and that woman did to you. It was unconscionable."

"By that woman, you mean my mother."

"Of course. Your mother. We mean no disrespect."

"We went to them to protest what they had done, but it was too late," interjected Zagam.

"Really! I must have missed that part."

"Ummm...missed?"

"Yes. It's rather odd, but you see...while I was in the Netherworld, I saw and heard everything you did. I don't remember you going to my Father or Mother on my behalf."

Zagam flushed a dark red.

"We started to. They wouldn't see us is what he meant," said Dagon.

"Oh. Well. That's different." She sneered. "That changes everything."

"Good. Good. We've thought a lot about you, Child."

"Did you, now? Well, I have to admit I've been thinking about the three of you. Especially you, Zagam."

Zagam fidgeted.

This isn't good! he thought.

"No, it isn't," she replied, making him take a step back. "I believe it was you who first lied to me about Adam."

"I misunderstood what I heard. Right?" he asked, looking at the other two for support.

"Yes. That's right," they agreed, glancing at each other.

"So I'm wrong to think you deliberately misled me."

"No...I mean yes. We wouldn't do that."

The Child didn't reply for several minutes while she examined each demon as if looking for something. Finally, focusing on Zagam, she scowled and then glared, her eyes burning with an inner rage. The other demons backed away, fearful of distracting her attention away from the Deceiver.

Smoke rose from his skin. He tried to scream. Writhing in pain, he clawed at his throat, his eyes imploring his companions to assist him. Paymon took a hesitant step forward but retreated when the Child gave him a warning glance. Cowering, the two demons watched as Zagam was slowly and sadistically incinerated into a pile of dust. Turning to look at the others, she smiled her satisfaction and walked away, then stopped and spun around.

"You two! Get rid of the dust and then come to my chambers. You serve me now. Only me," she commanded.

"But we are free minions."

"Were, Dagon. You forfeited that right the moment I was set free."

"For how long?" Paymon asked, hesitantly.

"Until I decide otherwise. And be forewarned, no one is to know this. Do you understand?"

Lowering their eyes, they bobbed their heads.

"Good. I have work to do. I will need loyal supporters. Obey me and you will be well rewarded. Disobey me and your life is forfeit."

307

"Yes, Mistress," they replied in unison.

The Child smiled her satisfaction. A new force walked the streets of the Underworld.

The End

About The Author

FRAN HECKROTTE lives in sunny South Carolina with her husband. She spent three years in Alaska enjoying hiking, camping, gold panning and working part time at a local ranch. After moving to the South she became a police officer for five years, then left law enforcement to become a carpenter. Now she owns a property management company. As time permits, she likes to travel to Montreal, Canada to ski and do some hiking.

About the Copy Editor

Cindy Burke has had a lifelong interest in journalism and fiction writing. She started as a newsroom assistant and has contributed several articles to local newspapers. Her science fiction book, "Intimate Space: A Feminist Utopian Romp Through the Galaxy," was published in 2015.

Burke was born in Savannah, GA and lived for several years in California, Georgia and Florida before moving to Upstate South Carolina in 1998. She is a social justice advocate and Vice President of the Clemson Alumni Society for Equality (CASE), an alumni group that has established two student scholarships.

Her family is spread across the Southeast, including two sons, a sous chef and a navy technician. She lives with her husband, a computer analyst and fellow sci-fi and fantasy buff.

Burke writes from their home located in the foothills of the beautiful Blue Ridge Mountains.

About the Cover Artist

Patty G. Henderson is an author, publisher and artist and all around bohemian at heart. An independent author, she launched her own publishing imprint, Blanca Rosa Publishing. She writes Gothic Historical Romances and has published four so far, THE SECRET OF LIGHTHOUSE POINTE, CASTLE OF DARK SHADOWS, PASSION FOR VENGEANCE, and SHADOWS OF THE HEART. She has also penned four Brenda Strange Supernatural Mysteries, Comfortable wearing several creative hats, Patty is an accomplished artist as well as author. She's done popular book cover artwork for many mainstream mystery and horror authors and lesbian authors via her graphic arts business, Boulevard Photografica, in addition to a nearly complete immersion in indie writing and publishing. You can reach Patty via her author web site: www.pattyghenderson.com or check out her graphics and book cover professional web site: www.boulevardphotografica.yolasite.com.

Other Titles by Fran Heckrotte

The Illusionist (First in the Illusionist Series)

DAKOTA DEVEREAUX, an investigative journalist, is on a mission to uncover the secrets of Yemaya, the Illusionist. However, in her quest for an exposé on this mysterious woman, she uncovers more than she bargained for. Dakota is targeted by a power hungry CEO determined to learn the Illusionist's secret at all costs, and a madman intent on fulfilling his perverted fantasies.

From Moldova, land of the legendary werewolf, to the Transylvania and the Carpathian Mountains, two souls must battle the dark forces of evil for their lives and their love.

* * *

Bloodlust (Second in the Illusionist Series)

YEMAYA AND DAKOTA have just returned to the Illusionist's homeland for a well-earned vacation when they are informed that several villagers have been savagely attacked and killed by something or someone. At the same time, a young Carpi woman is found lying unconscious near the outskirts of Teraclia. Comatose, she is unable to tell anyone what has happened and science can provide no answers. Two small wounds on her throat raise the old specter of the vampire, a legend the locals of the Transylvanian community are very familiar with and still believe to this day.

The Illusionist and her partner search for the truth behind these attacks. Will they fall prey to the murderous bloodlust that surrounds them, or will they succeed in stopping this heinous reign of terror?

* * *

Lilith (Third in the Illusionist Series)

YEMAYA, the Illusionist, and her journalist partner, Dakota, find themselves embroiled in a search for the person responsible for the rape and torture of a young Carpi woman attending a university in the States. When they decide to visit a local nightclub for "women only," they find the owner and her employees unusual. Dakota feels mysteriously attracted to one of the clientele while Yemaya recognizes a kindred spirit in Lilith, the club's owner. Spiritual ancestors, missing whores, a sadistic exporter and new acquaintances lead the two lovers into an adventure of Biblical proportion.

Lilith! She was a demoness, as old as humanity itself. Now she is the owner of a "women's only" nightclub and part owner of the Sisterhood, a small group of whores who have banded together to create a better life for themselves. It is her job to protect the women who are putting so much trust in her. When a local pimp decides to eliminate his competition, Lilith and her two demon partners want revenge and no one knows better how to exact it than demons. This is a revelation of the past, the present and the events that forever changed the course of human history.

* * *

Les Gris, The Shadow People (Fourth in the Illusionist Series)

THEY WERE LES GRIS, the Shadow People, and they are as much a part of us as we are them. As children we talked to them, played with them and disclosed our innermost fears, secrets and dreams; and they patiently listened, comforted and encouraged us. In time, though, most humans outgrew their *imaginary* friends and eventually forgot them. For those few who didn't, humanity's very existence would be determined by the strength of the bond between a small group of women and their life partners, the *les gris*.

* * *

Saira (Fifth in the Illusionist Series)

SAIRA WAS A TRAVELER. Even her name meant 'traveler'. Her entire existence was dedicated to making the journey to seek answers to the questions that plagued her. Sometimes she felt as if she were a pawn in a game she didn't understand but knew her destiny was hers to decide. She chose to let the uncertainty of time make the decisions for her. Unfortunately, her curiosity not only gets her into trouble but creates a series of events that affects not only the mortal world but the spirit world too. Yemaya, Dakota, Mari and Maopa will find their lives turned topsy-turvy and Saira will learn an emotion she had never experienced before...fear

* * *

Warrior Demoness (Sixth in the Illusionist Series)

SHE WAS SABNOCK, a demon, who, like the Phoenix, lived and died many times because she chose to live amongst mortals rather than spend eternity babysitting the legions of the Underlord. There were no longer battles to be fought in the Underworld so the ex-commander left her realm to live with the humans as a human. Falling in love, she now had to choose between her vow to live and die as a mortal or love and live as a demon, not knowing if her lover could accept the truth. The wrong decision would condemn her to a life of loneliness—and for a demon, life was eternity.

* * *

Solaria (Futuristic Science Fiction)

THE FIRST AWARENESS of existence was a chaotic flash of colors, meaningless and yet in an odd way logical; why, she wasn't sure. Birth is the most significant event in life, and yet it is never memorable; at least not for the newborn; but then she really wasn't a newborn, even though it was the first day of her life. She was 1A526, the first of her kind, an artificially intelligent blend of technology and bio-mechanics. Created to serve humans, Solaria and her AI programmer, Carley, soon discover the company funding the Hubot Project had more sinister motives. If Solaria were to fulfill the hopes of the woman who had given her existence meaning, she would have to become the human her programmer had dreamed of and take down Future Dynamicon, the company that created her.

* * *

Future Perfect (Sequel to Solaria)

PRIMERIS WAS a Hubot, designed to serve humans. Her existence depended on her ability to complete her assignments... which she always did with a cold, emotionless detachment. Now, her perfect record was going to be tested to its limits. In her attempts to find and capture Solaria, another Hubot, Primeris is forced to either disobey her directive of obedience or become the human she never wanted to be.

The Order of the Healers was exactly that, healers. Their mission was to move humanity forward, even if it meant saving the worst of mankind. Chantelle is a Singer, a member of a small sub-group of Healers, whose latest calling takes her on a mission that will test her gift to its limit, and leave her wondering if her success will lead to humanity's downfall.

www.ingramcontent.com/pod-product-compliance
Lightning Source LLC
Chambersburg PA
CBHW061538170626
46811CB00001B/23